THE SANDMAN

A JOHN MILTON THRILLER

MARK DAWSON

LONDON

1

Belmarsh, in southeast London's Thamesmead, was a Category A holding prison and one of the more modern additions to Her Majesty's criminal justice estate. It was adjacent to Woolwich Crown Court, and that, together with its modern amenities and impressive security, made it home for some of the most dangerous and notorious prisoners in the United Kingdom.

The High Security Unit took that security and improved upon it. It was the only prison-within-a-prison in Great Britain, a separate facility within the walls of the prison and distinguished by its own twenty-foot-high concrete perimeter wall and separate security measures, including doors that could only be opened remotely by central control. The HSU had forty-eight cells, and if the main estate was secure, the HSU was inescapable. The unit was used chiefly for those suspected or convicted of terrorism offences, but it also accommodated those who would be at risk if released into the general prison population or those who were deemed to be particularly valuable.

Prisoner A4224AA was in the latter category. Tristan

Huxley had been charged with a host of offences, including human trafficking and the sexual exploitation of minors. Quite aside from the risk that his notoriety might inspire attacks from other inmates, the government had decided that he had made enough enemies during his career as an international fixer that an attempt on his life would have been likely if he was given a cell in one of the main wings. He had secured arms deals that had favoured countries at the expense of their neighbours; the armoured vehicles that had been purchased by his Israeli clients had killed Palestinians in the Gaza Strip; the Starstreak surface-to-air missiles he had supplied to the Indian military had been used to bring down a Pakistani jet over disputed Kashmir. At the time of his arrest, Huxley had been working on a deal that would have supplied Russian armaments to the Indians. The Pakistani secret service had already failed in several audacious bids to kidnap and then kill him in attempts to end the transaction, and British intelligence was of the opinion that they would try again and that, this time, they would make sure that they were successful. After all, this time they knew *exactly* where he was. It would be simple enough to find an inmate who was prepared to open his throat with a shiv in exchange for money and favours to be showered upon loved ones outside.

Beyond that, Huxley had been examined by a court-appointed psychiatrist, who had come to the conclusion that he was a potential suicide risk. The solution to both problems was to assign him a solitary cell in the HSU.

He sat on the bed now and cast his eyes around the room that had been his home for twenty-three hours every day for the last two months. The inmates and guards referred to the cells as 'boxes,' and each was small, with plain whitewashed walls and simple furniture. Huxley was kept away from the other prisoners and allowed to exercise for an hour before being locked away again. His money and influence had not been sufficient to secure his liberty, but they had provided him with a handful of luxuries and amenities that made his incarceration a little less unpleasant. He had a television and he had managed to secure boxes of cereal, confectionary and Pot Noodles, all preferable to the slop they served at mealtimes. The luxuries helped, but they could not hide the fact that he had been buried deep in the penal system, that there was no prospect that might change and that he was utterly alone.

He turned his attention back to the legal papers that he had been asked to review. His lawyers were due to appeal the decision not to grant him bail, and they needed him to approve his witness statement before it was submitted. His money had enabled him to assemble a dream team of the very best minds in the English legal profession, including solicitors from Magic Circle firms and the barrister with the planet-sized intellect who had recently set the record for the highest hourly fee in the United Kingdom. The cost was eye-watering, but Huxley didn't care about that. His best advantage was a bottomless well of money, and he was prepared to spend every last penny if it bought him his freedom. His barrister had suggested that the decision not to grant bail might have been improperly reached, and, if they were able to demonstrate that, the court would have no choice but to release him. The hearing was scheduled for next week, and —even though the lawyers had told him that the odds were against him—Huxley had started counting down the days to the moment when he would be able to leave the HSU and conduct his defence from outside.

He heard the sound of footsteps approaching and looked up from his papers to check the time. It was just after five, and he wasn't due to be given his dinner for another thirty minutes. He expected to hear the footsteps pass by along the corridor, but they didn't. They stopped, and then he heard the sound of the key in the lock.

He stood and faced the door.

One of his regular guards was standing outside. He was carrying a tray with a covered plate and a plastic beaker. There was a camera in the corner of the room. The guard stepped into its field of vision, his back to the lens so that it would have been impossible for anyone to see his face.

"You're getting out tonight," he said quietly.

"What?"

"Take the pill."

Huxley felt self-conscious with the camera on him, but he couldn't leave it like that. "What does that mean?" he said quietly, masking his concern with a forced smile.

The guard paused and stared at Huxley in a meaningful way that left him in no doubt that he wasn't being given a choice and that there would not be a discussion.

"Enjoy your meal."

The guard backed out of the cell, keeping his face hidden from the camera, shut the door and locked it. Huxley listened to the sound of his footsteps as they echoed away along the corridor. He went to the desk and lifted the plastic cloche that covered his plate. Tonight's meal was a cheeseburger, fries and a salad with apple juice in a covered plastic cup. Everything looked normal, until he lifted the bun and saw a single pill had been placed on top of the burger. It was blue and the size of the nail on his little finger.

He plucked up the pill with his thumb and forefinger and hid it in his hand while he took a handful of fries with his other hand and ate them. Apart from his money, Huxley was fortunate enough to have leverage over a large list of contacts with huge political power in countries all around the world. He had passed messages by way of his lawyer to his contact in both the Russian and Indian embassies and appealed for their help in getting him out. His lawyer had told him that an attempt would be made to extricate him, but that had been six weeks ago, and nothing had come of it. He had stewed on the snub ever since and had been thinking about how he might up the ante in an attempt to shake them out of their inaction; he could ruin people with a simple leak to the press, and he had come to the conclusion that he was going to have to remind them of that.

But now this? There had been no suggestion that his plea had been taken seriously, far less what any attempt to get him out would involve. He didn't even know who was responsible for whatever had been planned, and now he was being asked to take a pill with no idea what it might do to him.

He felt nauseous as he realised that it might be something else: what if, he thought, it was *not* an attempt to win his freedom but an attempt to end his life? He didn't know the guard. Who was he? Who had paid him? Huxley turned so that his hand was shielded from the camera and opened his fist; the pill sat there in his palm, the skin now clammy with sweat, offering either freedom or death and with no way for him to know.

Doubt swamped him. He went to the door and banged his fist against it.

"Hey!" he yelled. "Hey! Come back!"

He knew he was making a mistake, but couldn't stop. He crashed his fist against the door again and again and again until he heard the sound of footsteps approaching, and the slat in the door was drawn back.

"What is it?"

It wasn't the guard who had delivered his dinner to him, but one of the others whom he recognised from the night shift.

He froze, his fist closed around the pill.

"What *is* it?" the guard repeated.

"Nothing," Huxley said.

"Didn't sound like nothing."

"I'm sorry," he said, backing away from the door. The pill in his hand felt red hot, as if he were squeezing a burning ember.

"Eat your dinner and shut the fuck up."

The guard closed the slat, and his footsteps echoed away along the corridor.

Huxley went to the bed and sat down. He opened his hand and looked down at the pill. His skin was stained blue; the tablet's colouration had been washed away with his sweat.

He stared at it, closed his eyes, put it in his mouth and swallowed.

2

Harry Cope signed into the prison, made his way through the first ring of security and then continued on to the High Security Unit. He scanned his fingerprint, waited for the door to unlock and then went through, pausing in the vestibule until the outer door had been locked again and the inner door buzzed open. He went to the ready room, opened his locker and took off his coat. He hung it on a hanger and reached for his keys and radio. He clipped the radio onto his belt, stopped at the door and looked at his reflection in the mirror: he loved how he looked in the uniform. The white shirt and dark blue epaulettes, the black tie and the boots that he kept clean and polished ... It reminded him of how far he had come in his career. Cope had been a guard at Belmarsh for five years and had been delighted when the governor suggested that he transfer to the HSU. It was a prestigious posting, and, although the inmates were often more dangerous, there were fewer of them than in the general population, and that made the job easier, on balance.

He had worked here for eighteen months and had developed a reputation as a hard-working, trustworthy and fair officer who was well liked by his colleagues and respected by the inmates. He saw his job as a mixture of security and welfare, making sure that those in his charge were secured while also doing everything that he could to make them comfortable. Many of the inmates were looking at long stretches inside, and the weight of those years was something that could lead to depression and other mental health problems. Ninety percent of Cope's job was talking and helping them to maintain a positive mental outlook.

He opened the door to the control room. Nat Shapiro was at the desk, looking at the feed from the cameras.

"Evening."

Shapiro turned. "All right, Harry?"

He grimaced. "Spurs lost."

"I saw."

"Kane's heart isn't in it."

"Wants to go to Man U, doesn't he. I was reading they might flog him in January."

"Maybe."

"Would you?"

"If they can get a hundred million for him? I probably would." Cope gestured to the screens. "How's it been?"

"Quiet."

"What about Hussein?"

"Good as gold," Shapiro said.

Suleman Hussein had been convicted of bombing a nightclub in Leicester and had been moved to the HSU after fomenting unrest amongst the other Muslim prisoners while he was being held in Wakefield. He was a nasty piece of work with an edge to him. He had recruited two other inmates to push a guard down the stairs while he was in the Monster Mansion—so called on account of the high-risk sex offenders and murderers there—and the governor had applied to have him moved here.

Cope picked up the clipboard from the desk and saw that it was time for the half-hourly check. "Want me to do the rounds?"

"You sure? I don't mind."

"I could do with the exercise."

"Go on then." Shapiro held up his finger. "One thing— Huxley was making an almighty racket earlier."

"Why?"

"Didn't say. Just thought I'd mention it in case he's playing up."

"He's harmless," Cope said. "Back in a bit. Put a brew on."

Cope made sure that his radio was switched on and working, and set off, waiting for Shapiro to buzz him into the main unit. The prisoners were all locked in their cells, but it still gave him a little shiver of nerves when he made his way along the corridors. Some of the men in the HSU were physically imposing, and most of them had no real incentive to behave. They were already in solitary confinement and had nothing to look forward to except years and years of the same treatment. Several had been given whole life sentences and knew what that meant: there would be no parole for them, and the rest of their lives were bounded by the walls of their cells and, for an hour a day, the exercise yard. Why would they be on good behaviour? How else could they be punished?

Cope started his rounds. The cells were identified by way of a stencilled designation above the door: Special Cell, and then a number from one to forty-eight. Cope reached SC1 and slid back the hatch so that he could peer inside. The occupant of the cell—a murderer by the name of

Stephen Locke who had been convicted of killing three people with a hammer—was asleep on his bed. Cope satisfied himself that everything was as it was supposed to be, closed the hatch and moved on.

SC2 was occupied by Neil Ironside, a journalist who was being held in the HSU while the American government sought his extradition. He, too, was asleep in bed with nothing to suggest that there was anything amiss. Cope had enjoyed long conversations with Ironside; he was intelligent and witty, and, though he was fighting extradition on the basis that he risked a lifetime behind bars in an American supermax, he was still excellent company. Cope didn't want to disturb his sleep and closed the hatch as quietly as he could.

The next cell was Hussein. Cope looked inside and saw that he was sitting cross-legged on his bed, reading from his copy of the Koran.

SC4 was occupied by Huxley, the disgraced financier who had been charged with sex trafficking offences. He was an unpleasant man who had reacted to his fall from grace with indignation, as if what had happened was an unjust imposition against a man of his standing that would soon be remedied. Cope had talked about him with the others, and they all shared the same opinion: he appeared to think that his money would mean that his predicament was temporary and that, in due course, he would be restored to his previous position. He was arrogant and reacted badly to discipline. He complained about being confined to his cell and didn't seem to understand it when he was told that he would be eaten alive if he were put into the general population.

Cope opened the hatch and looked through it. Huxley often read in the evening, but, this time, he wasn't at his usual place at his desk. He was sprawled across the floor, his back against the edge of his bed and his arms hanging loosely at his sides.

"Shit. *Shit.*" He thumbed his radio to transmit. "Cope to Control. I need you at SC4. Possible unresponsive inmate. Over."

Standard procedure was to wait for a second guard before going into a cell, but Cope wasn't frightened of Huxley, and it looked as if he might not have the luxury of time, even if Nat got a move on. He unlocked the door and stepped inside. Huxley was unmoving. Cope knelt down next to him, and, after checking that his hands were empty, he reached over and rested his fingers against the side of his neck. He could feel a pulse, but it was weak.

"Bollocks."

Cope turned and saw Shapiro in the doorway.

"Might be a heart attack," Cope said.

"Pulse?"

"Faint. Call the doctor."

Shapiro ducked outside the cell and spoke into his radio. Cope reached for Huxley and checked his airway, then very gently lowered him into the recovery position. He hoped that he had found him in time. Huxley had left victims all around the world, and they were all owed the chance to see him pay for what he had done to them.

3

Cope held on to the side of his seat as the ambulance raced through the London streets under blue lights. Huxley was strapped to the stretcher on the other side of the ambulance with the prison doctor—a man called McClaren—alongside him.

"Still breathing?"

McClaren nodded. "Yes."

"What do you think?"

"He's not out of the woods, but his vitals look better than they did."

"What was it?"

"My money's on his heart. I gave him heparin—it'll thin the blood and work on the clot if he has one. They'll take him into coronary and take a look."

Cope exhaled. "Thank fuck for that. Can you imagine the shitshow if he died before he got to trial?"

"You thinking of Epstein?"

"It did cross my mind. We'd be dealing with the aftermath for months."

Cope couldn't see anything to gauge their progress from

the back of the ambulance. He pressed the intercom to speak to the driver. "How much longer?"

"We're here."

The ambulance slowed and bumped over something as it left the road. They came to a stop, and McClaren opened the doors to let in the stark fluorescence from the lights set beneath the awning of the Accident and Emergency Department. They were met by a doctor and two porters. Huxley's stretcher was wheeled out of the back of the ambulance, lowered to the ground on the ramp and then quickly pushed through the corridors to a specialist ward. Cope hurried along behind them.

"Who's the patient?" the doctor asked him.

Cope looked at the badge that hung from a lanyard around the man's neck and saw that his name was Fry. "Tristan Huxley."

Fry must have recognised the name, but was too professional to react to it. "What do you think?"

"Heart attack," McClaren said. "He's had heparin."

"Good."

The porters pushed the stretcher through the hospital, diverting around the Accident and Emergency Department and continuing deeper into the interior of the building.

"Where are we going?" McClaren asked the closest porter.

"A secure ward," he said.

The porters turned left, passing signs for pathology and then radiology, then turned left again. Cope was quickly lost.

McClaren looked confused. "Where's the ward?"

They reached a lift. "Just up here."

One of the porters called the lift, and Huxley was pushed inside. The car was large, designed to have enough space for a hospital bed, and there was plenty of room for all five of them. The doors closed, and the lift started to descend.

Cope frowned. "We're going down?"

Fry nodded. "That's right."

"You said it was up."

The porters turned away from the stretcher. Cope went for his radio, but didn't get the chance to switch it on. Both men reached inside their tunics and pulled out handguns that had been fitted with suppressors. The porter to the left aimed at McClaren and fired. The suppressor muffled the sound of the shot, but only a little; the gun barked out, the sound ringing back off the walls. The porter was too close to miss; McClaren jerked as the bullet tattooed him in the centre of the chest. Blood splattered onto the dented and scratched metal wall behind him.

Cope had nowhere to go. He raised his hands.

"Please," he said. "I have kids."

The porter ignored him. He aimed his pistol and fired.

Cope felt the bullet in the stomach. It didn't hurt as much as he might have thought it would; it was as if he'd been punched. The strength ran out of his legs, and he fell to his knees. He fumbled for his radio and felt something warm and wet and sticky against the plastic; he pulled his hand away and held up his fingers and saw that they were red.

The lift slowed, and the doors opened. Cope felt a tide of fatigue wash over him and tried to keep his eyes open as the wheels of the stretcher went by his head, one of the castors squeaking from a lack of oil. Cope turned his head and followed it; Fry had hurried ahead to a waiting truck while one of the porters manoeuvred the stretcher to its loading platform.

The driver of the truck was waiting. He said something to the porters, but not in English. Cope didn't recognise the language, but then the porter replied with '*Nyet*,' and he knew it was Russian. He coughed and felt the blood in his mouth. He tried to spit it out, but didn't have the strength.

The porter took his pistol and aimed down at McLaren. Cope watched, helpless, as the man pulled the trigger for a third time. He aimed for the doctor's head and didn't miss. McLaren spasmed for a moment and then lay still.

Cope fought to keep his eyes open. He reached for his radio again, his fingers brushing against the stubby antenna as he probed for the button he needed to press to transmit. He tried to speak, but couldn't tell if he had said anything or whether the noise in his head was just another moan of pain.

He blinked his eyes and saw the porter's scuffed boots just inches away from his head.

The truck's engine rumbled to life, and the platform wheezed as it started to ascend. Tristan Huxley disappeared from view.

Cope tried to crawl away.

He didn't get far.

4

Huxley opened his eyes and realised he had absolutely no idea where he was. He was lying on his side in a dark space and might have concluded that he was in a windowless room were it not for the sudden jolt of movement that told him that he was in a vehicle. His eyes felt heavy, and his head throbbed as if someone had fastened a strap around his temples and then tightened it. He blinked again, and then, feeling a churning in his gut, he sat bolt upright, jerked over to the side and vomited. All he had in his gut was bile; it rushed up his gullet and filled his mouth. It was hot and acrid, and he spat it out, the stench of it unpleasant in his nostrils.

The voice was to his left. "Are you okay?"

"Where am I?"

"In the back of a van," the voice said. "We're taking you to the airport, and then we'll get you out of the country."

The man spoke with a Russian accent.

"Who are you?"

"I'm Maxim. My colleagues and I have been sent to get you out of the country. Please—sit back."

He felt a hand on his shoulder and allowed himself to be moved back so that he was leaning up against the side of the vehicle.

"Who do you work for?"

"The Russian government."

"What? The GRU?"

"Yes—that will do for now."

The detail could wait until he had reached wherever it was he was being taken. "What happened to me? I remember... I was given a pill..."

"It causes symptoms that resemble a heart attack. We needed to remove you from prison before we could get to you. I'm sure it was unpleasant—I'm very sorry about that, but there was no other way."

"'*Unpleasant*'? That's an understatement. I feel *awful*."

"It is wearing off now, and I am assured that there will be no side effects. You will be able to sleep again once we are on the plane. By the time we reach Russia, you will feel—how do you say—right as...?"

"Rain," Huxley finished for him. "Where in Russia?"

"Krasnodar. We have a facility nearby. It was decided that would be the best place for you to recover. I am told that you will be taken to India once your strength has returned."

Huxley had tried to win the cooperation of both the Russians and the Indians with the implied threat of what he knew, but the motives for their wanting him out were even more prosaic than the risk of embarrassment: for the Russians, it was avarice; and for the Indians, the desire to dominate. Western sanctions after the invasion of Ukraine meant that Moscow needed the money, and the stalemate with Pakistanis in Kashmir meant that the Indians needed the weapons. Huxley was the go-between who had brokered the deal, and he guessed it had been decided that the effort expended in getting him out would be worth it if it meant that renegotiation could be avoided.

The van slowed down and turned to the left, then stopped for a moment. Huxley heard the sound of a gate being wheeled out of the way, and then they started ahead again.

"We're here," Maxim said.

The van stopped once more, and Huxley heard the sound of footsteps approaching from outside. The doors opened, and Huxley looked out onto a wide-open space that was lit at a distance by overhead lamps. There were a series of hangars behind the van and a tower to the right. There were two runways, side by side; one was grass and the other —wider and longer—was a strip of smooth tarmac. Huxley recognised North Weald airfield. He had flown out of here before, and, at least compared to the other smaller facilities that were used by wealthy outsiders—Farnborough, Elstree, Blackbushe—this one was small and private, yet still large enough to fly a Gulfstream in and out.

Maxim hopped down and helped Huxley to join him. Huxley was able to see the Russian better in the artificial light; he was a little taller than him, with closely cropped hair and a neat beard. He was wearing the green scrubs of a hospital porter with a name badge hanging from a lanyard around his neck. He took Huxley by the elbow and guided him out onto the taxiway. A Gulfstream G550 was waiting for them, the stairs unfolded and the pilot making his way around the aircraft, performing the final checks that needed to be undertaken before he was ready to take off.

KRASNODAR

5

H uxley managed to get some sleep on the plane, although he awoke twice in the teeth of a nightmare. It was the same dream that had tormented him ever since the shoot-out at his home: the Pakistani agents in the darkness outside the swimming pool, the gunshots that tore through the glass, the escape, and then, worst of all, Milton's betrayal. He sat up in his seat, his forehead slick with cold sweat, and struggled to relax again. He gave up after the second time and, seeing that they would be landing soon, went to the bathroom at the front of the cabin. He relieved himself and then doused his face in cold water.

Krasnodar had its own airport, and, as the pilot lined them up and began the descent, Huxley could see that it was more than big enough to accommodate larger private jets like the Gulfstream. The plane touched down smoothly, and the pilot taxied to a private part of the facility while the crew readied the plane for arrival. They came to a stop, and, as Huxley undid his safety belt, he watched through the porthole window as a BMW drew up alongside.

"Come," Maxim said.

Huxley stood and followed him to the door, the stairs were deployed, and he made his way down to the tarmac. The driver of the BMW—another man with military bearing—opened the door at his approach.

"The base is a short drive to the west," Maxim said.

Huxley got into the back of the car. He was tired—he suspected that his body was still recovering from whatever it was that had allowed him to feign the heart attack—and all he wanted to do was sleep. Maxim lowered himself onto the seat next to Huxley. The driver closed the doors, got into the front and pulled away.

Huxley fought to keep his eyes open as they continued to the south. The road led them along the western shore of a large body of inland water before they reached a town that was identified by the road signs as Mol'kin. They drove to its southern edge, then turned off the main road and followed an unpaved track beneath a bridge until it stopped at a checkpoint. The way ahead was protected by a tall chain-link fence and a barrier operated by soldiers in a small guardhouse. A billboard to the right of the gate bore a large poster of a helicopter swooping over a line of tanks.

One of the soldiers emerged from the gatehouse to check their credentials. Huxley saw that he was armed with a holstered pistol, while the man who observed from inside the hut had an AKM-47 automatic rifle. The driver showed them an identity card, and, after a brief conversation between the two men, the guard lifted the barrier, and they drove on. They carried on through what was obviously a military base. Huxley saw armoured personnel carriers lined up in a row and an open hangar with helicopters inside. It was past midnight but still busy, with soldiers in camouflage making their way between the buildings on foot and in the backs of UAZ-469 light utility vehicles. The scale of the place was large, and it looked haphazard and disorganised.

The driver reached a junction where, if they turned to the left, they would continue into the main body of the base. Instead of that, though, he turned right and carried on along the unpaved track to a second facility to the north of the main one. This one, in contrast to the facility that they had just passed around, looked more professional. It was compact, with a series of low-slung buildings set around a paved courtyard. There was a small collection of military vehicles—jeeps and armoured personnel carriers—all painted in khaki green. Behind the complex, perhaps half a kilometre away, Huxley's eye was drawn to a helicopter that was slowly descending to land. He recognised it as a Ka-52—an Alligator—one of the Russian army's best attack aircraft. The rotors clattered as the pilot bought the chopper down to land, the noise abating as the rotors disengaged and the engines were shut off.

The security was more thorough here, too, and there was a second checkpoint. They drove on, passing through gates in two separate fences. The driver pulled up next to a single-storey building and got out, going around the car and opening his door for him.

"Welcome to Krasnodar," Maxim said. "I expect you would like to sleep?"

"That can wait," Huxley said. "I need to speak to your commanding officer."

"My father will be here the day after tomorrow," Maxim said.

"Your *father*?"

"I am Maxim Sommer," he said.

"Your father is Otto?"

Maxim smiled and nodded.

"You're in the Unit?"

"That's right. And this is our facility."

Huxley had heard of Unit 29155, although most of it was apocryphal. They were the equivalent of Group Fifteen, and the fact that they were involved told Huxley that Moscow had taken his plight very seriously indeed.

"What about Timofeyevich?" he said.

"My father and the minister will be travelling from Moscow together."

"Two days?" Huxley protested. "I can't wait that long. I need to see them now."

Maxim rested a hand on Huxley's shoulder. "*Please*, Comrade Huxley. You have had a very difficult few hours. The doctor is waiting to see you. I suspect he will prescribe sleep. Recover your strength. I know you have much that you want to discuss—much that you will want us to *do*—but you will do yourself no favours if you do not allow your body to recuperate."

Huxley wanted to argue, but he knew that it would be churlish. He was tired, and a delay was not going to mean the end of the world. He had the Unit to do his bidding; Christiaan Cronje, John Milton and Björn Thorsson could have another few hours of oblivious ignorance before he turned their lives upside down.

JOHANNESBURG

The meeting of the Fellowship was held at St. Francis in the Forest, a church just to the south of Johannesburg Zoo. Forest Town was a leafy suburb that was home to commuters and the local businesses that catered to them. The weather forecast had suggested that it would be a hot day, and John Milton had taken the opportunity to enjoy a leisurely early morning walk from his hotel. He had been troubled ever since he had arrived from London two days earlier and had hoped that the walk and then the meeting would give him the opportunity to find a little clarity about what he had travelled here to do. The sun on his face had been pleasant, but the exercise hadn't given him the stillness of mind that he had been looking for. He needed the meeting to deliver.

He arrived early and walked up and down Talton Road for twenty minutes, trusting that the website had been accurate and that the advertised meeting was still going ahead. He approached the junction for the third time and saw, to his relief, that a woman had opened the gates and had hung the familiar blue and white sign on one of the pillars. That sign—the two white *A*s inside a blue triangle, together with the motto of Unity, Service and Recovery—was familiar to Milton from meetings the world over. It promised peace and quiet and a chance to reinforce the insulation that he relied upon to keep away his guilt and the fear that, otherwise, he would deal with by drinking himself senseless.

He made his way through the gate and the wooden doors that led into the church. A table had been set up in the vestibule with an urn of hot water, a pile of stacked enamel mugs, jars with ground coffee and tea bags and a plate of biscuits.

An elderly man was behind the table. "Morning. Haven't seen you before."

"First time."

"First time here or first time?"

"First time here."

"Welcome, then. Tea or coffee?"

"Coffee, please."

The man took one of the mugs, tipped in a heaped spoonful of coffee and filled it with hot water. "Help yourself to milk and sugar."

"Thank you."

"What's your name?"

"John."

The man put out a hand. "My name's Eric. You can go through if you like—the meeting starts in five minutes. I know who's sharing today. Her story always makes me feel better about myself. Hope it'll be the same for you."

Milton took a seat at the back of the room. Five rows of ten chairs had been arranged in the hall, but only fourteen people were here. Milton didn't mind that. The room was tranquil, and, with one of the windows open, he had the benefit of the sun on his face. There was a breeze, too, a gentle wind that rustled the banner with the Twelve Steps where it had been hung from a nail in the wall.

The secretary opened the meeting, and, after the comfort of the familiar preliminaries was out of the way, he ceded the floor to the speaker who had been invited to share her story. She introduced herself as Alice and said that she worked in finance in the city. She explained that she had started drinking to excess after she discovered that her sister was having an affair with her husband. Her alcoholism made her unsuitable as a mother, her husband taking custody of the children once it became clear that she was incapable of looking after them. He and her sister had moved in together, and over the course of several months,

Alice had started to see the woman as the cause of all her problems.

"I used what I thought she'd done to blind myself to the real problem—my drinking. You all know how it is— everyone else was to blame for what was happening, and none of it was me. It was stupid. I'd been drinking too much for years, and it was because of *that* that my marriage fell apart. My sister and my husband only got together because of it—because I was intolerable. I treated them both like shit, and it gave them something in common. I still think that they betrayed me, but I know that I had my own role to play in what happened. It's taken me ages to accept that. And for the longest time—for *months*—all I could do was think about how she had betrayed me and how I was going to get my revenge on her."

Alice went on to talk about the campaign of abuse she had waged against her sister: confected accusations that she was unsafe around her children, that she had a conviction for assault, that she had cancer and was hiding it, that she was a drunk driver who had killed a pedestrian in an accident years earlier, and other slanders that were even more outrageous, none of them true.

"They got a protection order against me in the end. I wasn't allowed to see my children for two years. It's only when I admitted that I had an illness and worked out how to live with it that I was able to have them in my life again."

She finished her story by extolling the virtue of the Rooms and how meetings had saved her life. The others thanked her, and the secretary opened the floor for those who wanted to share their reactions.

To his surprise, Milton found himself raising his hand.

"My name is John, and I'm an alcoholic."

"Hello, John," the others responded as one.

"I was listening to what Alice was saying, and I could see similarities with the feelings I have at the moment. I don't usually share at meetings—I'm the one at the back, like this, keeping myself to myself—but I've been coming long enough to know that I get more out of them when I share, too, so"—he spread his arms—"here I am, sharing."

"Well done," the secretary said. "Go on."

Milton cleared his throat. "Alice was talking about how she felt when she was betrayed, and how she felt when she found out that her sister wasn't who she thought she was. I knew someone, once, back before I stopped drinking, who I might have said was a friend. Maybe not a friend, but someone who I could get along with. An acquaintance. I worked for him. He was rich and generous, and, because we got on well and he trusted me, he'd take me out to clubs and parties, and we'd get drunk together. I was younger then, and I didn't know any better. The thing is, I saw parts of his personality that I didn't like, but, because it was my job and because I liked the perks of being with him—the drink and the women and the famous people I saw—because of all of that, I persuaded myself that I could ignore the rest. And then, after a few months, the job came to an end, and that was that. I went and did something else and forgot all about him."

Milton paused, concentrating hard on choosing his words with care. He wanted to be honest, yet there were details about what had happened that he couldn't reveal. He looked down into the dregs of the coffee in his mug until he became aware that the others were waiting for him to carry on.

"It was ten years before I heard from him again. He had another job, and he said the only way he could do it was if I was there to look after him again. I don't know why he wanted me specifically. I think, probably, it was because he thought I'd turn a blind eye to the things that he was doing in the same way that I'd turned a blind eye to it all before. I should've said no, but I didn't, and it turned out that if I thought he was bad before, he was much, *much* worse now. I don't need to go into the details, but I found out that he was doing things that were wrong on so many levels. And the more I've thought about it, the more I can't help thinking that if I'd acted on what I saw before—done something to stop him—then a lot of people who came across him wouldn't have been hurt in the ways that they were."

"You can't blame yourself for what someone else does or doesn't do," Alice offered.

"I know that," Milton said. "But people like us love to blame ourselves for everything that goes wrong, and, with this man, a lot of things went *badly* wrong, and a lot of people suffered."

He paused again. The others could tell that he wasn't finished and let him gather his thoughts.

"There was another man—someone else who worked for my friend. And this man, it turns out, did things to help my friend hurt others. And while my friend is going to be punished for what he did, this other man has managed to get away without any consequences. And that's why I've come here. I can't allow that to happen."

"John," the secretary said, a note of wary caution in his voice, "I'm not sure about you, but I think Alice made it very clear in her share that revenge is never the answer. You're not going to—"

"I'm not going to hurt him," Milton interrupted, annoyed with himself for going too far. "I just want to confront him with the things that he's done, the hurt that he's responsible for—I want him to know that *I* know."

Alice raised her hand. "There was something else I wanted to say, and I forgot," she said. "It's about revenge. I can't remember who said it, but there's so much truth in it: there's no revenge as complete as forgiveness. I would've said that was the stupidest thing I'd ever heard, but, after everything that's happened since and the way I've thought about my own behaviour, I'd say that was worth thinking about. It's not going to be easy to forgive my sister, but I have a better understanding of why it happened now, and I'm going to try."

Milton nodded and joined in the shared sentiment that it was good advice even as he knew that it wasn't in his gift to offer forgiveness to Christiaan Cronje after everything that he had done. That was a choice that only Huxley's victims could make, and Milton knew them well enough to know that they were interested in justice rather than absolution. There was a line between justice and revenge, but it was blurred. Milton knew that staying on the right side of that line was what had been troubling him, and had hoped that the meeting might help him to define that line a little better. It hadn't. He was here to deliver justice for the victims because, without him, they would be cheated of it. Cronje could have surrendered to the police and taken his medicine like Huxley, but he had run. Milton had no choice now. The only way for Cronje to pay for his crimes was for Milton to take his life. Milton told himself that Cronje's decisions had led him to this juncture, and that he himself had no choice. He clung to that as a justification, but murder was still murder, and, even though it had to be done, he knew that he was going to suffer for it.

He would normally have stayed behind to help the secretary clear the room, to put the chairs and tables away, but he wasn't in the mood. He kept thinking about what he had heard, and it made him feel uncomfortable and agitated. He had tried to be better, to make more compassionate choices that might go some way to making up for the things that he had done in the years he had worked for the Group, but now he was going to dip his hands in blood again.

Men like Huxley and Cronje could not be forgiven for the things that they had done or allowed to be done. They deserved punishment, and, however much it might corrode what was left of his soul, Milton knew that he would be the one to deliver it.

8

M ilton walked back into the city, following quieter roads to the south that kept him away from the buzz of the traffic until he was in the centre. He was staying in a hotel on Anderson Street that lacked the glitz and glamour of some of the newer buildings that had sprung up to accommodate the burgeoning tourist trade. His room was cheap and a little unpleasant: the duvet cover on top of the bed was tired and bore a blemish that the cleaning staff had evidently tried—and failed—to remove; the wallpaper was brown, with whorls of grey that looked more like stains than decoration; the windows were covered by the slats of a plastic blind that tried—and failed—to look like wood, with shafts of bright sunlight exposing the dust that hung in the air. The temperature outside had climbed up into the high thirties, and the air conditioning unit was too feeble to do anything to alleviate it; it was hot and sticky and Milton found that the fabric of his loose cotton shirt had stuck to his skin.

There was a knock on the door. Milton was unarmed and would have been concerned were it not for the fact that

the man he had contacted had told him that he would be
coming. Milton looked through the spyhole: his visitor was
in his late middle age, with a beard and wispy hair that had
retreated all the way back on his head. He was dressed in an
unironed shirt and was carrying two bags, one in each hand.
The bag in his right hand was larger than the one in his left.

Milton opened the door and stepped back.

"Good afternoon," the man said, his voice weighted with
a harsh Afrikaans accent.

Milton returned his greeting with a nod. "Come in."

The man stepped inside, shut the door and made his
way to the bed. He hefted both bags onto the mattress and
unzipped them. He was focussed on business and uninter-
ested in pleasantries; that was not unusual for a man in his
particular position, and it suited Milton very well. Milton
had worked with quartermasters all around the world,
although not since his retirement years before. Some of
them were more talkative than others; this one was on the
more taciturn end of the scale.

He addressed the larger of the two bags first. The rifle
would usually have been transported in a case, but that
would have attracted too much attention. The quartermaster had broken the weapon down so that it could fit in
the bag. He took out the lower portion and extended the
bipod so that it could stand on the mattress. He removed the
pins, tugging back on the bolt to take out the one nearest the
front of the weapon. He took the upper part of the gun, slid
the barrel all the way out and fastened the upper to the
lower. He withdrew the bolt all the way, replaced the two
pins and stepped back.

"There you go."

It was a Barrett M107 and Milton checked it from front to
back.

The quartermaster watched him. "All good?"

"Very. Ammunition?"

"The other bag."

Milton opened the second bag and took out a plastic box. He worked off the lid and looked down on two dozen very large calibre rounds. They were Raufoss Mk 211 anti-matériel projectiles that were made for .50-calibre rifles. They were made by a Norwegian company and identified by a coating of white paint with a green circle around the tip. Milton had trained with the round in the SAS and had used it to lethal effect during missions where he had no choice but to snipe his targets, including one of his more ostentatious assignments in Pyongyang.

"You sure that's what you want?" the quartermaster said.

"Used them before. I'll only get one shot—want to be sure it counts."

"That'll count," he said with a grim chuckle. "It'll take the head off an elephant."

That was true enough. The rounds were designed for use against both soft and hard targets, with enough power to punch a hole through light armour. Each cost around sixty-five dollars, restricting their use to government agencies for whom expense was not an issue.

The quartermaster reached into the smaller bag and took out a pair of Zeiss Classic 60mm binoculars. Milton took them and saw that they were brand new.

"Perfect." He laid them on the bed next to the rifle.

"And this," the quartermaster said, handing over a satellite phone.

"Thank you. What about ID?"

The quartermaster reached into his pocket and took out a South African passport. The photograph inside was of Milton, one that had been taken in London before he left. The name of the bearer was listed as Francis Worthington.

"That'll do." Milton put the passport in his pocket.

The quartermaster started to disassemble the rifle. "Anything else?"

"That's everything."

The quartermaster finished with the rifle and zipped up the bag. "Good luck, then. I'm here if you need me."

Milton thanked him, led him to the door and stood aside so that he could exit into the corridor. He went back to the bed and looked at the two bags. He took them and his luggage down to the basement parking garage, walked to the rental that he had parked, opened the boot and put the bags inside. He had a long drive ahead of him before he got to the ranch, and he couldn't really see any point in waiting.

If he left now, he could be in Stellenbosch in time to scout the area tonight so that he could work out a plan of attack tomorrow.

9

Milton drove southwest, following the N1 through the bush until he reached the coast. It was a fourteen-hour drive through spectacular scenery, and he found that his thoughts turned to what had happened to him over the last few weeks and to what he would do once he had tied up this one remaining loose end. Control had promised that his return to the Group was a one-time deal, a requirement that was necessary because of Huxley's specific request for Milton to manage his security, and the obligation had been extinguished once Huxley's true nature had been revealed. Milton would attend to Cronje, and then he would melt away again, secure in the knowledge that he had a powerful ally—an uncomfortable ally, perhaps, but an ally nonetheless—in the Group who would see to it that he would be warned if British intelligence came after him again.

Milton had been provided with a dossier on Cronje. He was forty-five and a native South African, schooled in England and then returning home to serve in the Recces, the country's special forces and counter-insurgency brigade.

He had been invalided out of the army after suffering an injury in an operation in Botswana and had built a career running safaris for rich tourists in KwaZulu Natal. That had not proven to be successful, and he had returned to the military world as a soldier-for-hire. He had seen action in Angola, Sierra Leone and Papua New Guinea and had eventually been introduced to Huxley by a mutual friend. Cronje had worked for Huxley ever since, until, it appeared, his head had been turned by an offer from the Pakistani intelligence service. Details were still subject to the investigation that was being carried out, but the preliminary findings were that Cronje had sold Huxley out. It was suspected that he had helped arrange the failed hijacking of Huxley's private jet and then had let the ISI agents onto his property to kill him, an attempt foiled by Milton and the Group Fifteen agents who had filled out the security detail.

Milton crested a hill and looked down at the open valley beneath him: he saw acres and acres of vineyards with the lights of a large town visible in the far distance. He hadn't given any thought to where he might go once he was finished here, but, as he looked out through the windscreen, he decided that he would stay on the continent for a while. Not in South Africa, perhaps, on account of the fact that it would be best to put a national boundary or two between him and the investigation that would follow after Cronje's death, but somewhere else nearby where he could enjoy the sun and slip into a relaxed pace of life. He had worked in Africa before, but had never had the need to visit. He remembered something that Michael Pope had told him; Pope had travelled through South Africa and Namibia and had said that the Kaokoland region around Epupa Falls was one of the most spectacular places that he had ever seen. The skies there were said to be so clear that the stars were as bright and sharp as anywhere on the planet. Milton knew that he would be able to lose himself there for a month or two without any bother at all.

Milton stopped for an hour in Hanover and then continued, driving for another six hours straight. He passed through Nelspoort and Rietfontein, stopped for another hour at a twenty-four-hour diner outside Laingsburg, and then, with midnight approaching, he passed his first sign for Stellenbosch.

Cronje had bought a large tract of land to the east of the town, using it to run luxury safaris for guests who wouldn't baulk at the prospect of dropping six figures on a week spent on horseback in search of big game. Milton suspected that he had also chosen to make his base here because it would be easier to maintain security; a big open space would give him a better chance to spot someone who might visit with the intention of doing him harm.

Someone like Milton.

He rubbed his eyes and decided that, rather than divert to the lodge now, he would find a room in a bed and breakfast in Stellenbosch and refresh himself. There was no need to rush. Cronje couldn't know that he was here, and he risked making a mistake if he went out when he was tired. He would sleep first, then get something to eat, then head back out to scout the reserve and find a place to do what he had come here to do.

STELLENBOSCH

10

Milton pressed himself flat against the rocky plateau and looked through the binoculars at the lodge on the other side of the valley. The main house was half a kilometre to the east, with the valley widening out between the arms of the rocky ridges and then extending for a full twenty thousand acres. The lodge was separated from the rest of the property by a post-and-rail fence. Milton could see half a dozen thatched cottages with viewing platforms where the guests could watch the zebra, wildebeest and impala as they grazed in the valley. There was a large infinity pool, several smaller outbuildings and a collection of vehicles that he supposed must belong to guests or staff. The main lodge was large, a brick building with a generous thatched roof. It was an impressive estate, and the analysts who had briefed Milton suggested that it was now worth five or six times more than the ten million rand that Cronje had spent when he purchased it a decade ago. Sixty million rand was three million pounds; Cronje was a very wealthy man.

And his property portfolio was not the extent of his

wealth. The analysts had identified two large multimillion-dollar payments that were made to Cronje's Swiss bank account during the last five years and had followed the money back to an account in the Caymans that was owned and controlled by Huxley. Milton knew that the relationship between the two men went deeper than what might have been expected of employer and employee, and the money was further proof—not that proof was needed—that Cronje had engaged in unpleasantness in order to keep Huxley's perversions hidden from view. Milton had spoken to some of Huxley's victims, including the mother of the girl who had killed herself following her own encounter with the financier, and they had told him that their silence had been won after threatening visits from a man with a South African accent.

Milton had all the evidence that he needed.

Cronje had gone out on horseback at just after six that morning. He had been at the head of a line of six horses, four of the others bearing tourists and the sixth, carrying another guide, bringing up the rear. Milton had watched as he led the guests down into the valley and then out into the veldt. They stopped at regular intervals so that Cronje could point out the animals around them. Both he and the other guide had rifles strapped over their backs in the event that they came across anything that might be dangerous.

Milton checked his watch: it was coming up to eight now. He doubted that they would want to be out once the sun was all the way up, and, just as he thought that, he saw movement from the direction in which the horses had gone. He reached for the binoculars and saw the six horses with Cronje in the lead. They were a mile away, and, with the horses moving at a leisurely trot, Milton guessed that Cronje would be in the target box within five or six minutes.

He put the binoculars down and put his eye to the rifle's scope. It had a 30mm tube, external windage and elevation turrets, and a fast-focus eyepiece. He chambered a round, adjusted the rifle until Cronje was suspended in the crosshairs, then watched as the South African put his heels against his horse's flanks, nudging him onto the track that led up to the top of the ridge. The party climbed up to the main building, where two grooms were waiting to attend to the horses. The guests made their way back to their cottages, and Cronje went to the outdoor bar and fixed himself a drink.

Milton took the satellite phone and switched it on. He waited the moment it took for the unit to acquire a signal and then pressed the button to call the number that he had stored in the phone's memory. He put the phone on speaker and rested it on the rock to the left of the rifle's bipod.

Milton put his eye back to the scope. On the other side of the valley, Cronje took out his own phone and held it to his ear.

"Hello?"

"Hello, Christiaan."

"Who's this?"

"Don't remember me?"

"No, I don't. And I'm too busy to be wasting time. Who are you, and what do you want?"

"It's John Milton."

Milton watched through the scope as Cronje paused. The magnification was powerful enough for him to see the confusion on his face.

"What do you want?"

"I know what you did."

"What does that mean?"

"For Huxley. I *know*." Milton slipped the index finger of

his right hand through the guard and positioned it so that the trigger rested between the second and third joints. "The women that you threatened. You made sure none of them spoke about what he did to them. That led to other women being hurt. You're responsible for that."

"Bullshit. You don't know the first thing about what I did for him."

Milton pulled back on the trigger, just a little, and felt it squeeze against its oiled springs. "I spoke to some of the women you scared. You made their lives hell until they swore they'd accept his payoffs and keep quiet."

"Piss off. You don't know shit."

Milton flipped the safety.

"I know everything I need to know."

Cronje's face blackened with anger. "I'll tell you what. You come and try saying that to my face. Say that to me when you're in front of me and see what happens."

"I am."

"You are *what*?"

"In front of you. I wanted you to know the reason for what's about to happen. And I want to see your face when you realise that the chickens have come home to roost."

Cronje looked left and right, the anger had turned into confusion, and Milton knew that panic would not be far behind. He had moments to act before Cronje realised what was about to befall him and tried to run.

He breathed in, held it, and watched through the scope as Cronje turned his head and looked right at him. He was too far away and too well hidden for him to have been visible, but Milton was pleased to think that, in his last moments, Cronje had realised what was about to befall him and why.

He pulled the trigger.

The report was thunderous. Milton felt the backwash of hot barrel gas coming back from the muzzle break and the kick to the shoulder as the rifle recoiled. He kept his eye to the scope and heard the ejected case strike the ground. He chambered a second shot but it wasn't necessary; the first had found its mark.

Cronje had been knocked over as the bullet struck him in the chest.

Milton moved with an efficiency that was born of practice and experience. He broke the rifle down, stowed it in the bag, found and pocketed the ejected case and hurried back to his car.

KRASNODAR

11

Huxley had slept for a full sixteen hours. He had been taken to a doctor on the night of his arrival at the base, and the man—a military medic, from the look of him—had given him a sedative and told him to rest. Huxley had been taken to a simple bedroom in the accommodation block where, lying on a comfortable bed, he had taken the pill, closed his eyes and drifted away. The sleep had been restorative, and, for the first time in weeks, he was untroubled by dreams. He awoke with a foggy head, but that was nothing that couldn't be solved by a long, hot shower and a mug of strong black coffee.

His room was large but austere: a double bed, a desk and a cupboard, with the furniture all made from the same cheap wood and the walls freshly painted in monotonous cream. Huxley was used to opulence and had stifled a protest when Maxim had brought him here; it was better than the tiny cell that had been his world for twenty-three hours a day, and, more to the point, Huxley knew that he was going to need the Unit in the days ahead. Better not to appear ungrateful, at least not until they had done what he was going to need them to do.

He finished his coffee and was about to pour another when there was a knock on the door.

"Comrade Huxley?"

It was Maxim. Huxley opened the door.

"Good morning," Maxim said. "How do you feel?"

"Better."

"You slept like a baby," Maxim said with a smile. "The doctor has asked to see you later to check that everything is as it should be."

"It is," Huxley said with a wave of his hand. "I'm fine."

"Right as rain?"

He was trying to make a joke, and Huxley humoured him. "Exactly."

"I am glad to hear it."

"No more wasting time," Huxley said. "Is your father here?"

"He is," Maxim said. "That's why I came to see you. He is with Comrade Timofeyevich. They wondered whether you would see them."

HUXLEY FOLLOWED Maxim into one of the buildings around the central courtyard. It looked as if it was also used for accommodation, with a series of rooms on either side of a central corridor. Maxim continued to the end of the corridor and opened the door that they found there; it opened out into a space that was evidently used as the mess. It lacked the charm that Huxley had seen in similar facilities at home, with an emphasis here on function over form. There were six tables, each with four chairs upholstered in material that bore a camouflage pattern. The Russian flag was hung at one end of the room and the Hammer and Sickle of the Soviet Union at the other. Two men were waiting for him: he recognised Nikolay Timofeyevich, but not the second man. Timofeyevich was the Russian foreign minister with whom Huxley had been negotiating, and as Huxley approached, he stood and smiled widely at him.

"Tristan," he said, "it is so good to see you."

"Nikolay," he said. "Thank you for taking care of this."

Timofeyevich waved a hand to dismiss Huxley's gratitude. "I'm pleased that we could help. What happened to you was a disgrace. I was shocked when I heard what they had done. You must have had an awful few weeks."

"I've had better."

Timofeyevich was shovelling on the bonhomie a little too enthusiastically. He could pretend that the two of them were friends, but they both knew that wasn't true. Timofeyevich had agreed to help Huxley not because of any closeness between them, but for two reasons: greed and fear. Greed on account of the huge sums that he stood to make if Huxley was able to bring the arms deal to a conclusion; and fear because he had been seduced by the illicit delights on offer when he visited Huxley's private island—and because of his knowledge that Huxley had recorded it all.

"Please—sit. You must be exhausted."

Huxley sat and turned to the second man. "Mr. Sommer?"

The second man smiled and extended a hand. "You must call me Otto."

Huxley had heard of Otto Sommer, but nothing beyond rumour and conjecture. He was a legend, but, such as was the case with most legends, it was difficult to know the line where truth blurred into fiction. Huxley remembered a conversation that he had had with a senior official from the Iranian Ministry of Intelligence. The spook had heard a rumour that Sommer and the Unit had been responsible for the assassination of the exiled separatist Chechen president Zelimkhan Yandarbiyev in Qatar, an expertly coordinated bombing that saw the culprits vanish into thin air. Huxley could recall other rumours that he had heard through the years, breathless whispers of an assassin so careful that there were no known photographs of him anywhere in the world. He was said to be almost supernaturally good, with no target that he could not reach.

Huxley looked at him now; Sommer was not at all as Huxley had imagined. He was of average height and slender build, with salt-and-pepper hair that he wore in a neat, short cut. Huxley knew a little about fine clothes, and he could tell that Sommer's suit was both bespoke and expensive. His brogues were polished to a high sheen, and as he shook his hand, he saw that his nails had benefitted from a recent manicure. His handshake was firm but not overly so, and his skin felt smooth.

"A pleasure to meet you, Comrade Sommer."

"And you. I'm sorry that we did not have time to brief you on what was planned to remove you from custody, but it was difficult to be sure that we would not be compromised. I decided it was better that you knew as little as possible."

"The pill," Huxley said. "What was it?"

"Something cooked up by the chemists at Shikhany."

"Shikhany? Where they make nerve agents?"

He chuckled. "They make more than that. I am told that the drug simulates a cardiac event very credibly."

"That's an understatement. I thought I was going to die."

"And evidently so did your guards. We knew that we would not be able to reach you if you remained in the prison. A hospital, though, and at such short notice?" He shrugged. "That changed the conditions in our favour. It wasn't so difficult."

Sommer's English was good, although his understated accent suggested that he was a native German speaker.

"You're not Russian," Huxley said.

He smiled again. "My accent? I never really lost it."

"German?"

"I was born in East Berlin. I served in the Stasi, and then, when the Wall came down, I made a new life for myself and my family here. The Unit includes men and women from the intelligence services and the military, but only the very best. I believe I command a group of the most effective agents in the world."

"You're very confident."

"With reason," Sommer said. "I won't tolerate mediocrity."

"I hope to put that to the test. Shall we get to business?"

Timofeyevich nodded enthusiastically. "Indeed." He gestured to the tablet on the table. "You gave us the names of three men that you wanted Otto to deal with: Cronje, Milton and Thorsson. Milton and Thorsson have been difficult to find, but not so with Cronje. Otto?"

"Yes," Sommer said. "He was at his ranch in South Africa. Two of my agents had him under observation, and then they saw this."

Sommer took the tablet, tapped the screen to wake it and rotated it so that Huxley was able to watch the video that had been cued up. The still image showed a man who was in the process of taking a drink. It looked as if the shot had been taken from some distance away, the image magnified through a telescopic lens. Huxley pressed play and watched as the man turned to the camera; it was Cronje. He watched as he put a phone to his ear and engaged in a conversation that, judging by the expression on his face, was vexatious. He looked confused and then angry and then, as the conversation continued, frightened. Cronje gazed out into the distance, as if looking for something, before something struck him in the chest with enough force to throw him backwards. Huxley heard the sound of a gunshot shortly thereafter, and then the footage stopped.

"When was this?"

"Two hours ago," Sommer said. "My men were reconnoitring the ranch and had decided to wait until Cronje went out again in the evening before taking action. Of course, that won't be necessary now. An ambulance attended the property, but the only useful thing the crew could do was to take away his body. His injuries were... well, let's just say they were considerable. He was dead before he hit the ground."

"What about the shooter?"

"My men said he fired from well over a thousand metres away. That's a challenging shot for any sniper. He knew what he was doing."

Huxley dragged his finger on the screen to scrub back through the footage, Cronje staggered upright, and the splash of red was sucked back into his chest. Huxley dragged back until Cronje had the phone to his ear and then let it play. "Who's he talking to?"

"We had an intercept on Cronje's phone," Sommer said.

He took the tablet, navigated to another file and tapped play.

"Hello?"

"Hello, Christiaan."

"Who's this?"

"Don't remember me?"

"No, I don't. And I'm too busy to be wasting time. Who are you, and what do you want?"

"It's John Milton."

"Fuck," Huxley said. "Did your men go after him?"

"The terrain there is difficult—the lodge is on an escarpment that sits above a narrow valley. My agents were on the same slope as Milton, but not close enough. They made their way to where the shot was taken, but found nothing. There is a track to the south, and they found fresh tyre prints there. It looks like he parked there, trekked to the sniping position and then left. I'm afraid we don't know where he is now, but you can be assured that we are looking."

"Why would Milton do this?" Timofeyevich asked.

Huxley thought of Milton and how he had changed in the time since he had first known him. He had been a ruthless, pitiless killer when they had worked together before, but the intervening years had seen him dig up a conscience from somewhere. He had insisted that Milton be assigned to protect him until the arms deal was signed between the Russians and the Indians; it was not lost on him that that decision, and Milton's reaction when he found out about the island, had very nearly cost him everything.

"Milton is a machine. Relentless. If he thinks you've done wrong, he'll keep coming until he thinks it's been made right."

"Then you think he will come after you?"

Huxley gestured to the tablet. "You saw what he did. He'll come after me—no question."

"Then we are fortunate that he doesn't know where you are."

"But we don't know where *he* is, either."

"We will," Sommer said. "The GRU has agents in South

Africa who are friendly with the police. They'll tell us if they discover anything else."

"What about Björn Thorsson?" Huxley said. "Is he there, too?"

"No," Sommer said. "We are in a better position with regard to him. He is in Finland with his girlfriend. Time off to recuperate from the injuries he suffered while he was working for you. A holiday."

Huxley held his eye. "You can get to him?"

"Of course."

"Don't underestimate him. He'll be cautious."

"I would not have lasted as long as I have if I made a habit of taking our targets lightly. Please—tell me that you would still like to proceed, and it will be done."

Sommer was confident, but, rather than diagnosing arrogance, Huxley knew that he was a man who could back up his words. The reputation of Unit 29155 was fearsome, and Timofeyevich had vouched for Sommer personally.

"Yes," Huxley said. "Yes, of course. I want it done."

Sommer stood. "Then that's that. Thorsson first and then Milton. I'll get onto it straight away."

Huxley stood, too. "There's one other thing."

"Yes?"

"I want them to know. I want them to know that they brought this on themselves. *Especially* Milton. I want him to know the cost of betrayal."

THE MEETING CAME TO AN END, and Huxley made his way back to his room. He was still tired, so he undressed and lay down on the bed. For the first time since his arrest, he felt as if he had a measure of agency over his life. Sommer was as impressive as advertised, and the Unit had demonstrated its effectiveness time and again. Huxley knew enough to know that the Kremlin had established a number of small groups over the course of the last few years. Western intelligence had only been able to get a sense of them, without anything substantial by way of details. Huxley had learned as much as they had through his own contacts both inside and outside of Moscow. He knew, for example, that the hackers of Units 26165 and 74455 had been responsible for breaching the servers of the American Democratic National Committee and the Clinton campaign, unearthing embarrassing communications and then publishing them for the world to see. And he knew that Sommer's unit—29155—was staffed by men and women who practised more direct forms of action, including sabotage and assassinations. Huxley was well connected, but even his queries had initially been rebuffed. The operations of the Unit were so secret that its existence was unknown even to other GRU operatives.

He chuckled. It was not lost on him that the collections of operatives were not dissimilar to what London had built over the last forty years. The Firm—and the fifteen groups that comprised it—had been put to uses similar to the ones that Moscow had now found for its own units. Milton had risen through the ranks of Group Fifteen until he had become its lead agent; Sommer would have an equivalent, and that man or woman would now be unleashed. There was a pleasing symmetry to it that appealed to him.

A poetic justice that what Milton and Thorsson had done to him would now be done to them.

Otto Sommer stepped out of the mess and went out into the courtyard. He crossed it and went into one of the other buildings on the other side. This one was reserved for planning and operational matters. He went through to his office, took off his jacket and hung it up.

His secretary was sitting at her desk outside the door.

"Could you ask Maxim and Lukas to come and see me, please?"

"Yes, sir."

He sat down at his desk, woke his screen and opened the file that Timofeyevich had sent to him when he had been tasked with working on Huxley's business. John Milton was out of reach for the moment, but the second target—Björn Thorsson—was not. He opened the folder with the photographs that had been taken of him and his girlfriend as they enjoyed their time together on holiday. The Icelander was an enormous man, and his girlfriend—a Russian by the name of Olya Sokolov—looked like a little doll at his side. They had been followed by a GRU team for the last week and had been photographed at tourist spots across the country: a visit to Rovaniemi to watch the Midnight Sun, a day trip to the Åland islands, watching the orcas off the coast of Finnish Lapland. Sommer knew that Thorsson would be cautious, but there was no reason for him to be concerned for his safety in Finland, and the men and women who would have been assigned to watch him were the best; they would have been particularly careful.

"Father?"

It was Maxim, his eldest son. His brother Lukas was behind him.

"Come in," Sommer said, gesturing to the two chairs that sat in front of his desk.

The two boys were twins. Both had been officers in the Naval Spetsnaz, serving in the 431st Naval Reconnaissance Brigade, until Sommer had requested that they be moved across to the Unit. They had served in Syria, first to provide training to Assad's forces and then in helping to secure the Latakia and Tartus naval facilities. They were both excellent soldiers with distinguished records.

They took the chairs on the other side of the desk.

"I spoke to Huxley," Sommer said.

Maxim cocked an eyebrow. "What did you make of him?"

"Spoiled and entitled. He speaks like a man who expects everything to be done for him. I don't like him at all."

"Neither do I," Maxim said.

"But we still have orders to do what he wants?" Lukas said.

"We do. We are to keep him safe and make him happy, and he wants us to go ahead. I think it is something that need not detain us for very long—Thorsson should be easy, and Milton just needs to be found. Neither of them has any reason to know that they are targets. Have you studied the file?"

"Yes." Maxim took out his tablet, selected a photograph of Thorsson and turned the screen so that his father could see it. "Are you sure? A serving British agent?"

Sommer waved away his son's concern. "It would hardly be the first time."

"And the Kremlin is happy?"

"Do you think I would have taken the job if it would have caused a problem?" He shook his head. "Of course not. Huxley might be an oaf, but he is important to them. Keeping him happy is worth a little turbulence with the British over the death of one of their killers. And the president sees this as a chance to make a point. Group Fifteen has been involved in Russian business for years. The decision has been taken that it cannot go on. We will deliver a message that that is unacceptable. A message they won't be able to miss."

"What does that mean?" Maxim said. "Not poison?"

"Not this time." He shook his head. "Something that can't be mistaken for anything else."

Lukas gestured to his brother. "Do you want us to do it?"

"No," Sommer said. "Alyosha."

Maxim frowned at that. "Are you sure?"

"This needs to be *obvious*. Your brother is many things, but subtle is not one of them." He leaned back and waved his hand at the two of them. "Anyway—he is already on his way."

Maxim and Lukas were evidently unconvinced, but they knew better than to argue with their father when he had made up his mind. They would both have done a more professional job than Alyosha, but Alyosha was more than capable of following these particular instructions. What was more, he had complained for weeks that he was not given the same work as his brothers. That was true; Alyosha's last assignment had been the assassination of Grigori Nikolaevich in London, and his botched preparation had meant that the aim—to make it look as if the oligarch had hanged himself—had not been met. There had been a struggle, and Alyosha had left contusions on Nikolaevich's face that made suicide an unlikely cause of death. Sommer had been reluctant to give him the more difficult work after that.

It wouldn't matter this time. He could leave as many marks as he wanted.

Lukas flicked a finger on the screen to scroll through to the next photograph. "What about this one? Milton?"

Sommer nodded. He hadn't heard of Thorsson, but the fact that he was Number One made it obvious that he was a dangerous man and worthy of their respect. But Sommer *had* heard of John Milton, although not by his real name. He had requested a search of the FSB files prior to taking the meeting with Huxley, and the photograph of Milton that had been supplied matched no fewer than six images that had been recorded and stored over the course of the last decade. He had been active in Russia and in countries where Russian interests were at play, working under a variety of different aliases: he had been Charles Turing, a teacher who taught Russian children how to speak English in St. Petersburg; Oliver Powell had crossed the border with documents that suggested he was involved in the export of vegetable oil; Julian Nightingale had visited Moscow under the pretext of selling vintage sports cars to oligarchs who were looking for ways to fritter away their money.

There was one constant throughout: regardless of his legend, Milton left a trail of death and destruction wherever he went. Turing had murdered the army general who had been responsible for the death by shelling of British embassy staff in Syria; Powell was suspected in the death of a Moscow businessman who had fallen to his death from the balcony of his apartment in Moscow's Neva Tower. The earliest file that Sommer had seen suggested that Milton, travelling this time as John Smith, had travelled to Russia to avenge the death of a Russian defector who had been shot to death in a sleepy English seaside town.

"Father?"

"Milton is dangerous. He will require *very* careful handling. Alyosha will be responsible for Thorsson, but the two of you have Milton."

Lukas nodded with satisfaction. "Of course. Where is he?"

"He was in South Africa this morning—he shot and killed the third man on Huxley's list. The FSB are looking for him there. I would send you now, but I doubt he will stay in the country. Be ready to move—as soon as we know where he is, you will both go. Put the jet on standby."

LOWESTOFT

13

Lilly Moon had been waiting in the reception area of Irwin Wilson Bishop for twenty minutes. She had arrived in plenty of time for the appointment with her lawyer, but was still waiting to be called through to the conference room. She had asked the receptionist if there was a problem, but the woman had given her a withering look and told her that Mr. Irwin was just finishing a phone call and would be with her as soon as he could. The woman had turned back to the magazine that she had been reading, and although Lilly had been tempted to tell her that she was a client and she expected better than to be kept waiting like this, she knew it would do more harm than good, and, with a tight-lipped smile, she went back to her seat and continued to wait.

She picked up a dog-eared copy of a gossip magazine and flipped through the pages. It was a parade of pointless vapidity, and it didn't hold her attention; she put it back on the table and stood up, walking over to the window and looking out onto Lowestoft High Street. It was a Wednesday morning, and the shops—the ones that were still open, at least—were quiet. It was a warm day, and the forecast was good for the next fortnight. Lilly had a job to do at work that would require her to be in London as soon as this meeting was concluded, but she had arranged for a week's leave when she returned and was planning on spending it with her daughter on the beach.

"You can go through," the receptionist said.

Lilly made the effort to thank her, but the woman's attention was already on her magazine again. Instead, Lilly opened the door to the conference room and went inside. Her lawyer, John Irwin, was just opening the ring binder that sat on the table in front of him. There was a box with other files on the floor, and, as she sat down, Lilly saw LILLY JANE MOON v JAMES ARTHUR MOON on the upward-facing spines.

"Morning, Lilly," Irwin said. "Sorry for the delay. Bit of a coincidence—your husband's lawyer wanted to speak, and I thought I'd better take the call."

She sat down. "Really? What did he want?"

He winced a little. "I'm afraid it's not good news. Jimmy is definitely going to make the application."

"You said he wouldn't."

"We didn't think he would, but..." He shrugged in what he might have hoped was a helpless gesture, but looked pathetic instead. "His lawyer won't tell me what he advised, but I'm about as sure as I can be that he would have told him not to do it. Whatever he said, it hasn't made a difference. Jimmy has clearly made up his mind."

Lilly swore under her breath and slumped back against the chair. "He's just doing it to score points."

Irwin winced again. "He says that he had decided that he

would agree to joint custody until he found out that you left Lola again."

"What?"

"Last week?"

"I had to work," she protested. "I left her with my *mother*."

"He's going to say that you're not at home enough to give Lola the attention that she needs."

"It's my *work*," she protested. "I don't have a *choice*. I want to stay at home, but I can't. I have to travel."

"Couldn't you see whether your employer could keep you here until the hearing is over?"

"It doesn't work like that. It's not that kind of job. Foreign travel was always part of it."

"All right," Irwin said, gesturing that she should relax. "All right. It'll be fine. We'll work around it."

"How does he know?"

"Sorry?"

"That I was abroad. I didn't tell him. How does he know?"

"I think it's very likely that he has a private investigator on his team."

"Come on. He's *watching* me?"

"It would be a good idea to assume that. He has a lot of money."

Lilly clenched her fists beneath the table. She had to be careful about her private security on account of her work, and the thought that Jimmy was paying someone to spy on her would have been funny if it wasn't so potentially dangerous.

"That does bring us to the other thing that I wanted to talk to you about," he said.

She sighed. "Money?"

Irwin shrugged apologetically. "Our advice was to reach an agreement with him before the hearing. It seems unlikely that that's going to be possible now, so we're left with no choice—we're going to have to start the preparation."

"And how much will that cost?"

"I'll be honest. A contested hearing isn't going to be cheap."

"Just spit it out."

He sucked his teeth. "Your husband has instructed a barrister from one of the more expensive chambers in London. We'll want to get someone who can go toe to toe with her. The minimum for that—the preparation and the hearing—is going to be twenty thousand. That's the *minimum*—it might be more."

Lilly closed her eyes. "Jesus."

"I'm afraid that's not all. We agreed not to charge you for the time that we've spent until later, but we've accrued a significant amount now, and my partners aren't comfortable with us continuing until that's been settled and we have some money on account to take us up to trial."

"How much do you need?"

"We've got a shade over twenty-three thousand on the clock, and they've asked me to get another ten on account."

"Thirty-three thousand."

"Plus a retainer for the barrister," he reminded her. "It's a little over fifty."

Lilly felt as if things were slipping away from her. "But when we win, Jimmy has to pay that back? Right?"

"Probably not. Courts very rarely make orders for costs in custody proceedings. Each side will have to pay their own fees." He smiled sympathetically. "I know it's a huge amount of money, and I'm sorry to have to ask—but do you have access to it?"

Fifty thousand? The question was so preposterous that Lilly wanted to laugh. She had supported Jimmy through all his asinine plans and schemes until he stumbled upon the opportunity that had finally made him rich. He had found an opportunity that enabled him to flog scammy cryptocurrency to anyone gullible enough to fall for his patter, and had been involved early enough to be near the top of the selling pyramid to be pulling down sixty or seventy thousand a month. He would never have been able to get there without her, and the injustice of what he was doing now—flinging the money that she had enabled him to make at his lawyers in a bullshit macho display to force her to buckle—was so unfair as to make her feel physically sick. He had moved back to Dublin, buying a vast seven bedroom mansion on the coast at Howth, and here she was, still struggling to make ends meet while fighting him court with both hands tied behind her back.

Lilly had been a soldier for most of her adult life, and that was a profession that was never going to make her rich. She had recently transferred to a new role that paid much better, but still... it wasn't remotely similar. She knew roughly how much she had in the bank and how much she could make if she cashed in her pension. She supposed she could ask her mother, but it wasn't as if *she* was well off, either, and Lilly hated the idea of being in debt.

Irwin was still looking at her. "Lilly? I'm sorry to have to press, but I think it's much better if we are completely transparent about what we're going to need if we're going to take this forward."

"It won't be a problem," she said, hoping that she had been able to put enough certainty in her voice to persuade him that she was good for it.

"Are you sure?"

"Not a problem."

"That's great. My secretary will prepare the invoice and email it to you this afternoon. If you could arrange for a bank transfer to be made before the end of the week, we'll get started."

The unsaid threat was obvious: if you don't pay us, we won't be able to work for you any longer. She would be left to face Jimmy's legal team on her own. She would have done it, too, save for the fact that the stakes were too high. Lola would be taken away from her if she lost. Jimmy had more money than he knew what to do with, and Lilly knew that he would shower it on their daughter and get her everything that she wanted. Lola had told her mother that she didn't want to live with him, but Lilly was terrified by the thought that he might be able to buy her love. How much would it take for Lola to forget about her?

Lilly's temples throbbed with the start of another migraine, and she closed her eyes again in the hope that it might pass.

"Lilly? Are you okay?"

She opened her eyes and forced a smile. "I'm fine. A little headache, that's all."

"It can be stressful," he said.

"I just want to get it over with."

"And we will. I'd still hope that we can settle before the hearing, but, even if we can't, that'll be the end of it. You have a good case. Everyone can see how much Lola loves you. I know it's been a long slog, but we're on the final straight, and I'm as confident now as I was when we started."

Lilly stood. "Anything else?"

"No," he said. "That'll be all for now. We'll need to start preparing your witness statement next week—I'll be in touch."

Lilly thanked him, left the room and continued through the reception and into the courtyard outside. The office was set back off the street, facing an empty building that had once accommodated the branch of a regional department store. It had closed down years ago, along with many of the other units on the street. There were benches outside it, and Lilly went over to one and sat down. She was still in something of a daze. That much money was so far out of reach that it might as well have been a hundred times more.

The worst thing was that she had brought all of this on herself. She had precipitated the end of their marriage with a mistake that she had immediately regretted, and had tried to make up for it by being honest with Jimmy. He had reacted badly, and that—her moment of madness—had been the start of a nightmare from which there seemed to be no emerging. Lola was the most important part of Lilly's life, and now Lilly's mistake risked losing her, too.

She blinked back the tears. *No.* It wasn't going to happen. She wouldn't let it. She wiped her eyes and, suddenly paranoid, looked up and down the street. The only people around were those whom she would have expected to see: an elderly man in a blue shirt sitting on the next bench along, a woman pushing a shopping trolley, a younger woman corralling two squabbling children. Lilly would have backed herself to spot someone who was surveilling her, and none of the men and women around her set off any of her warning signs. The thought of it—and the thought that Jimmy's paid help had been spying on her with Lola—filled her with anger and a determination that she was not about to give up.

It was a lot of money to find, but she would manage.

She had overcome longer odds than this to get where she was in her career; a vengeful husband using their daughter against her was not about to beat her. She straightened out her jacket and checked the time. It was a little after nine, and her car to London wasn't due yet.

She still had time to see Lola before she needed to set off.

WILDERNESS

14

Milton had been driving for five hours when he decided that it was time to stop. He had been following the coastal road and had just reached the small town of Wilderness, fifteen minutes east of George. He saw a sign for the Old Post Office Lodge and pulled over. The building had an open hatch that offered food and drink from a small Italian restaurant. There were tables beneath a shaded veranda; Milton decided that a strong espresso and something to eat were just what he needed. He parked and locked the car and crossed over to the restaurant. The waitress was busy with another diner, so Milton took a seat in the shade and waited for her to become free.

He had given thought to his route as he had left the ranch. Cape Town was the closest airport, but Milton had decided against it for that very reason. It would be the easiest and most obvious way for him to leave the country, and he would rather put a little distance between himself and the ranch before he took the risk of subjecting himself to airport security. He dismissed Johannesburg as too large and well organised, as well as being the next most obvious choice. Durban and Nelspruit were too far. He settled for Port Elizabeth: an eight-hour drive along the famous Garden Route. The road was bordered by the Outeniqua and Tsitsikamma Mountains, with the road passing a panoply of picturesque lagoons and coves and crescent beaches of untrammelled white sand. It had been a pleasant drive, and the scenery had distracted him enough that he hadn't dwelt too much on what he had just done.

He had decided to fly to Madagascar. He had considered driving across the border to Namibia, but concluded that it would be better to put a little more distance between himself and the investigation to find out who had shot Cronje. He had read that it was possible to swim with whale sharks off the coast of the northwestern island of Nosy Be, and, after that, he would spend time exploring Antananarivo, the island nation's chaotic, vibrant capital city. The investigation would be stymied by the time that he had seen everything he wanted to see.

"Good morning, sir," said the waitress, handing him a menu. "Can I get you something to drink?"

"An espresso," he said, "and a glass of water."

"Of course."

There was a television on the wall inside, and the hourly bulletin had just started. Milton watched it as the waitress went to the coffee machine and prepared his drinks. The presenter ran through the headlines: a fire had broken out in the parliament building in Cape Town; the life of a beloved archbishop would be celebrated at a memorial service; hundreds of big cats had been seized after an investigation into a worldwide trafficking ring. The waitress delivered his coffee and water and had just removed her notebook to take his order when the newsreader cut to the final story.

The backdrop was a picture of Tristan Huxley.

"Excuse me," Milton said, pointing at the screen. "Could you turn that up for me?"

The waitress found the remote control and turned up the volume so that Milton could hear what was being said.

"...was being treated for a suspected heart attack when he was taken by armed men who shot and killed the prison staff who were with him. Huxley was facing charges of sex trafficking and blackmail, and, given his wealth and influence, his trial was expected to be of significant interest later this year. Police have reported that they do not have any idea who took him or where he might be."

The presenter handed over to the sports reporter, and there followed a piece on the Springboks' most recent Test against Australia. Milton stared at the screen, his thoughts still fixed on what he had just seen. He had followed the updates on the case in the news, and from what he read, it was expected that Huxley would be found guilty and given a minimum of twenty years behind bars. Milton had not expected that the quest to deliver justice to the victims would be straightforward. Huxley was rich beyond reason and had assembled a powerful legal defence team that would have presented all manner of challenges to the lawyers from the Crown Prosecution Service who would make the case against him. But now this? He thought of the victims; what about them? What about Hazel Lewsey, the mother of Roxanne and the widow of Rufus; her family had been destroyed by what Huxley had done, and Milton knew that she—and the others who had been tormented by Huxley's perversions—needed their days in court.

What would they be thinking now?

"Sir?" the waitress said.

"I'm sorry," Milton said, smiling at her. "Million miles away."

"Awful, isn't it," she said, nodding at the screen. "Are you English?"

"Yes," he said.

"What he did was a pretty big story here—can't imagine what it must be like over there."

"It's a big story."

"And now he gets out? That's not right." She took out a pen. "Anyway—what can I get you?"

Milton ordered a bowl of pasta and a salad and stared up at the screen as the bulletin came to an end. He wondered what he should do, and concluded that there was no point in doing anything until he was safely out of the country. He would find a meeting when he arrived in Antananarivo and use it to try to find a point of balance from which he could assess his options. He would speak to Thorsson, too, and find out who the intelligence services thought might be behind what had happened. And then, once he had that, he would locate Huxley. He would have been better served staying in prison and accepting his fate. Milton had given him that choice, and Huxley had refused it.

Now Milton would have to deliver justice the *other* way.

HELSINKI

15

Björn Thorsson woke up, and for a moment, he couldn't remember where he was. He looked up at an unfamiliar white ceiling and then turned his head to the left to the open window, a gentle breeze sending ripples through the fabric of the thin curtain. He looked to his right and saw that he was alone in bed, although the covers were disturbed, and he could see the indentations against the mattress that said that he had not slept by himself. He closed his eyes again and exhaled, smiling as he remembered that he was in Suonenjoki and that he had come here with Olya. He breathed in and out again, heard the sound of activity from the kitchen and smelled fried bacon. He remembered: she had teased him about his cooking last night and had promised to prepare breakfast for them both today.

The two of them had only been together properly for a month. She had known his sister, and he had always thought her a bad influence on her until he had grown to know her better in the aftermath of Gudrún's murder. Thorsson had been flattered that someone as good looking as Olya might be interested in him, and it had taken him six months before he had accepted that her attraction was real.

This week had been the longest time that they had spent in each other's company, and Thorsson was surprised—and pleased—to find that they had got along together so well. He had had little doubt that they would be compatible in a physical sense—he knew *he* was attracted to her, in any event—but he had always found her a little brash before and had worried that they might have clashed. That hadn't happened. He was lacking in emotional intelligence, but even he could see that the brash exterior was a mask that Olya wore to hide behind. She was tender and kind and intelligent and pretended to be a bitch in order to deflect the attention that she received from men whenever she went out. He had seen the way they looked at her, and had made a point of ensuring that it was obvious that she was with him. Thorsson was a big and daunting presence, and other men quickly turned away when they realised that he had clocked them.

He swung his legs out of bed, wincing from the pain as he pushed himself to his feet. He had been caught up in the explosion from the suicide bomb that had been intended for Huxley, and, although the wounds were healing nicely, he was still sore. He stood and looked around. The cottage was a tiny place, with just a single bedroom, but it had been perfect for them. They had spent the last week getting to know one another, getting up late each morning and then driving out to visit places that Thorsson knew that she would enjoy. There was a hot tub on the deck, and they had spent their evenings in it, drinking chilled champagne and talking until the nights turned to dawn.

He pulled on his dressing gown and went through into the living room. "Good morning."

"About time. I thought you were never going to wake up."

"Late night," he reminded her.

"Hungry?"

"Starving."

She took three of the rashers of bacon that she was frying on the stove, laid them on a slice of freshly rye cut bread and slathered on a decent amount of mustard. She added a second slice of bread and put the sandwich on a plate. "Here."

She made a sandwich for herself, and they took their food to the dining table to eat.

He took a bite out of the sandwich. "One day left. What do you want to do?"

"We'll need to pack."

"That won't take more than an hour, will it?"

She shook her head.

"So we can do that tonight. We have the whole day before then. I was thinking this?"

He handed her his phone and watched as her face lit up.

"Dogsledding? But it's not snowy enough."

"They pull carts in the summer," he said. "You said you like huskies."

"*Love* them," she cut across, correcting him.

He took another bite. "There we are, then. That's settled. They do two-hour trips with a stop for lunch—we just need to get there for eleven."

She looked at her watch. "That's three hours. What could we do until then?"

She grinned at him, put her sandwich down, reached out for his hand and tugged him back to the bedroom.

16

Thorsson said that it would take forty minutes to get to the place where the dogsledding took place. He showered and dressed and then waited for Olya to get ready.

"Come on," he called out. "We don't want to miss it."

"I take longer than you," she complained.

That was true, he thought wryly. He had never spent that much time on how he looked. He supposed it was something that had become habitual after his time in the Regiment. The personal ablutions of a soldier could be boiled down to three things—shit, shower and shave—and he had never really shaken the routine even though he had been out for years. He had tried to hurry Olya along before they went out for dinner in Helsinki on the first day that they arrived in the country, and she had very quickly disabused him of the notion that she could abbreviate the time that she needed.

There was no television in the cottage. Thorsson had insisted on that when they were looking for somewhere to stay; he wanted to be disconnected from the news as much as possible and just spend the time getting to know Olya. He hadn't taken any sort of break for years, and he had known that he would enjoy it more if he didn't have to worry about the things that were happening in the world that might end up requiring his involvement. He would have liked to leave all his devices behind, but there was always the possibility that he might be needed. Being completely off the clock was not something that he could entertain, at least not until the day when he was moved from the Group.

Olya emerged from the bedroom wearing a monochrome outfit of top and leggings and a scarf with an outsized Chanel logo.

Thorsson rolled his eyes.

"What?"

"We're going *dogsledding*."

"So?"

"It's not the Oscars."

She pouted. "I don't see anything wrong in trying to look my best."

"You'd look lovely in a sack."

"I can get changed if you like," she said, a sparkle in her eye.

"That's all right," he said. "We need to get going. We're cutting it fine as it is."

They went outside. Thorsson locked the door as Olya made her way down the path to the Mercedes convertible that they had hired.

"I'm driving," she called out.

"Fine."

"*And* it's my turn to pick the music."

He followed her. "Are you sure? Didn't you—"

"I had to put up with Sigur Rós on repeat yesterday. I

made a playlist on my phone last night when you fell asleep. We're listening to that."

"Fine," he said again, smiling.

She got into the driver's seat and opened her handbag to look for her phone. Thorsson went around to the passenger side and opened the door.

"Shit."

He lowered himself into the seat. "What?"

"My phone. I left it in the house."

"Where?"

"Kitchen counter."

"I'll get it," he said. "But I can't promise I won't drop it on the way back."

He swivelled around so that he could get his legs out. He loved the car, but it wasn't the most practical. He was six-four and big with it, and even with the seat pushed all the way back, there was still only just enough room for him. He wasn't just tall, though; he was wide, too, and the seats were designed for normal-sized people. It would have made much more sense for him to have rented a larger vehicle, but they had both been taken by the thought of doing it in style. The weather had been kind in that it hadn't rained, but it was still cold. That hadn't stopped them from lowering the roof, and Thorsson was hoping that they might be able to get away with doing the same today.

He went back to the cottage, took the key from his pocket, unlocked the door and went inside.

They hadn't washed the pots and pans after their meal last night, and Thorsson had to search to find Olya's phone. It wasn't on the kitchen counter but, instead, was on the edge of the sink in the bathroom. He picked it up and tapped the screen, unable to stop his smile as he saw the photograph of the two of them that a stranger had taken in front of the Pihtsusköngäs waterfall. The picture of the two of them with their arms raised, tons of water from the seventeen-metre drop crashing into the plunge pool behind them, was one of his favourites. The screen faded to black, and he made his way back through the kitchen, snagging the last *korvapuusti* from the bag they had bought at the bakery yesterday morning and munching on it as he stepped out of the house.

"Got it," he called, holding up the phone before turning back to lock the door.

"My phone or the bun?" she called back through the open window.

"It was the last one," he protested. "You said you didn't want it."

She shook her head in mock exasperation and then reached for the ignition.

Thorsson saw the flash, a bloom of bright yellow light that seemed to shine from the bottom of the chassis before engulfing the car, and then he found himself lying flat on his back, his eyes screwed tight shut and his ears ringing.

He was totally disorientated.

He could feel intense heat and smell burning. He levered himself up into a sitting position and forced his eyes open. There was a wreck in front of him and he realised that it was the car, obliterated, engulfed in a roiling cloak of sooty yellow flame.

He climbed to his feet and staggered unsteadily towards the fire before the heat and the realisation that there was nothing he could do stopped him in his tracks.

He stood, staring into the flames, slack jawed with shock.

17

T horsson saw someone in the tree line across the track that led to the road.

"Help!" he yelled.

It was a man. He was standing in the gloom between the trunks of the tightly packed trees. He just stood there, and as Thorsson blinked his eyes back into focus, he saw him raise a submachine gun and take aim. He threw himself to the ground as the gun barked. Bullets streaked out, thudding into the wall of the cottage and blowing out the kitchen window.

Thorsson was shielded by the burning car and obscured by the pillar of smoke, but knew that was only a temporary reprieve. He got to his feet and, staying as low as he could, ran for the cottage, shouldered his way through the door, and fell inside. He had no idea what he was facing—the identity of his attacker, nor how many there were—and until he knew more, the only tactical choice that he could make was to get as far away from the property as he could.

He made his way to the back of the cottage, pausing at the door to the kitchen until he could be as sure as possible that the door to the deck had not been breached. He could still smell the breakfast that Olya had prepared, see the plates stacked up in the sink ready to be washed later when they had returned. He crouched down low and hurried to the counter, selecting a chef's knife from the knife block and holding it in his right hand, the handle tight against his palm and his fingers up against the guard.

He closed his eyes for a moment and tried to bring his pulse back under control. Who was outside? He wasn't naïve —he had made a lot of enemies in the years that he had worked in the Group—but he had always been scrupulously careful with his personal security, and, at least as far as he knew, only Olya knew of their plan to come here for a break. He hadn't told anyone, and, although he had warned her that it would always be better to be careful with the information she shared with anyone else, he found himself wondering whether she might have said something to give them away. He had warned her against using social media; might she have ignored him? Thinking of her led to a flashback of what he had just seen—the transformation of the car into a pyre in less time than it would have taken him to click his fingers. She had been strapped inside, dead from the blast or the flames or the smoke.

She was gone, and she had died because of him.

He thought that he heard the sound of the broken front door; the hinges were in need of oil and they squeaked a little each time the door was pushed back. He pressed himself against the wall, painfully aware that he was presenting a target to anyone who might be on the deck, yet unable to leave until he was sure that he wasn't making himself vulnerable to a shooter approaching along the hall. He slowed his breathing and tightened his grip on the knife; he thought he heard the pad of a footstep, and then, as he looked up at the fridge-freezer that was directly opposite, he saw a flash of movement in the polished stainless-steel door.

Thorsson heard another footstep, then the sound of a breath, then saw the slatted muzzle break of a submachine gun as its bearer slowly edged into the kitchen. He saw it bit by bit: the front sight, the gas cylinder above the barrel. The gun was held professionally, left hand cradling it beneath the barrel jacket. Thorsson let the man continue inside, and then, as he revealed his forearm and then the side of his shoulder, Thorsson angled the knife and plunged it into the man's chest. The blade scraped against his sternum, and Thorsson yanked it out and stabbed again, this time leaving it where it was. The man tried to call out, but Thorsson clamped a hand over his mouth and grabbed him, heaving him all the way into the kitchen and then down onto the floor. The man was wearing black tactical pants and a black jacket. He reached for the handle of the knife and tried to pull it out; Thorsson helped him, then turned the blade and slashed it across the man's throat.

The weapon was a modified PP-19 Vityaz submachine gun. Thorsson took it and frisked the man quickly, finding two stun grenades in pouches that were attached to the jacket. He took both and stood, glancing around the edge of the doorway and into the hall just as a second man came through the door. He swung back again as a barrage of automatic gunfire punched a neat collection of holes in the door of the fridge.

"Come out," a voice called.

"You come in here."

"You're outnumbered. Let's not make this difficult."

The man had a distinctive accent: Russian.

"Are you sure about that? I just killed your friend."

Thorsson glanced out of the window into the rear of the

property and saw nothing. He might have an opportunity to escape that way, but if he did—and he couldn't be sure— then it wouldn't likely be available for long. He took one of the grenades from the dead man's pouch, pulled the pin and tossed it into the corridor. It exploded, sending out a starburst of white light and a thunderclap that added to the ringing in Thorsson's ears. The men who had attacked him must have been professional operators, and, while Thorsson didn't expect to cause panic with the blast, he knew that there was a chance that the man would have been blinded by the flash.

He cradled the PP-19 in both hands, slipped his finger through the trigger guard and turned into the hallway. The man who had been there must have taken shelter when he saw the grenade; Thorsson used a quick salvo to persuade him of the good sense in staying where he was, then turned and ran. He kicked down the flimsy rear door, rushed by the hot tub where he and Olya had spent so much time, then bounded down the steps of the deck and stumbled on the loose gravel path before finding his balance.

A path led through the woods at the back of the house. It descended to the shore of Lake Kuvansi, and Thorsson headed for it.

PORT ELIZABETH

18

Milton checked the time: he still had nearly two hours before he needed to make his way to the gate. He hadn't rushed the drive, trying to stop his thoughts about Huxley as he followed the Garden Route along the coast. It hadn't been entirely successful, but as he passed around Buffels Bay, he found a radio station that was playing eighties rock, and the music—Foreigner and Blondie and Whitesnake—gave him the peace of mind he needed.

Milton sipped his water and looked around the waiting area. There were plenty of families, some parents were struggling with fractious babies and toddlers, and others pacified older children with cartoons and games on their tablets. There were also single travellers, like Milton, most likely passing through the airport on business. He found himself thinking of all the airports that he had passed through while he was still working for the Group, of the broken families that he had left in his wake, the bereaved wives and husbands and the children from whose lives a parent or parents had been erased. He thought of the job in the French Alps that had triggered his crisis of conscience.

"Mr. Milton?"

Milton turned and saw a man approaching him quickly from behind. He was dressed in a grey suit, a white shirt and cheap shoes.

"I'm sorry?"

"John Milton?"

Milton was caught off guard, he was travelling as Francis Worthington, and there was no reason why anyone here would know who he was. But this man clearly *did* know who he was, and Milton could see there was no sense in disputing it. "Who are you?"

"My name is Brody. I work at the consulate. We had a call from London that you would be at the airport, and I was asked to come and meet you."

"How did you know that?" he said, and then, thinking better of it, told him not to answer. "How can I help?"

"I'm afraid I'm the bearer of bad news. You need to fly to London."

Milton shook his head. "Why?" he said. "Is this about Huxley?"

"No," he said. "At least, I don't think so. That's not what I was told. Do you know a man named Björn Thorsson?"

"What about him?"

"He was attacked this morning." The man took a step closer and lowered his voice. "His car was bombed, and then he was shot at by two men."

Milton stood, took the man by the elbow and guided him to a quieter part of the gate. "Is he dead?"

Brody shook his head. "He escaped, but his girlfriend was killed."

"And they think it was Huxley?"

Brody shook his head. "They didn't say. But they thought you'd want to know."

Milton exhaled and drummed his fingers against the handle of his carry-on. Thorsson wasn't what Milton would call a friend—he didn't really have *any* friends—and he didn't owe him anything. But he had turned out to be a straight shooter, and Milton didn't wish him harm. And it might not have been Huxley. Thorsson was Number One, filling the same role that Milton had filled before he had quit. The Icelander, like Milton, would have made enemies over the course of his career; Huxley was just the most recent. But it was a coincidence that an attempt had been made on his life just after Huxley had been broken out of custody. Milton didn't like coincidences. And if it wasn't a coincidence, if it was Huxley, then it would mean that Huxley would come after him, too.

That changed things.

Brody nodded to the gate. "I'd hate for you to think I was being presumptuous, but since you're at the airport already..."

"You have a ticket?"

He held out an envelope. "And a new passport. You leave in an hour."

KRASNODAR

19

O tto Sommer got up from his desk and went to the window that looked out onto the missile range. A group of his agents were exercising with Kornet anti-tank missiles. The system was more diffi-cult to master than the Western Javelins, but just as effective; he watched as a missile was ejected from the launcher, its engine igniting and sending it in a straight line that ended with a direct hit against the hull of the derelict T-72 tank that was being used for target practice. He heard the whoop of jubilation as the agents surveyed the aftermath of the clean strike.

Sommer nodded in satisfaction. The men and women who were recruited to Unit 29155 were the best of the best and were deployed only where nothing else would do. The biggest jobs of the state could be serviced by the merce-naries of the Wagner Group and the other PMCs that had sprung up to fill the Kremlin's need for deniability, leaving the Unit to attend to the more difficult assignments that required deeper planning and more skilled operators. It also provided Sommer with the power and prestige that he would not have thought possible when he had been left penniless and homeless after the end of the Stasi career that came with the lifting of the Iron Curtain. He often thought back to that time: the death of his father at the hands of a British agent, the days filled with the frantic burning and shredding of documents and files, and then running from the mob as they stormed and occupied the East Berlin head-quarters. Sommer had fled into Russia and had lived hand to mouth for weeks until his application to join the KGB had been accepted. That had been difficult enough, but to then be caught up in events as the KGB, too, was dissolved made for another six months of uncertainty.

He was a survivor, though, and had managed to right himself. The KGB became the FSB, and there were opportu-nities in the new organisation for those prepared to be as ruthless as he was, and he had made sure to take advantage of every single one. He had been sent to South Ossetia for the war and had traded on a number of intelligence successes to reinforce and then advance his position. He had worked hard to ensure that a *silovik* president—an officer with a background in the Soviet *nomenklatura*—won the election, and then stayed behind to eliminate those who sought to discredit the result.

And now? Money and power. Sommer owned properties in Cap d'Antibes, St. Barts and Salzburg; the MV *Angela*, a two-hundred-foot-long yacht named for his youngest daughter; a private jet and a fleet of cars. His salary would not have been enough to afford the annual cost of fuelling the yacht, but President Putin was a generous man who rewarded those within his circle, and Sommer had done more than enough to ensure that he was showered with roubles. His father had been a Generalleutnant in the Stasi and had enriched himself with the loot that he had hidden in the basement vault beneath the Pfarrhaus on Roedelius-platz that had been his headquarters. Sommer had thought that his own chances of enrichment had been taken from him by what had happened, but, by dint of ruthlessness and hard work, he had built a life that was the equal of anything that his father had managed. He had reason to be satisfied with what he had achieved, but it wasn't enough; he still wanted more.

One of his female agents—Tatiana Tesershkova, he thought—fired a second missile; it streaked across the range and crashed down onto the battered T-90.

There was a knock on the door to the office.

"Yes?"

The door opened. Sommer's aide-de-camp, a former FSB agent called Dmitri Morozov, came inside. He looked anxious.

"What is it?"

"I'm sorry to bother you, sir."

Sommer stopped, saw that it was more than just anxiety that was making Morozov uncomfortable, and felt sick. "What is it? What's happened?"

Morozov swallowed. "It's Alyosha."

"What's he done now?"

"I'm sorry, sir. He's been killed."

"No. That's impossible."

"It's..." he stammered, then paused to gather himself. "I've just been sent this from a contact in Finland."

He was holding a printout of what looked to be a police report. Sommer saw lines of text, in Finnish, but gave them only a moment's attention. His eye stopped on a photograph that had been taken of a dead man. The body was lying against a wall, with a bloody wound sliced across the throat.

Alyosha.

Sommer put the paper down and bit against the inside of his lip.

"I'm very sorry, sir."

Sommer mastered himself. "What happened?"

"We're not sure. He was found inside the cottage that was being rented by the target."

"Alyosha wasn't alone, though, was he?"

"No, sir. He was working with Aleks Sergeev."

"So why are *you* telling me what happened to my son rather than *him*?"

"Sergeev stayed where he was and waited for your orders."

"My *orders*? My orders were to terminate the target. Did he at least manage that?"

Morozov shifted from foot to foot. "No, sir. He reports that Thorsson wasn't in the car when the bomb was detonated. Alyosha pursued him into the cottage and..." He stopped, the sentence unfinished.

"And?"

"And there was a struggle. Thorsson stabbed him to death."

Sommer stared at Morozov, but he wasn't really looking at him. The image of Alyosha was fixed in his mind, and he couldn't erase it. His youngest son had been on at him for weeks for a chance to prove himself. He lacked the sophistication of the twins, but a job like this—two men against a target who had no idea that he was under threat—should have been a simple thing.

And now he was dead?

"Sir?"

He brought his attention back to the room. Morozov was still in front of him.

"What?"

"What do you want me to do?"

"Get Sergeev back here. This should've been easy. I want to know how he could fuck it up."

"Yes, sir."

"What do we know about Thorsson? Where is he?"

"We don't know."

"Find out. And find the twins—I want to speak to them. I should've known not to listen to Alyosha. They wanted to do it—I should've listened. I won't make the same mistake again."

LONDON

20

M ilton was tired when he finally arrived at Heathrow. He had tried to sleep on the flight but his concern about what he had learned about Huxley had made it impossible. He paid to access the in-flight Wi-Fi in the hope that he might be able to find out a little more, but there was nothing beyond what he already knew. Milton guessed that the story had been suppressed on the grounds that his escape was embarrassing. He could imagine the furore it would have created in the intelligence community. An operation like that would not have been easy to plan and execute. Huxley had access to almost limitless funds and so would have been able to hire the very best in the world to get him out, but there was also the possibility that this might have involved agents from hostile states. The Pakistani ISI had already tried—and failed—to get to him in an attempt to stop the arms deal. Could it have been them? And if not, then who? The Russians and the Indians would both want to conclude the deal, and having Huxley working on it again would make that more likely. What about third parties? Huxley had *kompromat* on important and influential people all around the world. Could he have called in a favour? Could it have been an inside job?

A driver was waiting in the Arrivals hall to collect him. Milton followed him to a car in the short-stay car park.

He got into the back. "Where are we going?"

"Vauxhall Cross," the driver said, pulling out into the queue of slow-moving traffic.

MILTON HAD NEVER EXPECTED to be back at the Global Logistics building, but here he was again for the second time in weeks. The red-brick office was the headquarters for Group Fifteen, the operations of its twelve agents cloaked behind the activities of the real company that did legitimate business inside its otherwise anonymous walls. The driver took Milton inside and handed him over to a woman whom Milton recognised at once as an agent. He hadn't seen her before, but she had the unmistakeable bearing of someone with time served in the military.

"Which one are you?" he said as he followed her into the lift.

"What?"

"What number are you? Five? Ten?"

"Twelve," she answered as she pressed the button for the third floor.

There was a little hesitation in her eyes; that she was Twelve meant that she was the latest addition to the roster, and Milton guessed that her recruitment had been triggered by the death of Number Six in the grounds outside Huxley's mansion. That was the thing about Group Fifteen: it was a closed shop, with only twelve positions available. One coming open usually meant that an agent had been killed and that everyone behind that dead man or woman would be moved up a slot. Her apprehension might also have been as a result of *his* standing. Milton took no pleasure in it, but he knew that his status as a previous Number One—and the notoriety that had followed his resignation and the manhunt that followed—added a little extra frisson to his reputation.

"A word of advice," Milton said as the lift slowed to a stop. "You'll last a little longer if you don't trust anything they tell you."

"If I need your advice, I'll ask for it," she said. The doors opened, and she gestured that he should step out. "This way, please."

"It's all right. I know the way."

He didn't wait for her, walking across the open floor that was set out with desks for the analysts who were channelling the information that flowed into the building. He carried on to the corridor on the other side of the floor, passing from the old vinyl tiles onto thick carpet as he followed it around to the right. The noise and activity behind him faded away. He faced a row of doors that were backed with green baize and picked the one at the end. There was a desk outside it from where a man Milton recognised from before guarded access to Control.

"Number One," he said.

"Not anymore. I forgot your name."

"Weaver."

"Weaver—that's right. She wants to see me?"

"She does." He gestured up to the green light above the door. "You can go in."

Milton shook his head in wry amusement; he had knocked on this same door a hundred times before, and he had thought—he had *hoped*—that he would never have the occasion to do so again. Huxley had brought him back the first time, and now the Icelander had brought him back again.

"Come in."

21

M ilton opened the door and went inside.
Control was sitting at her desk, her chair
turned so that she could look out of the wide
picture window at the Thames beyond. The glass was dusty
and smeared with a white streak of excrement from one of
the gulls that swooped over the water.

"Mr. Milton," she said.

"Control."

"How was your flight?"

"Long. And annoying."

"I'm sorry to inconvenience you, but you'll agree that
this is necessary." She gestured to the chair on the other side
of the desk. "Please."

Milton sat down as Control called Weaver and asked
him to bring through a pot of coffee. She steepled her
fingers on her desk and looked over them.

"You did what you needed to do in South Africa."

Milton nodded. "He got what he deserved."

"So I understand. A .50-calibre round?"

"I wanted to make sure."

"You certainly did that," she said. "The quartermaster was helpful?"

"He was. Thank you for arranging it."

"And did Cronje know it was you?"

"We spoke beforehand. He knew."

She wouldn't be fazed by what he had just told her. Dealing out death was her business. Milton wondered how many red-lined files had passed across her desk to be distributed among the agents under her command.

There was a knock on the door, and Weaver came in with their refreshments. Control took the jug and poured coffee into two cups. She handed one to Milton and took the other for herself.

Milton took a sip. "You'd better tell me what's happened."

Control stood, went to the window and looked outside. "You know about Huxley," she said. "He was found unresponsive in his cell and was taken to Queen Elizabeth Hospital for treatment. The guard and the medic from the prison were killed, and he was taken."

"Unresponsive?"

"Heart attack—at least that's what they thought. He was taken to the infirmary, and the doctor who saw him said that was what had happened. On reflection, though, knowing what we know now... no. I don't think so."

"Faked?"

"That would be my guess."

"He'd need help to do something like that."

"I agree—he would. It was well planned and executed. It was a professional job."

"But who?"

"We don't know."

"No idea at all?"

"All we can do is speculate. Someone who's afraid of what he might have on them or someone who can profit from his business. We both know how well connected he is."

"And how much dirt he had."

"Quite. It could be anyone."

"Any idea where he's gone?"

"None. We've analysed activity at all ports and airports, and we haven't found anything."

"It'll be a private flight."

"Yes, and we're looking. We're working through everything that left the country to see if there's anything that might give us an idea."

Milton sipped his coffee. "You don't know very much at all, do you?"

"No," she said. "I don't."

"Tell me about Thorsson."

"That's why I wanted you here. I owe it to you to be completely honest. I'm concerned that you're in danger." Control took a tablet from her desk, woke the screen and swiped to a photograph. "Look at this."

Milton took the tablet. The photograph showed the blazing wreck of a car. The bright yellow flames and thick black plume of smoke rising from the fire obscured most of the detail.

"That's Thorsson's car?"

"Yes."

Milton swiped left and looked at a photograph of the same car that had been taken after the blaze had been extinguished.

"And his girlfriend was inside when it went up?"

Control nodded. "Olya Sokolov. At least she wouldn't have suffered."

"Definitely a bomb?"

"The Finnish police are still investigating, but Thorsson is clear: there was an explosive device under the driver's seat that detonated when she started the engine."

Milton stared at the picture of the burned-out car. "What about him?"

"He went back into the house because she'd forgotten her phone. He was on his way back when the bomb exploded."

"And then?"

"A shoot-out. He thinks there were two men. He killed one of them and got away."

"Where is he now?"

"Still in Finland. I would have preferred for him to come back, but he wouldn't have it. He wants to find who did it."

"It doesn't have to be Huxley. He'll have other enemies."

"That's true, but I think it's unlikely. Until we know otherwise, I'm assuming that the two events are linked. Huxley has the money. And he has the influence and connections."

"And a motive."

"A very good one. You can see why I wanted to warn you."

"You think he'll come after me."

She nodded. "Don't you? That's why I thought you might like to be involved."

"I'm not worried about myself," he said. "Someone will get to me eventually—him or someone else. But the thought of him escaping justice for the things that he's done?" He shook his head. "I have a big problem with that."

"What would you propose?"

"Find him."

"And then?"

Milton held her gaze. "What do you think? What I

should have done before. I'm assuming you wouldn't have a problem with that?"

"Would it make a difference what I thought?"

"No."

She chuckled. "You're a free agent, Milton. I'm not responsible for anything that you might or might not do. And if you were to get a copy of the report that Number One filed this morning... that wouldn't have anything to do with me, either."

There was a printed document in front of her. She pushed it across the desk.

Milton took it. "Does this have the location of the attack?"

"Yes. Why?"

"I want to go and have a look."

"I was hoping you'd say that. Do you want a lift? I'm flying there this afternoon." She looked at her watch. "Now, actually. You can come with me if you like."

22

The government jet was waiting for them at Biggin Hill. Weaver drove them onto the airstrip and opened the door for Control. Milton stepped out, too, and looked over at the Gulfstream that would deliver them to Helsinki. The captain was conducting a visual inspection of the plane as they crossed the tarmac, climbed the steps and boarded. Weaver came too, exchanging words with the crew and then going to his seat as the steps were brought in and the door closed.

Milton sat on the port side of the aircraft and looked out as the captain cycled up the engines and waited for permission to taxi out to the runway. This, too, brought back memories that he would have preferred to keep buried. He had used similar aircraft, usually owned by companies that could not be traced back to the government, to fly into and out of the countries where he actioned the files that he had been given. At least this time was different. He was choosing to take action, rather than blindly following orders.

Control sat down in the seat on the opposite side of the aisle and buckled herself in as the plane began to move.

She glanced over at him. "Tell me about my predecessor."

"Pope?"

"No. Before him. Harry Mackintosh. What was he like?"

Milton frowned and didn't quite know what to say. It was as if she were trying to engage him in small talk, and the effort—so unusual, both from his limited interactions with her and his longer experience of those others who had held her role—was confounding.

"He was Control for all of the time I was in the Group," he said.

"He selected you?"

"Him and the Number One at the time."

"Beatrix Rose."

Milton nodded. "He wasn't particularly social. It was always all business with him."

She steepled her fingers. "I studied his career. It was never obvious why someone who was as well regarded as he was would go bad like that. There was never even the slightest suggestion of impropriety. None."

"He was greedy, and he saw a way to make a lot of money. I don't think you need to dig any deeper than that."

The jet turned onto the runway.

Control was looking at him. "What about you?"

Milton shook his head. "There's not much to say."

"Why did you leave?"

He had no desire to talk about himself. She might pretend to be convivial, but Milton was not naïve enough to think that there wasn't an agenda to the conversation. "I'm sure you've read my file."

"Of course I have. The psychologists had a field day with you, as you can probably imagine. But I don't think I knew much more about you after I'd finished reading it than I did before."

"I'm afraid you won't find out anything interesting today, either."

The engines roared as the jet raced down the centreline. Control leaned back in the seat and looked out of the window as they took off, climbed quickly through the mist and drizzle, passed through the clouds and emerged into the cold blue afternoon.

HELSINKI

23

Milton and Control were met at Vantaa by a driver from the embassy. He opened the doors for them and they set off, navigating the snarl of traffic around the airport and then cutting through the city to the south.

"Have you been here before?" Control asked him.

"Once," Milton said.

"For a job?"

He nodded.

"My mother worked here during the Cold War," she said. "I went to school in Helsinki for six months before they sent me back to England to board."

He nodded again, uncomfortable with her candour and unsure what she wanted him to say.

"I remember it being cold and dark," she went on. "And having the Soviet Union over the border gave her work an edge you didn't find anywhere else. She liked it, though. My parents bought a summer house here after they retired." She looked out of the window with what Milton took to be a wistful expression. "It's the kind of place I could imagine ending up once all this is over. Do you ever feel like that?"

"Like what?"

"Like you might enjoy a life away from everyone and everything? Their place was in the middle of nowhere. You could go days without seeing anyone else."

"That does have a certain appeal."

She laughed, as if realising that she had just said something foolish. "Of course—stupid of me. You've been doing that for years."

THE EMBASSY WAS a large building that looked as if it might once have been the residence of a well-to-do Finnish family. It had been painted pink with white window frames and a grand white-painted portico. The driver stopped at the apex of a turning circle, and they got out, climbed the stone steps to the entrance and went inside.

The ambassador was waiting for them.

"Good afternoon," she said to Control. "How was your journey?"

"Fine," she said. "Where's my agent? I'd like to get started straight away."

"He's waiting for you inside. This way, please."

The ambassador led the way through the building to a conference room. Thorsson was sitting at a large table with a view of the gardens.

He noticed them and stood. "Ma'am."

"Are you all right?"

Thorsson nodded. "Fine."

He looked from Control to Milton, and, for a moment, the two of them locked eyes.

"Sit," Control said. "I'm sorry about your girlfriend."

"Olya..." Thorsson started. "She forgot her phone. I went back to get it and..." He stopped again, looked down, bit down on his lip and then looked up at them; his eyes burned with anger. "I went back to get it, and the bomb went off when she started the engine. I couldn't get her out."

Milton's inclination was to tell him that it wasn't his fault, but he knew it was trite and that Thorsson would not appreciate it. "You said there were two of them?"

"At least two. I killed one and then ran." He looked at Control. "It was Huxley, wasn't it?"

"We don't know yet," she said.

"It must be him."

"We're trying to confirm it."

Thorsson turned to stare at Milton. "We should have popped him when we had the chance."

"We don't know that it has anything to do with him," Control said before Milton could agree. "You've been in the job long enough to have made plenty of enemies."

Thorsson ignored her and kept his eyes on Milton. "Is he the vindictive type?"

Milton nodded. "Vindictive, with rich, powerful friends."

"Do you think it's him?"

"I do."

Control raised both hands. "There's no point in speculating. I agree—it's likely. There's a good chance it is him, and we're looking into it. We *will* find out."

Thorsson looked as if he was ready to retort, but held his tongue.

"I've read your report," Milton said to him. "Is there anything you didn't put in it?"

He nodded slowly. "I've been thinking about it. The second shooter spoke to me when they came after me in the cottage. I've been trying to place his accent. Might have been Russian."

"Anything else?"

"No. That's it. Everything else is in the report."

"What about the local police?" Control said.

"They've asked me to come for another interview this evening. Beyond that, though, nothing. They won't speak to me about it."

Control stood. "Unacceptable. I'll speak to the ambassador. We'll run our own operation separate from theirs. London is taking this very seriously."

Thorsson eyed her. "Not as seriously as I am."

"No. Of course not."

"What do you want me to do?" Thorsson said.

"Go to the interview. The problem with the police will be sorted by the time you're done."

Thorsson stood, too. "Thank you, ma'am." He turned to Milton. "You didn't say why you were here."

"You're right. We made mistakes before. I'm going to make sure we don't make them again." He got up. "I'll come with you."

24

M ilton and Thorsson went outside and got into the car that the embassy had supplied. Thorsson started the engine and glanced into the mirrors as he backed out of the parking space. "Huxley, then?" he said.

"It could be."

"What about his head of security? The South African?"

"Cronje?" Milton shook his head. "No."

"Why not? He got shot—there's his motive."

Milton held Thorsson's eye. "It's not him."

Thorsson gave a slow nod as he understood what Milton was implying. "You said you were going to visit him."

"I did."

"And?"

"He threatened the women and their families. Huxley wouldn't have been able to get away with what he did without him." Milton shrugged. "He got what was coming to him."

The headquarters of the Helsinki Police Department was to the north of the embassy. It was housed in an ugly building of concrete and glass, with a row of police vehicles lined up on the road outside it. Thorsson had to drive around the block until he found somewhere to park, and then the two men walked back to the entrance.

"What have they said so far?" Milton asked as they went inside.

"Not much. The detective told me that they only get seventy or eighty murders a year, and most of those are domestic. A bomb like this? Couldn't be more out of the ordinary."

"They're out of their comfort zone?"

"It took them a day to find someone who knew anything about explosives. They had to get a sapper from the army."

They reached the desk, and Thorsson explained to the officer sitting behind it that he had an appointment to see the detective investigating the murder. The man looked at his screen, told them to take a seat and made a phone call.

They didn't have to wait long. A woman made her way from the interior of the building and came over to them.

"Stefan Jóhannsson?" she said, looking from one to the other.

"That's me," Thorsson said. Milton was not surprised that he was using an alias.

The woman looked at Milton. "And you?"

"John Smith," he said, using his own old legend.

"I'm here to see Detective Kekkonen," Thorsson said.

"There's been a change of plan. You can speak to him later."

"I'm sorry—who are you?"

"Johanna Räikkönen."

"I'm sorry. I don't—"

"I'm the chief of the Helsinki Police," she cut over him. "I just had a call from the Minister of the Interior. I've been told that we have to cooperate with you."

It was evident from the tone of her voice that she had been given instructions and wasn't thrilled about having to follow them.

"I promise we won't get in the way," Milton said, trying to mollify her.

She snorted. "You're already in the way."

"We just want to help."

"We can manage," she said, then, perhaps thinking better, shook her head. "Never mind. What do you need from us?"

"Where are you with the investigation?"

"No witnesses and no motive," she said. "Unless you could help me with that—have you been able to remember anything?"

Thorsson shook his head. "Nothing more than I've already told you."

"Forensic evidence?" Milton pushed.

"Nothing," Räikkönen said. "The autopsy on the dead man is tomorrow morning, not that I can say I'm expecting much."

"Could we be there?"

She grimaced. "The pathologist can be cranky with outsiders."

"We'll stay well out of the way."

"It won't be pleasant. How's your stomach?"

"We'll be fine," Milton assured her.

"Whatever," she said. "I'll make the arrangements. Anything else?"

"Do you think we could go to the cottage?"

She shrugged. "I don't have time to take you—if you want to go, you'll have to drive yourselves."

"Of course."

"I'll call ahead and let them know you're on your way. When do you want to go?"

Milton looked at his watch. "It's nearly seven. It'll be dark soon."

She smirked at him. "No, it won't. It's summer, Mr. Smith. White nights. There will be barely any darkness here for another month."

25

M ilton's last visit to Helsinki had been in winter, when there was barely any sunlight at all. He hadn't thought of its obverse, the summer months when the sun remained above the horizon for almost all of the day. The difference between day and night was marked only by the change in the nature of the light, the sun took on a reddish-yellow tint, and everything was washed in a warm, bright light.

Thorsson was quiet as he drove them to the cottage. Milton wasn't about to start a conversation, happy to let him dwell on his thoughts, but, as they left the city limits, the Icelander tapped his fingers against the wheel and then glanced across the cabin.

"I haven't been back there yet."

"You don't have to. I can take care of it."

Thorsson frowned angrily. "That's not what I meant. It'll be better if I show you what happened rather than let the police make a mess of it."

"I'm just saying—there's no shame in taking a back seat."

"You ever had anything like this happen to you?"

"People I care about? Yes. More than once."

"What'd you do about it?"

"It's not about—"

"Did you take a back seat?"

"No," Milton said. "I found out what had happened and…" He let the sentence drift.

"Exactly," Thorsson said. "I don't know why you'd think there'd be any difference between the two of us."

He was angry, and Milton understood why. Thorsson fell back into a gloomy reverie once again. The atmosphere in the cabin matched the bleakness of the Finnish landscape outside: icy blue lakes, grey hunks of volcanic rock and flat terrain that stretched all the way to the horizon.

～

MILTON COULD SEE why Thorsson and his girlfriend had chosen the cottage: it was a cosy little building, but it was its position—on top of an escarpment that offered a glorious view of the landscape beyond, the forest and then a vast lake —that made it so attractive. The bucolic charm was spoiled today, though, by the burned-out wreck of a car and a police patrol car that was parked next to it. Two officers stood outside the cottage, one was speaking on the phone, and the other was smoking a roll-up cigarette. Thorsson pulled up alongside, and Milton got out.

The officer put out his cigarette, flicked the butt away and raised a hand in greeting. "Good evening," he said in excellent English. "The chief called to say that you would be on the way. I'm Detective Saarinen."

"You're in charge?"

Saarinen nodded. "It's my case. My colleague over there is Detective Litmanen. Are you Smith or Jóhannsson?"

"John Smith," Milton said. He pointed to where Thorsson was unfolding his frame from the cabin of the car. "That's Jóhannsson."

"I've been told to let you have whatever you need."

"That would be very kind."

"So? What would you like to do?"

Milton looked over at the cottage. "I wouldn't mind just having a look around, if that's all right?"

Saarinen pointed to several cardboard boxes of disposable gloves and overshoes that stood on a table that had been set up just before the first stretch of crime scene tape. "You'll have to wear those, though. Can't have anything being contaminated."

Milton crossed the road and approached the cottage. The exterior walls bore the evidence of gunfire, with a series of holes chewed into the wooden facing. The panel in the door had been shot out, with jagged remains of the glass still stuck in the frame. He went to the table, took out a pair of nitrile gloves and overshoes and pulled them on. Thorsson greeted the two officers, joined Milton at the table and put on gloves and shoes.

Saarinen drifted over to them as they signed the crime scene log.

"What can you tell me about the bomb?" Milton asked him.

"What do you want to know?"

"Composition?"

"TNT. But there was a blast and then the fire... finding evidence is proving to be challenging. Nobody will say anything for sure until the forensic investigation has been carried out."

"The arming mechanism?"

"It was connected to the ignition of the car."

"Where are the remains now?"

"At the laboratory. Do you want to see them?"

"No," Milton said. "But it would be helpful if the results could be sent to London."

"I've already been told to see to that. They'll be sent as soon as we're finished with them."

The two detectives waited outside the cordon as Milton lifted up the crime scene tape and stepped underneath it. Thorsson followed, pushing open the remains of the door of the cottage so that they could make their way into the hall.

"What do you think?" Thorsson asked him once they were out of earshot.

"TNT? Standard filling for most legacy Russian mines and shells. It's not something you'd find on its own in western munitions."

Thorsson shrugged. "Doesn't have to be Russian. A lot of older Finnish equipment is based on Russian designs."

"True. Then again, it could also have been a bag of loose TNT flake or powder. They'll have a better idea in London."

Thorsson nodded. "The man who came after me sounded Russian. You think it could be the GRU?"

"Too early to be sure," Milton warned, "but maybe."

Thorsson ignored Milton's note of caution. "Huxley was working on a deal with the Russians."

"That doesn't mean it's them."

"But they could have got him out and then done this."

"Maybe."

Saarinen came inside, and they shared a look, both knowing that discretion was preferable to honesty.

Milton gestured around the room. "You've checked for prints?"

Saarinen nodded. "Of course. Nothing."

Milton saw the remains of a stun grenade on the floor

and knelt down to examine it. It was around twelve centimetres tall from top to bottom, a bulbous sphere attached to a longer stem. The pull ring had been yanked out.

Saarinen looked at Milton. "Do you recognise it?"

"It's a flash-bang," he said. "A stun grenade."

"It's a Zarya-3," Saarinen said. "We checked. The Russians use it."

Milton led the way into the kitchen. The body had been removed, but not the bloodstains that told of what had happened here. Bullet holes studded the stainless-steel door of a large and expensive-looking fridge-freezer, and the windows had been shattered by stray rounds. There was a knife on the tiled floor, the blade marked with dried blood.

"The shooter came into here," Thorsson said.

Milton pointed to the knife. "You used that?"

He nodded. "Twice to the chest and then across his throat. I took his weapon and went out through the back door and into the woods."

"What did he have?"

"A PP-19."

Milton nodded. The Vityaz submachine gun was Russian, too.

"Let's go out the front again," he said.

They ducked under the tape, pulled off the gloves and overshoes and dumped them in a box that had been reserved for trash. Milton walked to the car. It had been thoroughly destroyed: the glass had fallen from the windows, the chassis had been buckled by the force of the blast, and then everything had been consumed by fire. Even the asphalt had been blackened, with spots bubbling up from where the heat had been the most intense. Milton had no experience in forensics, but wondered whether it might be useful to have the Group send a bomb technician to look at the wreck.

He turned to Thorsson. "Where was the shooter?"

Thorsson pointed into the trees. "There."

"Show me."

Thorsson led the way across the road and into the trees. There was an oak tree and, behind that, a screen of heather. The vegetation had been pressed down just to the left of the tree. Milton turned to face the cottage and knelt down. The spot offered a good vantage of the building; it was obscured by the low plants but still offered an excellent line of sight.

"Looks like they both waited here," Milton said. "Look at the vegetation. It's wide enough for two men, not just one. And there's this." He pointed at the remains of two cigarettes, then indicated the dog-end to the left. "I smoke. That one looks like a Marlboro. And that one"—he pointed to the right—"is a roll-up. I don't know many smokers who'd smoke both." He turned to Saarinen. "I'm surprised you didn't collect the butts. Have you searched this area properly?"

Saarinen frowned. "I was told that it had been done, but I can see that it wasn't done properly. I'll see that it's checked again."

"It might be worth running a DNA check on the cigarettes."

"They'll be tested."

Milton stood and parted the bushes so that he could get back to the road.

"What do you think?" Thorsson said.

"Whoever was waiting there was sloppy. I wouldn't have left evidence like that. You know the routine—you pick up everything when you leave."

"It didn't go like they planned. They might have been thrown off by what happened."

"Come on. That's no excuse. You're either professional or you're not."

Saarinen caught up with them. "Do you have any idea who it might've been?"

"No."

"Russian, though?"

"Possibly."

Milton thought it very likely that the men were from across the border, but that didn't mean that they had been sent by the state. Could they have been from one of the mercenary groups who were brought into theatre when the government wanted space between themselves and its operatives? There were plenty of them; the Wagner Group, most obviously. Whoever it had been, they had made a series of elementary errors. They had left evidence of their presence in the woods, and, even more damning, they had failed in doing what they had come here to do. They had the advantages of surprise and numbers over Thorsson, and, given that, a bomb was an unnecessarily flamboyant way to kill him. They could have broken into the cottage at night or ambushed him on the road.

It should have been easy. Why had they made it more difficult?

Were they trying to make a point?

Saarinen's phone rang, and he stepped away to answer it.

"How about the Indians?" Thorsson suggested. "They wanted that deal to go through."

Milton shrugged. "Huxley has enough money to hire private contractors. He has connections in Latin America. There are plenty of groups who'd take his cash for something like this."

"The ISI?"

Milton thought about that. The Pakistanis had sent agents to kill Huxley, and two of them had been shot and killed. One of their agents had gone to ground; could he have been given orders to avenge the deaths? "We can't rule anything out."

Saarinen rejoined them, tucking his phone back into his pocket. "The post-mortem has been brought forward to eight tomorrow morning. Do you still want to go?"

ISLAMABAD

26

A bbas Kader waited in the lobby outside the conference room and picked at the edge of a nail. He had been an operative of the ISI for many years, with experience of hazardous operations all around the world, yet he was still nervous to have been summoned to the compound today.

Kader had returned to Pakistan in the aftermath of the aborted assignment to capture Tristan Huxley. The attack at the financier's vast mansion in the English countryside had been a bitter failure; despite Kader having the advantage of a man on the inside, the agents of Group Fifteen had still been able to remove Huxley from his grasp. What was worse was the loss of the two agents he had trained for the mission; Nadia and Nawaz had been eliminated by the headhunters who had very nearly accounted for him, too. Kader had flown out of the country aboard the light aircraft that they had planned to use to exfiltrate Huxley, an igno-minious withdrawal that had seen him return to Islamabad in disgrace.

The door to the conference room was guarded by a

member of staff who was seated at a desk to the side. The woman—glacially cool and dressed in military uniform— observed Kader with a blank expression as he got up and paced back and forth across the carpet. He had been placed on indefinite suspension upon his return and had been left in no doubt that his fate was not likely to be pleasant. Did the woman know that? Definitely. Failure was a stink that not even the most vigorous scrubbing could remove. The reek of it would stick to him forever, and everyone would smell it.

The telephone on the desk buzzed, and the woman picked it up. She listened for a moment, replaced the handset in its cradle and turned to Kader.

"You can go through now."

The message to come to the compound had been delivered late last night, and there had been nothing to accompany it that might explain why he had been summoned. He had been unable to sleep and, as his thoughts swirled, had concluded that the only reason he was required in person was so that he could be interrogated again as to what had happened. He had looked around his apartment before leaving this morning with the dread that he would not be returning.

He walked to the door, took a breath and, hoping that his discomfort wasn't too obvious, reached for the handle.

Lieutenant General Chaudhury Ali Khan and Iskander Nazimuddin were waiting for him inside. Ali Khan was the director general of the ISI and had a reputation within the agency for ruthlessness. Nazimuddin was the head of the counter-intelligence wing, and was known for a brutal attitude toward those who he felt had fallen short in the performance of their duties. Kader knew that Nazimuddin had been responsible for the punishment that had been meted out to Kader's previous commanding officer; Brigadier Subhani Rashid had been put under house arrest and charged with incompetence.

"Abbas," Ali Khan said, "thank you for coming."

Kader bowed his head. "Of course, sir."

Nazimuddin looked up from the sheet of paper from which he was reading. "You're probably wondering why we have asked to see you?"

"Yes, sir."

"You've heard what has happened to Brigadier Rashid?"

"I have."

"And perhaps you think the same treatment is about to be meted out to you?"

"I don't know, sir."

"Your record was unblemished. What happened with Huxley has been difficult for us to deal with. I doubt you realise just *how* difficult it has been. Two agents were killed and left behind. You've worked in intelligence for many years, Abbas."

"All my life."

"So you'll know about the discomfort the mess caused in the embassy. If we've been lucky at all, it is that the agents who were killed were not known to the British. The fact that they were cleanskins is the *only* reason we have been able to deny involvement even when it is perfectly obvious that they worked for us. The British need to maintain a cordial relationship with our government, and we've been able to give them enough freedom of movement that they can say that there is no proof that the agents were ours. They know otherwise, of course, but there is deniability. It is the only reason you still have a career—the only reason you haven't found yourself sentenced to the rest of your life in Sahiwal."

Kader heard the word 'career' and wondered if he was about to be handed the chance to win a reprieve.

Ali Khan looked at Nazimuddin and raised a hand as if to ask him to stop. "That's not why you're here. The failure of the assignment is a cause for regret, but the reasons for its failure go beyond your own culpability. Rashid, in particular, will pay for what happened. But you still have value to the agency."

Nazimuddin looked down at the paper again. "You told the investigators that you consider the agents who were lost your responsibility—correct?"

"Yes, sir."

"You are angry about what happened?"

"Very."

"And you would like to avenge them?"

"I would."

"Good," Ali Khan said. "In that case, we will give you that chance. You will be returned to the field with immediate effect."

"With what orders?"

"You have probably heard—Tristan Huxley has escaped from custody. We are still trying to discover exactly what happened and who was responsible, but we know *why* it happened—the deal between the Russians and the Indians is still alive, and both parties need him to complete it. We have intelligence that Huxley will shortly be taken to Delhi, where he will convene the parties to agree the final details of the deal. We want you to make sure that he does not get the chance to do that."

"Where will he be in Delhi?"

"Our source does not have that information yet, but he promises us that he will have it soon—you will be told immediately."

"Somewhere secure," Kader offered. "They'll know that the deal is vulnerable until it is signed."

Ali Khan nodded. "Of course."

"What support will I have?"

"None. This will be an operation inside Indian territory. We can't take the chance that our involvement is known. As far as we are concerned, in the event that you are captured or killed, the conclusion that will be drawn is that you are a rogue agent seeking revenge for the deaths of your protégés. We will deny all involvement. Once this meeting has concluded, and save the provision of intelligence, you will be operating alone. Will that be a problem?"

Kader knew that an assignment like this, in a hostile environment without any support, probably amounted to suicide. Even the remote possibility of success would not secure his own future. Reaching Huxley and stopping the deal would be difficult, and, even if he did manage to achieve his goals, he had no doubt that the agency would want him to disappear immediately thereafter. They would have tasked an agent to murder him just as they had aimed him at his own targets over the course of his career. But Kader found that that didn't matter. This would give him the chance to launder his reputation and gain revenge for what had happened to Nadia and Nawaz. He would deal with whatever came afterwards later.

"Abbas," Nazimuddin pressed, "is that a problem?"

"Not at all. Thank you. I appreciate the opportunity. I'll leave for Delhi at once."

HELSINKI

27

M ilton took a room in the Holiday Inn in West Ruoholahti. It had still been light when Thorsson had dropped him off at eleven the previous night, a reddish dusk that cast a rusty glow over everything. The room had been equipped with curtains and a blackout blind, and Milton had quickly fallen asleep, waking to his alarm at five so that he could work out for an hour in the hotel gym. He showered and changed and grabbed a coffee from the café on the ground floor and leaned against the side of the building as he waited for Thorsson to arrive to pick him up.

He took out his phone and flipped through the news, then Googled Huxley's name to see what else came up. He found himself navigating to less reputable sites where conspiracists posted theories on what had happened to him: he had been killed by the political elite whom he had been blackmailing, one site suggested, the attack in the hospital used to cover up the fact that he was dead; another site said that he had been spotted in London, and that the intelli-

gence services had broken him out of custody so that they
could reap the benefits of his blackmail for themselves.
Commentators pointed out that Huxley had long been
rumoured to have ties to various intelligence agencies; one
site suggested Mossad were involved; a rival put it down to
the GRU; another pinned the blame on Pakistan.

Milton heard the sound of a car's horn and looked up;
Thorsson had pulled over on the other side of the street.
Milton put his phone away and crossed over to where the
car was waiting.

"Morning," Thorsson said. "How's your stomach?"

"Fine," Milton said as he lowered himself into the seat.
"Why? Yours isn't?"

"This is going to sound weird," he said. "But I've never
actually seen an autopsy before."

"Don't say you're squeamish."

"I don't know," he said with a snort. "We'll see, I
suppose."

The post-mortem was due to be carried out by a pathologist attached to the University of Helsinki on Haart-
maninkatu, a road that ran through the centre of the city.
The faculty building was a modern construction that looked
sleek in comparison to the post-war monoliths that
surrounded it. Thorsson found a space to park, and they
made their way inside. Saarinen was waiting for them, and
the detective led the way to the pathology department. He
explained that the National Institute for Health and Welfare
was responsible for carrying out autopsies in Finland, and
the pathologist split her time between teaching students
and conducting the few examinations that were required in
a city with such a low murder rate.

Chief Räikkönen was waiting for them in a reception
area before the entrance to the faculty.

"Saarinen said you saw the cottage last night," she said.

"We did," Milton replied.

"And?"

"I don't have any better ideas than you do."

She watched his face carefully. "Nothing at all?"

"No."

Saarinen sucked on his teeth. "But you had an idea about the explosive they used."

"I think it might have been Russian."

"And the grenade in the cottage?"

"Yes," Milton said. "That was Russian, too."

"And the weapon," Saarinen added.

"Someone from over the border, then?" Räikkönen said.

"Either that, or someone who wants you to think it was."

"What do *you* think?"

"I really couldn't say."

She was obviously dissatisfied with his answer, but let it go and gestured to the room behind the door. There was a nameplate next to it that announced the name of the occupant: Professor Päivo Häyhä.

"She wants to show us something before she gets started on the post-mortem. Are you ready?"

Milton looked over at Thorsson. The Icelander gave a terse nod.

"Lead the way."

THE EXAMINATION ROOM beyond was a study in white tile and steel. The floor and walls were tiled, and the harsh overhead light flashed back at them from the two polished steel tables. There were pathology workstations, a necropsy table, and a cadaver lift that had been wheeled to the side of the room. One of the autopsy tables was empty, but the other bore the body of a man. Professor Häyhä was dressed in a white smock with a pair of blue nitrile gloves on her hands. Her surgical equipment was arranged on a pedestal next to the table, and a microphone and camera were suspended on an articulated arm that hung down from the ceiling.

Räikkönen introduced Milton and Thorsson.

"Good morning," Häyhä said.

"I told them that you've found something you'd like to share," Räikkönen said.

"I have. And it's very unusual indeed."

She reached down and removed the cover from the body. The man's clothes had been removed, and Milton was able to see the damage that Thorsson had inflicted during their struggle. There were two stab wounds in his chest that had been clogged with congealed blood, and a crescent-shaped incision that ran across his throat from one ear to the other. Milton looked at his face but didn't recognise him.

"Here," Häyhä said.

She took the dead man's right wrist, raised his arm and turned it over so that the hand faced upwards.

Räikkönen muttered a curse.

The dead man had no fingerprints.

"I've never seen anything like this before," Häyhä said. "It's not accidental, either. He's burned himself so that the basal layer of his epidermis has been disrupted. Fingerprints are complex things. They're formed by friction ridges, and they're usually hard to damage. I've had burn victims in here that we've been able to identify by peeling off the burned skin like a glove—the prints are still intact beneath. But this is different. Heat has been applied in a deliberate way to damage everything all the way down to the junction between the dermis and epidermis." She took the man's index finger and held it up; the tip was waxy and shiny. "What's left still leaves an identifying mark, but if his old prints were taken at some point in the past, then we wouldn't be able to match them with him."

"How extraordinary," Räikkönen said.

Häyhä laid the hand down. "That's not all. I'll be able to tell you a little more once I've opened him up, but he's had extensive plastic surgery that goes way beyond his fingerprints. Look at his cheekbones. Look at his nose and lips. His chin. There's Botox in his forehead, and he's had rhinoplasty to change the shape of his nose." She took her scalpel and held the point of the blade against the man's chin. "Look here—the shape has been altered, probably with an implant. And it's not the kind of work that's been done because he wants to look better. It's much more comprehensive than that. Enough work has been done to alter his biometrics. He doesn't want to look like he used to look."

Räikkönen turned to Milton. "Does that tell you anything?"

Milton shook his head.

Räikkönen looked back to the pathologist. "Anything else?"

"No," she said. "I'll have a look at him now, but I'm not expecting to find out anything that isn't already obvious, at least when it comes to cause of death." She pointed to his wounds. "There's no mystery there."

Milton made his way around the table so that he could look at the body more closely. A large swathe of skin from his shoulder down to his elbow was discoloured, with puckering around the edges.

Häyhä noticed that Milton was looking at it. "He's had a tattoo removed."

Milton pointed. "Scarring from the laser?"

"That's right."

Milton took out his phone and, gripping the cold flesh of the man's wrist between his thumb and forefinger, turned over his hand so that his fingertips were visible. He took a picture of them.

Räikkönen watched him. "What?"

"I'm just curious about why he would have done something like that. I'll have someone in London check it out."

Milton knew more than he was prepared to say, and, despite his best efforts to pretend to the contrary, it appeared that Räikkönen's suspicion had been aroused.

"I'm just making sure again, Mr. Smith—we're all agreed that you'll share everything with me, aren't we?"

"Of course."

"Because I'm getting the impression you're holding something back."

"I'm not."

Räikkönen stared at him, obviously unconvinced. Milton stepped back and took a photograph of the man's face. He looked at the screen, then down at the dead man, and confirmed that—as far as he knew—he had never seen him before.

Häyhä went over to the pedestal and looked down at the instruments that were arranged there. "I'll get started, then. Are you staying?"

"I think we can leave you to it," Milton said. "Thank you."

Räikkönen went to the door and held it open for them. Milton followed Thorsson outside, swiping back through his photographs to the shot of the man's fingers. He might not have recognised him, but he *had* seen fingertips like that before, and he knew that investigating the reasons why the prints had been removed would be their best chance of finding out who the dead man was and for whom he was working.

28

M ilton and Thorsson climbed into the car. Räikkönen and Saarinen convened on the pavement behind them, both officers aiming distrustful glances in their direction.

Thorsson started the engine and pulled away.

"Well?" he said. "What was it? The fingertips?"

"That's part of it."

Milton paused for a moment, wondering whether he should tell Thorsson what he suspected. There was no real reason to keep it to himself; he was concerned that they were both in more danger than they might otherwise have suspected. Milton would need help in confirming his fears, and, if he was right, he would need Thorsson's help in holding Huxley to account for his crimes. Despite the fact that Thorsson worked for an organisation that had chased him for years, Milton trusted the taciturn Icelander. Finally, and most important of all, Thorsson deserved to know. His girlfriend had been killed, and he was entitled to seek redress for that.

"Have you heard of Unit 29155?"

"No."

"They call it the Unit. It's a GRU group. Subversion, sabotage, assassinations. Elite operators—their best."

"Reminds me of someone."

Milton nodded. "It's the Russian equivalent of the Group."

"So why haven't I heard about them?"

"Because you've never been put in the field against them. You know what it's like—it's need to know."

"And you have?"

"I saw a man with no fingerprints like that in Berlin once, just before I left the Group. I was babysitting a journalist who'd been investigating Russian assassinations in London. She'd been a thorn in Putin's side for years, and we heard that he'd had enough. We were told that he'd sent someone to put an end to her. An agent came—and I sent him back to Moscow in a body bag. He'd had plastic surgery to change the way he looked. And his fingerprints had been burned off."

Thorsson cursed.

"The Unit has ties to the Moscow elite and close connections with the Spetsnaz. They're discreet, and they don't usually miss."

"And they're working for Huxley?"

"Why not? He's resourceful—maybe he used the arms deal as leverage into them getting him out and settling his scores. Maybe he's got *kompromat* on someone in the GRU. It doesn't matter—it's worth looking into."

"How?"

"The journalist," Milton said. "She knows more about them than anyone. She moved to Riga. I'll confirm she's still there, and if she is, I'll go to see her."

"Can you handle it alone?"

"It has to be me. She won't speak to someone she doesn't know."

"I need to make the arrangements to have Olya's body repatriated." Thorsson stared across the cabin at him. "If it *is* them, if you find out who did it, you leave them to me —understand?"

"I will. You can have them. But Huxley is mine."

RIGA

29

M ilton sat back in his seat and gazed out of the porthole window as Latvia appeared through the clouds beneath the 737. It was only a short one-hour hop between Helsinki and Riga, and Milton had booked a return ticket with the intention of making his way back to Finland after the meeting with Anna Grigorieva.

It had been simpler than he had anticipated.

He had spoken with Ziggy Penn and asked him to trace Grigorieva for him. Ziggy had grumbled and moaned about how many favours Milton *already* owed him, but he had done it anyway and in double quick time. He confirmed that she was still living in Latvia and had provided a phone number and email address. Milton had messaged her and said he needed to talk; she had called him back, and after a moment to reacquaint themselves, she had invited him to come and visit. Milton had gone straight to the airport and booked a flight. Thorsson was staying behind to take care of the practicalities of repatriating his girlfriend's body, and Control, as far as Milton knew, was meeting with the

Finnish intelligence services in order to ensure that cooperation between the two bodies continued to be frictionless.

The flight was too short for a meal to be served, so Milton took out the sandwich and drink that he had bought in the departures lounge and made do with those. His thoughts ran to the Unit and what it would mean if he was right about who had been responsible for the attack on Thorsson's life and the operation to free Huxley from custody.

The Russians had increasingly turned to deniable operations in order for its agendas to be met; that was especially so when the aims of those operations were murky and tainted by the self-interest of the elites who ordered them. He remembered what Anna had told him before: she was sure that the Unit had been behind the destabilisation campaign in Moldova, the poisoning of an arms dealer in Georgia and then the attempted coup in Montenegro. Much more had happened since then that also bore the hallmarks of their involvement. Milton kept abreast of the news as much as he could. He had observed the poisonings of Alexander Litvinenko, Alexei Navalny and Sergei Skripal and would have placed generous bets that the Unit had been involved on those occasions. And then there was the campaign against the exiled oligarchs who had fled to London as Putin consolidated power by eliminating all opposition to his presidency. Billionaires with multimillion-pound security details who died of unexpected heart attacks while out jogging or by apparent suicide. And then there were the lawyers who served them and the journalists who investigated their unexpected ends; many of them were dead, too.

The Unit was beyond secret, but Milton hoped that Anna would be able to furnish him with a more detailed picture of its operations and, perhaps, confirm that his suspicions of their involvement in this case were well founded.

MILTON TRAVELLED without a bag and so was able to pass quickly through the airport and find a taxi to take him into the centre of Riga. The Latvian capital had changed since the last time he had been there. Soviet Latvia had been as grim and foreboding as the other countries within the Kremlin's ambit, and it had taken time for the dour atmosphere to be shrugged off and replaced in the time since independence had been won. Now it was a vibrant, busy, cosmopolitan city, unafraid to acknowledge its heritage while looking forward to the future.

Anna had told Milton to meet her at an event that was being held at the Stockholm School of Economics in Riga. The gathering had been arranged to provide an opportunity for exiled Russian journalists to meet with one another, there had always been a steady flow of dissidents out of the country, but that flow had become a torrent since Moscow had taken the decision to impose its military will on its neighbours. The journalists who had fled had all been critics of the regime, but their voices had been stifled for fear of persecution. They were able to be more vocal here. Milton had visited the website for the organisation that was hosting the symposium and had read through the resumés of some of the men and women who were attending. There were eminent Kremlinologists who had made their names in efforts to report on the often-baffling power struggles between those jockeying for the president's favour; fact-checkers who debunked the propaganda that filled the schedules of Rossiya 1 and Russia 24; podcasters who provided commentary to help Western audiences understand Russian policy.

They reached the venue, and Milton paid the driver and got out of the car. A banner had been draped across the front of the building and, in bad English, it announced: "You are warmly welcome to Riga." He went inside and looked around. It was busy; Milton estimated that there were fifty or sixty people in the hall, with a member of staff ministering over coffees and teas and another fixing the bunting that had been draped from one side of the room to the other. There was a courtyard between the buildings, and Milton could hear the sound of a ping-pong ball as children played together. The French ambassador was slated to deliver a speech later on, and a musician was preparing his balalaika to provide entertainment and a reminder of home. The atmosphere was laid-back, the sound of frequent laughter rising and falling over the steady hum of conversation.

Milton saw Anna at once. She was talking to two older men, her colourful dress a stark counterpoint to their dour grey suits. He remembered her penchant for colour from when they had first met. It had been winter then, and the Moscow streets were full of grey sludge from where the snow had been sprayed with chemicals and then pushed into ugly drifts by the boiler-suited crews. Her vivid yellows and oranges and greens were chosen, she had said, as an antidote to the monotony of the winter months, with the snow and the rain and the cold and the hours of darkness that often seemed interminable. She was in her forties now —forty-five, Milton thought—but could easily have passed for ten years younger. Her hair was cut fashionably short, and her skin was still smooth, with lips that quirked up at the edges as if she was always about to laugh.

He picked a path across the room, stepping around two older men who were debating Russian foreign policy. Anna saw him when he was halfway there. Her eyes widened as she put a hand to her mouth in a failed attempt to hide her surprise. She said something to the man with whom she had been speaking and left him standing.

"You came," she said.

"You didn't believe me?" Milton said, unable to stop the smile from spreading across his face.

She reached out and hugged him. "How long has it been?"

"Too long."

The smell of the floral perfume that she wore was a trigger that took him back to Berlin, when he had been in the service of the Group. They had both been younger then, and, thrown together for weeks after the plot against her life was uncovered, there had been a mutual attraction that Milton had struggled to ignore. But he *had* ignored it, knowing that anything less than his most assiduous protection could get her killed; she had been put out by his rebuff, but then had enjoyed herself by teasing him about it incessantly.

"How have you been?" she asked him.

"I'm fine."

"You look good."

"I look old."

"Distinguished," she corrected him, her eyes sparkling.

"That's worse." He gestured at the men and women who had come to the meeting. "It's busy."

"Putin has made Russia an uncomfortable place for anyone who is more interested in the truth of what is really happening rather than parroting his propaganda." She pointed to a man with thick black-rimmed spectacles. "He runs a website that was involved in the investigation that proved the GRU has been poisoning dissidents outside Russia. He'd be killed if he went back." She pointed to a clutch of others, younger than the rest. "He's a tech entrepreneur—built an encrypted messaging app that the opposition uses and wouldn't give the GRU the keys when they asked for them. You can imagine how well *that* went down." She pointed again. "She's an actress, and he's a designer—they don't see a future at home, so they all chose exile. There are others like them—many, *many* others. Putin is turning Russia into a failed state. Until there's a change in leadership, it will just get worse."

"And you?" he said. "What have you been doing?"

"The same," she said. "Still writing. There's no shortage of things I want to say."

She guided him over to the table where the refreshments were being served and got them both plastic cups of coffee.

"You wanted to talk to me."

"I did."

"It must have been important for you to fly here straight away."

"I think it could be."

"This is to do with British intelligence?"

"No," he said. "I don't do that anymore. I retired."

She scoffed. "*No*, you didn't. I don't think I ever met anyone who identified with their work as much as you did."

"Look at me," he said with a wry smile. "I can't keep up with the younger ones anymore."

A man approached them, smiled at her and put out his hand. "Anna," he said, "this is a wonderful event. Thank you for organising it."

She waved the praise away. "It was a joint effort." She

turned to Milton. "This is my friend John Smith. John—this is Aleksandr Kovalev."

She used Milton's legend with an ease that Milton didn't remember from before.

"Good to meet you," Kovalev said. "What do you do?"

"I work in exports," Milton said. "What about you?"

"Journalism. How do the two of you know each other?"

Anna laid a hand on Milton's shoulder. "We used to be engaged."

Kovalev was evidently taken by surprise. "You never mentioned that."

"John broke my heart. It took me years to get over it."

Kovalev was silent, clearly unsure what to say. Anna took advantage of the moment by telling him how nice it was to see him, and then she placed her hand on Milton's elbow and angled him away.

"'Broke your heart?'" he said when they were out of earshot.

"But you *did*," she said, winking at him.

Kovalev stood awkwardly where he was for a moment, caught between two groups of conversing guests, before shuffling over to the refreshments and helping himself to a coffee. Milton found that he was enjoying Anna's playfulness. He had thought it childish before, but now, to his surprise, he found it flattering.

"What do you need to ask me about?" she said.

"The Unit."

"Right," she said. "I see."

"Are you still following them?"

"Writing a book about them. I have a very good source."

"How good? On the inside?"

"Maybe."

Milton looked over Anna's shoulder and saw that

Kovalev was looking in their direction. "Is there somewhere else we could talk about it?"

"You could buy me dinner," she suggested. "I don't have any plans tonight."

Milton knew that he should really say no, that he needed to get back to Helsinki, but he found that the prospect of spending a little social time with Anna was something that he would enjoy. "Where and when?"

She gave him the name of a restaurant and told him she would see him there at eight.

HELSINKI

———

30

The eight-hundred-mile land border that Finland shared with Russia had lent the country an importance in European geopolitics that ensured that there was a steady stream of MI6 agents and British military making their way to and from Helsinki and its environs. Control had been stationed here before and had been responsible for helping the Finns to monitor the activity of the FSB agents who operated in the country. She had enjoyed several successes, including the unmasking of a mole in the government who had sold classified information on the Finnish army's integration with NATO. Beyond her professional successes, her time here had been enjoyable. She had met her husband at a gala in the capital. Tuomas was Finnish, and the couple had kept a property here so that he could return whenever he wanted to visit his elderly parents. They enjoyed their time in the country and had kept the property even after Tuomas's parents had passed away.

Control had a busy evening ahead of her. There had been no problem in arranging for her own agents to have access to the investigation into the attack on Thorsson, the head of the Finnish Security Intelligence Service had invited her to dinner to discuss the case, and she had been happy to accept. Teemu Koskinen was an old contact from years past, and, apart from the good sense of maintaining a cordial relationship for the good of the two intelligence communities, she had always enjoyed his company. He had a lakeside house in Savonlinna, and he had promised her a dinner of salmon soup and cabbage casserole during which they could discuss what could be done to ensure that the flow of information continued in both directions.

She had met Thorsson earlier that afternoon. He had updated her on the discovery that he and Milton had made at the post-mortem of the man whom he had killed. Milton was of the opinion that the man might be a member of Unit 29155, the GRU group that had been responsible for a campaign of destabilisation all across Europe. She had sent an urgent flare to London and was waiting to be briefed. That would be something for later, though. Time was getting on, and they had a three-hour drive to reach the venue for dinner.

She descended the steps and crossed over to where Weaver was waiting by the car.

"All set, ma'am?"

"All set."

Control had a file of papers that she could review on the way. She got in, Weaver started the engine, and they pulled away.

THEY LEFT the capital and headed to the northeast. Control concentrated on her papers for the first hour; the entire apparatus of the intelligence service had been put to work in trying to work out what had happened to Huxley, who had authored his escape from custody, and who had attacked Thorsson. To lose a man of Huxley's notoriety had the makings of a national scandal, and nothing was being spared—neither money nor manpower—in the attempt to track him down.

Her phone buzzed, and, expecting a call from London, she was surprised to see that it was Flora, her elder daughter.

"Hello," she said.

"Where are you, Mum?"

"I told you, darling. I'm in Finland."

"For how long?"

"I don't know. A day or two. Why?"

Flora stifled a sob. "I just wanted to speak to you."

"What is it?"

It turned out that her two girls had had an argument. Flora was interested in one of the boys in the swim squad, but Clementine had said that one of her friends had overheard him laughing about Flora and saying that he was just messing her around. Flora had taken the news badly and had said that she didn't believe it; she was convinced that Clementine's friend was interested in the boy herself and was stirring things up in an attempt to get her out of the way. The two sisters had squabbled about it, and now both were in tears.

"Can't you speak to your father?"

"Seriously, Mum? He's not going to understand, is he?"

"Try him," she said. "You might be surprised."

"Ma'am," Weaver said.

Control covered the phone. "What is it?"

"I'm not sure." He glanced in the mirror. "Might be nothing."

"But?"

"There's a black Mercedes three cars back."

She turned in her seat and looked behind them. "What about it?"

"I'm a little concerned that it's been following us."

She took her hand away from the phone. "I've got to go, Flora. Speak to your dad. If it's still not sorted by the time I'm back, I'll sort it out."

They were approaching the town of Vierumäki, the lights glowing on the horizon ahead of them. The four-lane road was long and straight and quiet, with no cars approaching them and just one car in the distance ahead. There was a wide central reservation, and trees had been planted on the embankments that had been made when the road was cut through the landscape. The car behind them was a black Mercedes GLS; she squinted through the gloom in an attempt to make it out.

"Driver and one occupant?"

"I believe so, ma'am."

They reached the junction for Vierumäki and Asikkala and carried on, passing underneath a flyover and then past the junction where northbound cars could merge with the main road. Control looked to the right and saw two cars that were parked on the hard shoulder, their lights flicked on, and they pulled out, quickly accelerating as they joined the little convoy. The driver of the Audi to the front of the pair put his foot down and picked up speed, passing them on the right and then turning into the fast lane ahead of them. The second car, a BMW, drew alongside and matched their speed.

Weaver looked into the rear-view mirror. "We're being boxed."

Control looked back and saw that the Mercedes had manoeuvred its way between the cars that had divided them so that it was now directly behind them. The Audi was to the front, and the BMW was to the side.

It was obvious. Weaver was right: they were under attack.

"Do we have any backup?"

"Not out here," he said.

"How far to the next junction?"

Weaver looked at the satnav. "Seven kilometres."

Control looked to the right. The rear windows of the BMW were tinted, and she couldn't see inside, but she could see the driver and his passenger in the front. They were male.

Weaver took out his phone and placed a call. "This is SWAN. Over," he said, using Control's cryptonym.

"Copy that, SWAN. This is Helsinki Station. What's your situation? Over."

"North of Vierumäki. Over."

The driver of the Audi touched the brakes, the lights glowing red in the darkness. Weaver had no choice but to slow down, with the cars to the side and rear mirroring them.

"We're about to come under attack. Over," Weaver said into the phone.

He reached into his pocket for his weapon.

"Can you break out?" Control said.

"I'll try. Get down, please, ma'am."

Control did as he asked, leaning over so that she was stretched out across the rear seats.

Weaver yanked the wheel, and they swerved to the right. She heard the crunch of metal on metal as they crashed into the BMW that was boxing them from the side. Weaver tried again, jerking the wheel around. Control was jostled by the impact and then flinched at the sound of a gunshot and the crack as the rear window fractured.

"Gun!" Weaver shouted. *"Get down!"*

Control covered her head with her hands as automatic gunfire tore through the window and passed through the cabin, slugs punching their way out again through the windscreen and the roof. She heard a grunt of pain from the front of the car, and when she opened her eyes and looked between the passenger and driver's seat, she saw that Weaver had slumped over the wheel.

His foot must have slipped from the accelerator because the car started to slow. There was a gentle bump from the front as the car touched the Audi's rear bumper, slowing it even more. Control unclipped her seat belt and crawled forward, looking between the seats into the front of the cabin. Weaver was bleeding from a wound in his throat. He was alive, though, and managed to collect his pistol from where it had fallen in his lap, his hand flopping down on the console with it. Control took it.

"This is SWAN," she yelled, hoping that the line to the embassy was still open. "Man down. We've been fired upon."

Control couldn't be sure whether her message had been received, and before she could repeat it, there was another crash as the car bumped up against the BMW that was boxing them from the side. She was thrown forward, her shoulder thudding against the back of Weaver's seat and the pistol falling from her hand.

The car crashed into the barrier that split the central reservation. Metal ground against metal until the car finally came to a rest.

Control looked for the pistol.

"SWAN," came a voice on the phone's speaker. "SWAN —come in. Over."

She heard the sound of car horns blaring, then doors opening, then footsteps.

"No one move," a voice called out.

Control saw the pistol in the footwell and tried to reach for it.

She heard a gunshot from the left and then another. Weaver's body flinched, and his head twisted to the side.

Control's door was opened, and she swivelled to look into the muzzle of a submachine gun. The man who held the gun was dressed all in black. His face was hidden beneath a balaclava.

"Out."

She shuffled along the seat, swinging her legs around. The man stepped back and gestured down to her; another man, also wearing a balaclava, grabbed her by the shoulders and yanked her out. She didn't protest or try to resist. It would have been pointless and might very well have seen her shot. She glimpsed the scene: their car was boxed in between the three cars and the barrier that separated the eastbound and westbound lanes. A van had come to a stop against the blockade, with the driver—who must have seen the shooting—trying to reverse so that he might get out of the way.

A woman, her face also hidden, covered the van with a submachine gun. She fired a controlled burst through the windscreen, and the van came to a stop.

The second man hustled Control to the Mercedes at the rear of the box. The door at the rear was open, and she allowed herself to be pressed inside. The first man got in next to her, shouldering her across the seats and then covering her with his weapon.

"I'm sorry about that," the man with the gun said.

"You're making a very big mistake."

"We have no interest in seeing you come to harm."

His voice was accented: German?

The door to Control's right opened, and the second man lowered himself inside. The two of them wedged her in the middle of the seat. The door slammed shut, and the driver put the Mercedes in gear and pulled out, using the hard shoulder to get around the blockage and accelerating away sharply.

The first man spoke again. "We've got a long drive ahead of us."

No, she thought.

Not German.

Russian.

"Where are we going?"

The man reached into his jacket and took out a long plastic case. "We'll be crossing the border."

Control knew what was about to happen even before he had reached into his pocket again and withdrawn a small bottle.

"That's not necessary," she said.

He opened the case, removed the syringe that was kept inside and carefully pressed the needle through the plastic seal at the neck of the bottle.

"Please—no."

He pulled back on the plunger, filling the barrel of the syringe. "I can't take the risk that you'll cause a scene before we're in Russia."

She struggled, trying to shuffle away from the man and the syringe, but it was futile. The second man was large, and, as he laid a heavy arm across her torso and held her back against the seat, she could feel his strength. She wriggled against him.

"Please. I have children."

"We know. Two girls: Clementine and Florence. And you'll see them again if you do what you're told."

The mention of her daughters' names shocked her into stillness. She had always kept those kinds of personal details hidden; it should have been very difficult indeed for anyone to discover them. She knew then that she had to be dealing with a state agency, the ambush had been professional and executed ruthlessly, they were going to cross into Russia, and they knew things that there was no way that they should have been able to find out.

FSB?

GRU?

Or perhaps Milton was right: the Unit?

She tried to force the man's arm down.

"Stop struggling," he said. "There's no point."

He was right. Trying to fight them was futile, and she would only end up hurting herself if she carried on.

"I'm diabetic," she said. "I have insulin in my purse. If I don't inject myself twice a day, I'll get sick."

"We know. Please don't worry. You're in very good hands. We have a physician waiting to see you when we arrive."

She slumped back into the seat, her muscles tense. The man jabbed her in the fleshy part of her upper arm and depressed the plunger. She caught sight of the label on the bottle and saw characters from the Cyrillic alphabet. She was wondering what the sedative might have been—propofol, ketamine, maybe thiopental or methohexital—and as she thought about that, her mind began to untether, and her thoughts ran free. She tried to remember the faces of her girls

—the fleck of gold in the blue of Clementine's eye, the chlorinated smell of Flora's hair after she had finished her training —but, soon, even those details became wisps that were sent away by the gentle zephyr that blew through her mind.

Her eyelids felt heavier and heavier. The last thing that she remembered was something muttered in Russian and the odour of sweat that came from the man to her left.

After that, there was nothing.

RIGA

31

M ilton put on the suit, shirt and shoes that he had bought in a store near the hotel and made his way through the city to the restaurant that Anna had suggested for their meeting. Vincent's was near Kronvalda Park and was, at least if you read the plaudits on its website, the 'best restaurant in the Baltics.' It was an upmarket area that was home to several embassies. The entrance was at the foot of a flight of steps that descended from the street. Milton was greeted by the maître d' and taken to the table that had been reserved for them. Anna had not yet arrived, and Milton took the opportunity to look around: the dining room was dominated by a large tank containing live langoustines that, according to the restaurant's website, had been imported from the Faroes. The place was busy, and he was scanning the other diners when he noticed Anna at the entrance. She raised a hand in greeting and picked a route between the tables until she reached his booth.

She gestured to his suit. "Pushed the boat out?"

"They wouldn't have let me in with what I was wearing before," he said.

"No," she agreed. "You *were* a little ripe."

Milton pulled out her chair, and she sat down.

"I could *die* for a glass of wine," she said. "What are you having?"

"Water."

"Sorry?"

"I don't drink."

She gaped.

"It's true."

"You *used* to. I mean, you used to *a lot*."

"I did," he admitted. "But I stopped."

"You had a problem?"

"It was years ago. It was getting out of hand, and I thought I'd better stop before I did something I might regret."

"How did you manage something like that?"

"Meetings," he said, not willing to go into too much more detail than that.

"Good for you," she said. "I drink too much, but not enough to make me think that stopping would be a good idea. The prospect of a drink in the evening is usually the only thing that gets me through the day."

Milton was relieved when the waiter arrived with their menus. "I'll give you a few minutes to choose."

"No need," Anna interrupted before he could leave. "We'll have the blinis and caviar to start and then the beef tartare and the langoustines."

"To drink?"

"A bottle of the Sorrentino," she said. "And a carafe of water for my abstinent friend."

The waiter thanked them and moved away. Milton

smiled at Anna, remembering that she had a confidence that could sometimes verge on the presumptuous.

"What?" she said, noticing the look he was giving her. "There's no point wasting time deliberating. Those are the best dishes on the menu, and, since you're paying, I thought we might as well do things properly."

"I'm paying?"

"You do want my help?"

Milton knew she was playing with him, but let it pass. Control would pay much more than whatever they spent tonight if Anna could help him confirm his suspicions about who had been responsible for the attack on Thorsson.

"I *do* want your help."

"The Unit. Why do you want to talk about them? You said you were out?"

"I am," he said. "But it's like you said—you can never get *all* the way out. I've been doing a little freelancing from time to time, and the Unit came up. You said you were still up to date on them?"

She chuckled wryly. "More than before, actually. The book is going to be spectacular."

"Is that wise?"

"Because of what happened?" She shooed away his concern with a flick of her fingers. "*Please*. No—they won't like it. Yes—Vladimir Vladimirovich would much rather I was a good girl and kept my mouth shut, but I'm not going to be bullied by the likes of him or the Unit. I let them frighten me before, and not writing what I wanted to write about them and that world has been the thing that I've regretted most in my career. It's never going to happen again." She eyed him with steely determination. "And don't think you should be worrying about me, either. I can look after myself."

"I never said you couldn't."

She spoke with iron conviction, and, even if Milton had thought that she might listen to him, he knew that it was none of his business and that she wouldn't change her mind. The atmosphere was a little tense for a moment before the waiter returned with a frosted carafe of water and the bottle of white. He poured and waited while Anna tasted it. She told him that it was fine, and he filled her glass, then set the bottle in an ice bucket next to the table. He poured Milton a glass of iced water, placed the carafe within Milton's reach, and turned to leave.

"I didn't mean to jump down your throat," Anna said when the waiter had made his exit. "I've been angry with myself for years, and I get defensive if I think people are about to tell me how stupid I am and the risks they think I'm taking."

"You're a grown-up. It's your choice."

She raised her glass and held it out in a toast. Milton touched his glass to hers.

"So," she said, "why are they relevant to you?"

"A colleague was attacked a couple of days ago. There was a bomb underneath his car, and his girlfriend was killed when it went off. My friend killed one of them and got away."

"And you think that the Unit might be behind it?"

"I noticed something that made me think of you."

He took out his phone and opened the gallery. He found the photo that he had taken of the tips of the dead man's fingers and laid the phone on the table so that she could look at it.

Her eyes went a little wide. "Oh. I see why you'd think it might be them."

"I remembered the man who came after you before. His fingers were like that. You said that was standard for them."

She nodded. "Anything else?"

"Plastic surgery to his face. Nose, cheeks, chin. Substantial."

"That would be standard for them."

"And they were using Russian military equipment."

"Right," she said. "It's all pointing in their direction apart from one thing—they're good. Your friend wouldn't have been allowed to walk away."

"He's resourceful."

"Shouldn't have made any difference. Did he know they were coming?"

"No."

She shrugged. "They don't usually make mistakes." She sipped her wine and replaced the glass on the table. "How much do you remember about them?"

"You said they were established after the Wall fell. An ex-Stasi man was behind it."

She nodded. "Otto Sommer."

"German?"

"East German," she corrected him, "born in Magdeburg. Working in the Stasi ran in the Sommer family—his father, Karl-Heinz, was very senior in Berlin. There was quite a story about him, as it happens. The rumour was that he had a vault beneath his headquarters where he kept loot and compromising material. They called him *die Spinne.*"

"My German's not the best."

"The Spider," she said, "on account of how easy it was to get caught in his web. Rumour has it that the vault was raided by a team from British intelligence—you ever hear about that?"

"Never."

"I've tried to find proof, but it's impossible. I should ask you to dig into it for me—it'd make a great chapter." She chuckled and shook her head, forestalling his protest. "I know. You can't. I was just saying..." She took another sip. "Otto followed in his father's footsteps and made lieutenant colonel just before the Wall came down. His history is colourful, to say the least. He was suspected of being a member of a death squad who killed state targets in the mid- to late 1980s. The Wall comes down, he's paranoid that he'll be found out and prosecuted, so he goes to Moscow and joins the KGB and then, when that folds, the GRU. What happened next isn't clear—it depends who you talk to about it. The version that I've always thought was most likely to be true was that GRU leadership asked him to set up a small agency that they would deploy for the most sensitive work. Something that they could keep under the radar. Something very much like Group Fifteen. Moscow is using them more and more. Syria and Libya, sub-Saharan Africa, Latin America, Sudan, Madagascar, Venezuela. Putin sent them after me when I exposed what they were doing—but you know that. They've been all around the world since then."

"Where are they based?"

"There's a camp attached to the location of the 10th Special Mission Brigade of the Spetsnaz in Krasnodar. They're well equipped. They've even got their own missile range."

"And Sommer still runs it?"

She nodded.

"But if he was in the Stasi, he must be... what, in his sixties?"

"Early seventies, not that you'd know from looking at him. He could pass for much younger."

"How many agents?"

"No more than thirty. You join by invitation only. They vet possible new recruits and only make an approach if they're certain that they meet the grade." She tapped her finger against the photo on Milton's phone before pushing the phone back across the table. "They've got a cyber warfare division, and they have them wipe the records of everyone who joins. The GRU is lazy when it comes to that these days—too many instances of civilian observers tracking down agents after they've done whatever they were sent to do. So they make anyone who joins a cleanskin. *Everything* is faked: birth certificate, identity documents, employment history. Perfect legends—better than anything you'd see with MI6 or the CIA. And they go even further. They have a plastic surgeon who works on new recruits— new faces, no prints." She gestured toward Milton's phone. "Just like your man. That's how serious they are about staying in the shadows. They're all single, no families. They live for their work."

The waiter arrived with their starters, and Milton paused until he had left them alone once again before continuing.

"Who would I go to see if I wanted to find out for sure whether they were involved?"

"That wouldn't be easy."

"But not impossible?"

"No, not impossible."

"You said you had a source."

"I do."

"On the inside?"

"He still works for them, although that's something he'd like to change."

"He wants to defect?"

"Yes. His view on the kind of work he's been doing has

changed over the years. They sent him to Syria. They abducted a leader of the local militia and beat him with sledgehammers. Then they cut off his hands and feet and head, strung up what was left of him and set it alight. They videoed the whole thing from start to finish—I've seen it. The things they asked him to do there changed the way he looks at the world. He's been my source ever since—I've been working to get him a way out, but you don't leave the Unit unless they want you to leave."

I know a little about that, Milton thought. "What does he need?"

"The things I can't get him. A new identity. Somewhere he can start again where they won't be able to find him. Enough money to do that."

"I might be able to help. The attack on my friend is probably connected to a job I was doing that I can't discuss—but it's caused a lot of noise in London. They want it cleared up, and if your contact can help with that..." He shrugged. "I don't think a new life would be a problem."

"What would he have to do?"

"Prove that the Unit was involved in the hit. Would he see me?"

"I don't know. Sommer doesn't mess around—he'd have him shot if he had even the slightest idea that he was thinking about flipping. He's *very* careful about his personal security."

"But you've met him?"

She nodded. "Now and again."

"Could you ask?"

She nodded. "I'll try. No promises, though."

THE BORDER

32

Control was jolted awake by a bumping beneath her body. She opened her eyes and immediately felt sick. She closed them and turned her head and vomited, unable to stop herself from bringing up the snack that she had had at the embassy before they set off. That memory brought her right back to the present, and, as she opened her eyes again, she wondered whether she was still lost in a dream. It was dark, pitch black, and she couldn't see a thing. She blinked, and then, as she lay in the darkness and smelled the smell of her own bile, she remembered.

The ambush.

The syringe.

She could easily imagine what had happened. She had already determined that her abductors must have been involved with the intelligence services of a major state—her best guess was the FSB—and guessed that they would have used a car with diplomatic plates. Knowing that there was no prospect of the vehicle being searched at the border, they had sedated her and put her in the boot.

She had no idea how much time had passed between her abduction and now, nor any idea where she was. She was jostled left and right as the car manoeuvred, and, when she closed her eyes and concentrated, she could hear the sound of traffic above the noise of the engine. That was it, though. She couldn't see where she was, nor could she use her watch to give her any idea of the time. She reached into her pockets and found, not to any great surprise, that her phone had been confiscated.

She gave a moment's thought to the prospect of making a noise, but quickly discounted it. There was no point. She had almost certainly passed over the border between Finland and Russia, and even if that were not the case, she doubted that anyone would be able to hear her.

No choice other than to be patient.

They would get to where they were going in due course, and that would be when they took her out of the boot. She would try to assess her circumstances then. Her only reason for optimism was the fact that they were obviously aware of her status: she had been taken because she was Control for Group Fifteen, and the fact that they hadn't killed her suggested that they wanted her alive. Her absence would already have been noted in London, and every diplomatic and military option would be expended in an effort to get her back. This escapade would already have very serious consequences for whoever was responsible for it, but, if anything more serious were to happen, those consequences would be multiplied a hundredfold.

It wasn't much to rely on, but it was all she had.

HELSINKI

33

I t was ten o'clock, and the reddish glow of the midnight sun shone through the window and into the room at the embassy where Thorsson was working on the investigation. He had gone there after leaving the post-mortem, but as he set up his computer and made contact with London, he became depressingly certain that no real progress had been made. The analysts at Group Two had taken the photograph of the dead man and run it through what Thorsson knew to be an extensive database of opera-tives and agents from all the intelligence services all around the world. No hits had been returned. The search had been broadened to include mercenaries and soldiers employed by private military corporations—anyone who might have taken the job in return for getting paid—but, again, there was nothing positive to report. They knew that the assassins had used Russian gear and that the man Thorsson had killed had used plastic surgery to hide his identity, but, beyond that, they had nothing.

Thorsson had reported Milton's suspicion that the man

might have been connected to Unit 29155, but, again, the results that were returned were uninspiring. The files that dealt with the secretive organisation were classified, and it had taken an intervention by the head of MI6 in order for them to be released for Thorsson to review. They were suspected of a number of operations across Europe and were considered to be an elite force that was reserved for the most sensitive work. Thorsson had told Milton how the description of the Unit matched the Group, and the more he read, the more germane that comparison became. The assessment was that the Unit was small and that they were deployed only when the ends mattered more than the means; again, like the Group. But that was the extent of the intelligence that was made available. There were no photographs of serving members and nothing to match with the dead man.

If there was a connection, it would be down to Milton to find it.

There was a knock at the door. "Excuse me?"

Thorsson shut the laptop. "Come in."

The door opened, and a woman stepped inside. She was an agent from MI6 who had been working under the cover of being a member of the embassy staff. "There's been a development," she said. "You're needed on a conference call with London."

"What development?"

"They didn't tell me," she said, "but they said it's urgent. They're waiting to speak to you in the bubble."

THE ATTENTION GIVEN to Finland by its eastern neighbour had continued following the fall of the Berlin Wall, and the paranoia of the twentieth century had stretched into the twenty-first. The embassy had been equipped with a Sensitive Compartmented Information Facility referred to as the SCIF by those who used it. The use of secure spaces had become a necessity after a Soviet bug had been found inside the Great Seal of the United States in the embassy in Moscow, and Helsinki had been provided with a sealed container that had been installed in the grounds. It was built to keep sounds, electronic emissions, and vibrations from escaping, and was almost impossible for unauthorised people to get inside. It included a secure data centre that prevented electronic surveillance and mitigated against the leakage of sensitive security and military information.

Thorsson waited outside the SCIF while the metal door was unlocked. The mechanism buzzed, and he opened the door and stepped inside; the door closed and locked behind him, sealing him inside. The interior of the container was austere: the walls had been fitted with soundproofed sheets to absorb the noise of conversation, there were no windows and the only furniture was a small conference table that was large enough to accommodate half a dozen people. A laptop had been left on the table, its screen showing the virtual lobby for the encrypted software that was used to ensure that communications to and from London were not easily intercepted.

Thorsson sat down, moused over to click on his name and indicated that he was present and ready to speak. The screen went black for a moment, and when it came to life again, it showed the stream from a single camera. The camera was in a conference room in London and showed a man and a woman sitting at a table. They were representatives of the Intelligence Steering Committee, the body responsible for overseeing the work of the fifteen groups that, together, comprised the Firm. It was staffed by mandarins from the main Whitehall departments and members of Cabinet. Thorsson recognised them both: the woman on the left of the shot was Elizabeth Cheetham, the director general of the Secret Service; the man on the right was Sir Benjamin Stone, the chief of the Secret Intelligence Service. He looked from Stone to Cheetham and back again, perplexed; the heads of MI5 and MI6 were two of the most powerful and influential figures in British intelligence, and he couldn't begin to think why they would want to speak with him.

"We have disturbing news," Cheetham said. "As you may or may not have been told, Control had arranged to have dinner with the head of the Finnish Security Intelligence Service at a house in Savonlinna. She didn't arrive. Her contact got in touch with the embassy, and we were able to confirm that she had departed, just as planned. The local authorities found her car three hours ago. Her driver was still inside—he'd been shot and killed. There was no sign of Control."

Thorsson gripped the edge of the conference table. "Abducted?"

"We are operating on that assumption," Stone said.

"By whom?"

"We don't know."

"I'm afraid we don't really know anything at all," Cheetham said.

"Her phone?"

"It went off-grid. The Finns believe she's been taken over the border into Russia. The border is eighty kilometres from where the ambush took place."

"The Russians would do something like that?"

"It's our working hypothesis," Cheetham said. "That's why we wanted to speak to you. I understand you think there might have been Russian involvement in what happened to you?"

"We think it's possible."

"Go on."

"John Milton thinks it might have been Unit 29155."

Stone nodded. "That's what we've heard. Where is Milton now?"

"He has a contact in Riga. He's hoping she'll provide additional information."

Cheetham frowned. "I'm not happy to leave this to a freelancer, and especially not someone with his reputation. You need to supervise him."

"He won't take kindly to that," Thorsson said. "He doesn't work for the Group. He's here because of Tristan Huxley. He believes that Huxley is ultimately responsible for what happened to me."

Cheetham and Stone shared a look.

"John Milton is not someone we are comfortable having anywhere near an investigation like this," Cheetham said. "I'm sure you've read his file—he's compromised in a dozen different ways, and the consensus among the professionals who spoke to him before he tried to leave the Group is that he is suffering from a number of potentially serious psychological conditions. You know, I expect, that he has been attending meetings of Alcoholics Anonymous for years?"

Thorsson didn't respond.

"The bottom line, Number One, is that he is not to be trusted. He does not have security clearance. The fact that he is out there at all is something that we will have to discuss with Control when she has been recovered. It shows dreadful judgement on her part."

"Do you understand?" Stone said. "I want us to be clear on this—Milton is *not* to be trusted."

"I understand."

"What's happened to Control has the makings of a major incident," Cheetham said. "Our focus is on her. We're sending people to lead the investigation, but they won't be with you until this evening."

"What if she is in Russia? We'd go in and get her?"

"Losing her would be worse than what happened with Philby. It doesn't matter where she is. We want her back."

The call ended, and the screen went to black. Thorsson stared at the black and white Royal Coat of Arms that flashed up and thought about what he had been told. The thought that Control might have been kidnapped was almost beyond credibility. There were conventions that governed the relationships between intelligence agencies, even when a bitter rivalry existed between them. To do something as serious as abduct someone like her was almost unprecedented. He wondered whether it was possible that Huxley had anything to do with it, or whether what was happening could be something else entirely. An attack by the Russians on British intelligence? Would they really do something as brazen as that?

And then he thought of what they had said about Milton. Thorsson knew about his history. Control had shared everything with him when he had been sent to the Hebrides to bring him in, and there had been additional briefings once it had been decided that they would both work together to protect Huxley. The two men had spent time together, and, while Thorsson knew enough to know that he could never trust him completely, Milton had shown him nothing to suggest that he was compromised. Might he have missed something? Did London think he was involved?

Thorsson sat back in his chair, deep in thought. It was obvious that Milton's reputation had not been rehabilitated, and Thorsson was going to need to remember that.

SAINT PETERSBURG

34

Control found it very difficult to gauge the passage of time in the boot of the car, but she guessed that it was another hour before the vehicle slowed and came to a halt. She lay quietly, doing her best to ignore the painful cramps in her thighs and shoulders from being kept in the same position for too long. She heard the sound of doors opening and then footsteps approaching from outside. A key fob blipped, and the lid of the boot popped open.

She found herself looking up into the face of the man who had administered the sedative. He had removed the balaclava, and she could see him for the first time: blue eyes, short dark hair, prominent cheekbones. She blinked, adjusting her eyes to the glare of artificial lights somewhere overhead, and looked beyond him to try to get an idea of where she was. There was no sign of any buildings or anything that might have suggested that she was in an urban area.

The man reached down with his hand, Control took it, and he helped her to sit.

"Where are we?"

"Levashovo air base."

"Saint Petersburg?"

"That's right. Here—let me help you out."

He took her by the forearm and gently helped her to climb out of the boot. She winced with pain as soon as she put weight on her feet.

"Are you all right?"

"Cramp."

"I'm sorry. Things will be much more comfortable from now on."

Control looked around. She could see the wire fence that marked the perimeter of the facility, together with an open gate through which she guessed that they must just have passed. There were several buildings on the other side of the airfield, including offices and large hangars. The runway was a single strip that ran away into the gloom, lit at this end but invisible after a few hundred yards. She looked out onto the apron nearest the car and saw a handful of military aircraft: Antonovs, a Tupolev Tu-134 and Mi-6 and Mi-8 helicopters.

"We're going to take a flight," the man said, pointing to the Gulfstream G550 that was taxiing out of a hangar onto the apron. "We still have three thousand kilometres to travel."

Control screwed up her face to try to hide the pain from her sore muscles. Each step was difficult, but she was not about to admit to weakness in front of this man and the others who had been involved in her abduction. They had all removed their balaclavas now, and she tried to commit their faces to memory: another man with a nose that was squashed close to his face, a woman with blonde hair tied back in a ponytail and emerald eyes. There were another half dozen men and women, but they were on the other side of the car, and Control couldn't see them clearly. The ones that she could see had one thing in common: they were all bland to look at and completely unmemorable.

"Where are we going?" she said as she followed the man across the tarmac.

"Krasnodar."

She remembered the name. There was a military facility there that was attached to the 10th Special Mission Brigade of the GRU.

"You're Spetsnaz?"

"No," he said.

The flight crew had lowered the steps that were integrated into the door of the G550. Control climbed up, aware that the man was behind her and that there was nothing that she could have done to try to get away. The interior of the jet was opulent, she had flown in Gulfstreams before, but those jets—usually owned by the government—were austere in comparison. This one's cabin was spacious and looked as if it would have been able to comfortably accommodate twenty passengers. It had been configured for half that number, with a lounge section up front, a conference table behind that and a divan in the aft portion. There was a galley and two lavatories, and the cabin was separated from the crew area by a bulkhead and wood-veneer sliding door.

Control was shown to one of the seats. She sat and strapped herself in. The man who had been talking to her took the seat on the other side of the aisle.

"So if you're not military," Control said, "what are you?"

"I'd much rather we waited until we reach our destination."

"I deserve an answer."

He smiled patiently. "It will be explained to you when we arrive. I promise—all of your questions will be answered."

The others boarded the jet and took seats around the cabin. They were relaxed, and, as the crew went through their final checks, they started to converse in Russian. They either didn't know that Control spoke the language or didn't care, discussing the bar that they would visit after they went off duty. She was more convinced than ever that they were either serving military or that they had military backgrounds.

The crew finished their checks and took their own seats. The turbofans spooled up, and the jet raced down the runway, launching itself into the air far more quickly than any commercial jet would have managed. Control raised the blind that covered her porthole window and looked down at the landscape below. The screen that served her seat had a map, and she could see that they were heading south. She saw the glow of the city as they continued their ascent and the red and white lights of other commercial planes that were being stacked for landing.

She felt alone and vulnerable. London would know by now what had happened to her, but she doubted that they would have any idea at all where she was. These operatives were professional, and, if this wasn't official state business, they obviously had the benefit of serious financial backing.

A uniformed stewardess made her way along the aisle and stopped next to Control. "Can I get you something to eat or drink?"

"I'm fine."

"You should eat," the man beside her advised. "We won't

arrive for another three hours, and the food is very good. Please."

She thought of her diabetes and tried to remember the last time that she had eaten. It had been a while, and, if she didn't have something, she risked hypoglycaemia.

"Some chocolate?" she asked.

"Of course."

RIGA

35

M ilton awoke early and went down to the gym for another workout.

He stepped onto the treadmill, selected a fast pace and lengthened his stride until he was able to comfortably match it. He thought back to last night. He had enjoyed Anna's company, but had been pleased to get back in one piece. She had finished the bottle of wine and, a little drunk, had tried to persuade him that it wouldn't do him any harm to have just one drink with her. Milton had felt his stoicism beginning to wobble, and, knowing that one drink would not mean just one drink, he told her that he was tired and needed to call it a night. She tried one more time, suggesting that her flat was close by; he compromised and walked her home but politely extricated himself after she had invited him in.

He looked down at the screen, saw that he had finished his first mile and turned the dial to increase his speed. He stood tall, putting his shoulders back so that he could breathe in all the way, and picked up his cadence. He wiped the sweat out of his eyes and increased the speed again.

HE RETURNED to his room dripping with sweat. He had just undressed for a shower when his phone buzzed on the table.

It was Anna.

"He'll meet you," she said. "What are you doing today?"

"Nothing."

"Good. You need to fly to Krasnodar. He'll meet you at the airport."

LOWESTOFT

36

L illy Moon unrolled the windbreak and drove the wooden stakes into the ground, arranging it around the picnic blanket so that they were sheltered from the light breeze that was kicking up little eddies of sand. The beach at Lowestoft was glorious, an unbroken mile of golden, stone-free sand that ran from the harbour up to the dunes at Pakefield and then beyond. It was one of the only things that the town had left to offer. It had once been a prosperous port, but the death of its fishing fleet and the unsatisfactory state of the roads that led into it had meant that it had fallen on hard times. Lilly had been born here, though, and despite the evidence of decline all around her, she liked to come back. Her mother still lived here, and despite Lilly's attempts to persuade her that she would have a better life if she lived closer to her and Lola in London, she had steadfastly refused to leave. Her stubbornness, while frustrating, did mean that Lilly and her daughter had somewhere to go whenever they fancied a visit to the coast, so they came often.

Lola was eight years old and had dealt with the breakup of Lilly's marriage with a stoicism that made Lilly proud. Lilly's mother, Victoria, had been indispensable. Lilly's work often required her to leave the country, and Victoria had happily looked after the little girl whenever required, even on short notice. Lilly knew that she wouldn't have been able to manage without her.

She paused for a moment and looked around. It was a typical English summer's day. The forecast was fair, but the promised blue skies had been obscured by dense patches of cloud. It was pleasant—and sometimes even warm—when the sun was out, but the temperature quickly dropped when it was hidden. The promenade was busy with older couples idling along, dog walkers exercising their pets, and elderly locals on mobility scooters edging between the pedestrians. It was early, but Lilly knew that later there would be queues for those wanting ice cream from the kiosk and those waiting for fish and chips from the pier. Lilly took out the bucket and spade that they had purchased in town and placed them on the sand in front of her daughter's feet.

"Do you want to build a sandcastle?"

Lola shook her head. "I want you to read to me."

"That's what we'll do, then," Lilly said. "Why don't you sit down on the towel. Do you remember what happened in the book?"

"Horrid Henry has a time machine," Lola said, smiling at the thought of the passages that they had read together in bed the previous night. "And he's going to send Peter back to the past."

"That's right. Sit down, sweetheart. I'll get the book."

She went to her bag and took out the rest of their things: the picnic blanket and the packed lunch that they had bought in Marks and Spencer's. She took out the book and noticed that her phone was flashing with an incoming message. She fished it out and brushed the sand from the screen. Her stomach dropped: the message had been sent from the office in London.

"What is it?" Victoria asked her.

"I've got to call in," she said, turning away before the resignation and disappointment on her mother's face angered her.

She dialled the number.

"Global Logistics," the woman in the office said. "How can I direct your call?"

"Dispatch, please."

"Who shall I say is calling?"

"Chelsea McKinney."

"Hold the line, please."

Lilly walked away from the windbreak, her feet sinking into the warm sand.

"Hello, Ms. McKinney."

"I had a message to call in."

"That's right. We've got a new contract. It's very urgent. You need to come in."

Her stomach dropped. "I just got back from the last contract."

"This is important."

"When?"

"Right away. There's a meeting this afternoon at two. You need to be there. We've sent a car to pick you up. The driver will be with you shortly."

Lilly ended the call and put the phone in her pocket. She looked down the beach at the families setting up for the day, children sprinting for the slick sands at the water's edge and one little boy wrestling with a kite as it was tugged by the breeze. She closed her eyes and took a breath, certain that Lola was going to be disappointed but knowing that there was nothing that she could do to ignore the call. Her employers didn't care about the inconveniences that the job imposed on their staff. The work was important, and it was made clear to new recruits that family life—and everything else—had to come behind it.

She turned back and went around the windbreak. Lola was on the blanket with Victoria. The two of them were playing with the dolls that Lola took everywhere.

Victoria looked up at Lilly, saw her daughter's expression and groaned. "No. Not *now*, surely."

She nodded. "Sorry."

"But you've *just* got back. They can't expect you to go off again."

"I don't get a choice. You know what they're like."

"So maybe it's time you found another job." She got to her feet, stepped closer to Lilly and lowered her voice so that Lola wouldn't be able to hear. "Think of her. It isn't fair."

"Do you think I don't know that?" Lilly said, with more heat than she intended. She took a step away from the blanket, indicating that her mother should follow. "The only reason I'm still there is because they pay me a lot of money. I'd get another job, but it'd have the same demands as this one, and the salary would be worse, and then I wouldn't be able to pay for the lawyers. Who else can I go to? Are *you* going to pay for them?"

"You know I would if I could," her mother said, turning away to hide her hurt.

"I'm sorry," Lilly said. "I didn't mean that."

"Doesn't matter." Her mother picked up the bucket and spade. "How long will it be for?"

"They didn't say. There's a meeting this afternoon in London. I'll know more then."

Lilly used to hate lying as a child, especially to her mother. Her family was religious, and they had gone to church every Sunday. She had squirmed on her pew at the thought of the untruths that she might have said during the preceding week, and promised herself anew that she would try harder in the days ahead to make sure that she did better. Things were different now. Lying came easily to her. She delivered the prepared lines of her legend easily and comfortably, and it made no difference at all that it was her own mother whom she was deceiving.

She picked up the sun cream, brushed the sand from the bottle and held it out. "Don't forget."

Victoria took the bottle. "Of course I won't."

"Thank you."

"When are you leaving?"

"I'll have to go now."

Lola heard that and looked up with wide eyes. "You're going, Mummy?"

Lilly crouched down and put her hands on her daughter's shoulders. "I have to, poppet."

"But you said we could spend the whole week together."

"I know I did, and I'm sorry. I promise I'll make it up when I get back."

"You said that last time."

Lilly felt the sting of tears in her eyes and stood up before her daughter could notice. She wiped them away with the back of her hand, reached down to pick up her bag and turned to her mother. Victoria nodded; there was nothing else to say.

Lilly felt a tightness in her throat and knew that the tears were close now, and that, if she didn't hurry, she wouldn't be able to stop herself from breaking down. She leaned down and kissed her daughter on the top of the head, breathing in the scent of the warm sand and the sun lotion. She straightened and turned, kissed her mother on the cheek and set off across the beach, her feet sinking in the warm sand as she aimed for the wooden steps that led up to the promenade.

KRASNODAR

37

Control woke up in an unfamiliar room. It took a moment to remember what had happened to her and where she was; she recalled the ambush, waking up in the boot of the car and the flight south to Krasnodar. She opened her eyes and looked around from the bed at the room. There was a window up high on the wall, and sunlight streamed through it in a bright shaft. She stared at the motes of dust that were picked up by the light, slowly spinning and turning as they drifted down to the floor. The window might have offered a way out of the room, but what would be the point? She was in a military facility deep inside the borders of Russia, presumably surrounded by soldiers and with no means of transport. Where would she go? They would find her in no time at all.

She remembered the final leg of last night's journey. They had brought her onto a military base and then to a barracks of some sort, a series of one-storey buildings arranged around a central courtyard. She had been led into one of the buildings, following a corridor from which a number of rooms could be accessed. Some of the doors were open, and Control could see that each led into a small bedroom. She was led all the way to the bottom of the corridor to the final door on the right-hand side. The room that she had been given was simple, but not uncomfortable. There was a single bed, a chest of drawers and a tiny adjoining bathroom with a toilet, shower and sink. She had been tired last night and had fallen asleep quickly; her dreams, though, were haunted by the faces of her husband and her daughters.

Control had no experience of being in a situation like this. She had been given hostile environment training, but a week spent with the Regiment in Hereford being kept awake for hours and having a red-faced sergeant major bellowing in your face was not the same as this. The training was always undercut by the knowledge that it was simulated, and that, in due course, she would be allowed to leave and go home. This was different. She still clung to the hope that whoever it was who had taken her hostage would have known that she was an important member of the security service, and that there would be the most extreme consequences if anything was to befall her. But even as she remembered that, there was the nagging doubt that they might not care. They had killed Weaver, and they had made no effort to prevent her finding out where she had been taken. If they were worried about the repercussions, surely they would have taken steps to make it more difficult to ascribe blame. Wouldn't they have blindfolded her? The fact that they had not done that—and that they had *told* her where they were going—was chilling.

Control's predecessor as the head of Group Fifteen, Michael Pope, had come from the SAS before he had been recruited to the Group. His predecessor, Harry Mackintosh, had also been in the military. Control tried to think what they would have done in the same situation. The standard Regiment response to being held captive in a hostile environment was simple: you recited your name, rank and service number for as long as you could until the enemy broke you. She had reviewed John Milton's file when she had considered bringing him back into the fold to babysit Tristan Huxley and remembered that he had been held captive on two occasions, and how he had managed to withstand brutal interrogation for days. She wondered whether that would be what would happen to her today; would she be drugged or beaten in an attempt to get her to reveal state secrets, or had she been brought here for another purpose that she couldn't yet discern?

LONDON

38

T he driver had picked Lilly up at the pier, turned around and set off back to London. He delivered her to a building on the banks of the Thames that looked for all the world as if it were a legitimate office. Indeed, anyone who was minded to look into what went on behind the dusty windows would have found an import/export business with employees who were often sent around the world to attend to existing customers and work to secure new contracts. Global Logistics was listed at Companies House and employed a hundred people who worked on real business from their desks on the first and second floors. It looked just as one would imagine, at least until one reached the upper floors. From there it was possible to see what went on behind the carefully maintained façade. The Group had operated from the building for years, with the twelve agents who comprised its active complement supported by analysts and technicians provided by the other groups that, when taken together, comprised the Firm.

Lilly went through the doors that opened onto the reception area and made her way to the desk. The man staffing it gave her a nod of recognition, went through the rigmarole of handing her a lanyard with a swipe card attached to it, and indicated that she should go through to the lobby, where the two wheezing old elevators offered access to the other floors in the building.

The meeting was held in one of the conference rooms on the fourth floor, and, as she pushed open the door and went inside, Lilly saw that four of her colleagues were already waiting for her. The agents in the Group did not know each other unless they had been sent out on a mission together, and, even then, they were under instructions not to reveal anything about themselves. They were never given each other's real names, referring to each other either by way of the legends that were crafted for them by the cobblers of Group Eight or by their numbers within the Group's hierarchy. Lilly saw three agents whom she recognised: Two was sitting at the head of the table, Four was standing at a window with his back to the door and Eight was looking at something on her tablet. She had never seen the other agent before: his skin was the deepest black, and he wore a languid expression that spoke of a sardonic wit.

Two turned in her direction as she came inside. "Number Twelve," he said, "you took your time."

He stared at her, his dark eyes shining with a mixture of desire and cruelty. Lilly's palms started to sweat; she closed her fists in the hope that might disguise her discomfort.

"Excuse me."

Lilly stepped out of the way as a man she had never seen before made his way inside. He went to the front of the room.

"Please," he said, gesturing to the seats. "Sit down. Let's get started."

The man took off his jacket and hung it over the back of

a chair. He did not sit. He had a harried look about him, and the dark bags under his eyes suggested that he had not slept.

"I realise it's extremely unusual for someone outside of the Group to deliver a briefing like this," he said, "but I'm afraid to say that we are operating in unprecedented times. You should all know who I am, but, for those who don't, I'm Benjamin Stone, and I'm the chief of the Secret Intelligence Service. Thank you all for coming. The five of you make up the available complement of active Group Fifteen agents. Your colleagues are in theatre, but we're looking at whether we can abbreviate some of their assignments so that they can also be available to assist with the situation that I am going to tell you about today. It's serious enough for us to do that."

The atmosphere in the room was tense.

"I'll keep it brief. There was an attempt on the life of Number One in Finland earlier this week. He survived, but the woman he was there with did not. Control travelled to Finland to lead the investigation into what happened, and, last night, the car that she was travelling in was ambushed. Her aide-de-camp was shot and killed, and she was abducted."

Lilly's mouth fell open, and the others were listening with the same obvious shock. She could see why she had been summoned here on such short notice, an attack on Number One would have been serious enough, but for someone to go after Control? That was *extraordinary*.

Two sat forward. "Do we know where she is?"

"We don't. We're operating on the assumption that she's been taken across the border into Russia, but we can't be sure. Of course, this is a matter of the utmost importance, and every available resource has been deployed and made available to the investigation."

"Is One still there?"

"He is. He's leading the investigation with help from John Milton."

"What?" said Two. "Milton? Seriously?"

"I'm about as happy with that as you are," Stone said. "There is the suggestion that this might have something to do with Tristan Huxley. It hasn't been made common knowledge yet, but Number One and Milton were involved in protecting Huxley's life while he was finalising an arms deal between the Russians and the Indians. I'm sure you've all read the papers and are aware of what Huxley has subsequently been accused of doing. One and Milton were involved in the events that led up to his arrest, and we think it is possible that what happened to One was inspired by Huxley. As you know, he has escaped from custody. It is at least possible that what happened to One—and perhaps what has happened to Control—is revenge for what happened to him."

"What do you need us to do?" Four asked.

"You are all to make your way to Brize Norton and wait to be deployed. You will each be provided with a full file containing everything that we have been able to ascertain about what happened—you'll need to read and digest it. I understand that Milton is investigating a potential lead. If that comes to anything, or if we're able to discover anything else that might give us a better idea about what happened and who we are dealing with, I have standing orders that you will be deployed immediately."

The agent whom Lilly did not know raised a hand. "With orders to do what, sir?"

"The priority is Control, Number Ten," Stone said. "Your objective will be to go in and get her."

"Do we know that she's still alive?"

"We do not. If we find out that she's been killed, your orders will be to exact such a heavy toll on whoever is responsible that they will never think of doing something so foolish again. Any other questions?"

The room was silent.

Stone rapped his knuckles against the table. "Good," he said. "Get to the airfield. Dismissed."

KERCH STRAIT

39

I t took Milton nine hours to fly from Riga to Krasnodar, taking a connecting flight in Moscow. He made his way through the small and rather dingy terminal until he found the taxi rank. The meeting had been arranged to take place aboard one of the ferries that plied the water between Port Kavkaz in Krasnodar Krai and Kerch in Crimea. The terminal was fifty kilometres to the west, and Milton settled back in the cab and watched the grim Russian landscape as it rolled by on either side.

Milton knew almost nothing about the man he was here to meet, save that he would go by the name of Yakim Vinogradov. Anna said that he was not prepared for Milton to know what he looked like and that he would take the meeting only if he was satisfied that it was safe to do so. The man was paranoid, but Milton could relate to that; he would have felt exactly the same if he had still been in the Group and had been asked to meet a Russian agent. Vinogradov had been Anna's source for years, and the only way he would have been able to ensure his continued longevity while betraying the Unit was to be very, *very* careful.

The traffic to the west of Krasnodar was bad, and, as the minutes ticked by, Milton looked at his watch with an increasing sense of trepidation. He wanted to ask the driver how long he thought it would take, but his Russian was limited, and he didn't want to give away the fact that he was a foreigner. He had to make do with the Google map on his phone and keep his fingers crossed that the red lines that signified heavy traffic would clear before they reached them. This was not the sort of rendezvous where tardiness would be tolerated. Vinogradov was bound to be twitchy, and Milton didn't want to give him any reason at all to abandon the plan and disappear.

If the ferry departed and he wasn't on it, Vinogradov would vanish, and there would be no second chances.

THE TAXI REACHED THE PORT, and, after paying the driver a fare that had almost certainly been inflated, Milton stepped outside and made his way to the terminal building. He bought a ticket for the next crossing and, conscious that time was running away with him a little, walked briskly down to the pier where he joined the other passengers who were waiting for the ferry. He looked around at the other men who had gathered in the waiting area and couldn't see anyone who deserved more than a second glance. If Vinogradov was waiting with them, Milton couldn't pick him out.

A member of the ferry staff spoke over the public address system and announced that the boat was ready to start boarding. Milton followed the others outside, and they all lined up again to wait their turn to ascend the gangplank. The name of the boat—*Glykofilousa III*—was painted on the prow. It was a modern roll-on, roll-off vessel, with cars and freight loading directly from the pier. It looked as if the crossing would be quiet; the newly constructed Crimea Bridge fifteen kilometres to the south had reduced the need for the ferries, and there was talk that these crossings would soon be discontinued.

The gate was opened, and the passengers, each showing the bored-looking member of staff their ticket, climbed the gangplank. Milton found his way to the observation deck, went outside and stood by the rail. It took another ten minutes for the last cars to be boarded. Milton looked around again at the others on the deck and started to harbour doubts that the rendezvous would happen at all. There was a young man and woman—a couple, judging by their comfortable manner; a man with two boys; a woman in her late thirties with a scarf around her neck; an elderly man wearing a pair of dark glasses in spite of the gloom.

The last truck rumbled onto the car deck, the door was raised, and, with a mournful ululation from the horn, the ship's engines pushed it out into the channel.

Milton rested his elbows on the rail and watched as the dock fell away from them.

The woman in the scarf crossed from one side of the deck to the other and stood next to Milton.

"Mr. Smith?"

He looked at her with annoyance at being duped.

"You're not what I was expecting."

"I like to be careful."

"Anna *has* met you?"

"She has. But she has instructions about how to refer to me. She said you'd understand."

"What do I call you? You're obviously not Yakim."

"And you're obviously not John Smith."

"No," he said. "I'm not, but it'll do."

"You can call me Yevgenia."

"Not your real name, either?"

"No. But it'll do."

Beyond the moment of surprise, Milton wasn't fazed in the least. The Group included women and always had; after all, he had been recruited and trained by Beatrix Rose. There were files that were always better handled by women. He knew of many targets who had made the chauvinistic mistake of underestimating the women who had been sent to deal with them, and it was a mistake that they didn't get to make twice.

She kept her eye on him. "I take it you were careful?"

"Of course."

"I have to be cautious."

"I can understand that. Thank you for coming."

She chuckled humourlessly. "We're just two strangers having a chat on the ferry."

"Anna told you what I want?"

"She did. You still have to persuade me why I should help."

Milton held her eye. "Because you need me just as much as I need you. You want a new life. Somewhere you won't be found. Enough money so you won't have to work. You want papers. I can arrange all of that for you."

"Why should I trust you?"

"I took a risk coming here. And Anna trusts me. You've already decided it's worth it—we wouldn't be meeting otherwise—so maybe we ought to get to business."

She eyed him for a moment and then, a decision made, gave a stiff little nod. "I'll hear you out. What do you want?"

"A friend was attacked by two men earlier this week. I want to know whether they were from Unit 29155."

Yevgenia cocked an eyebrow. "Where?"

"Finland."

"Why do you think it might be us?"

"One of the men was killed, and I've seen his body. He had a lot of plastic surgery, and his fingerprints had been burned off. I remember something similar from something I was involved in before."

She turned her hand over so that it was facing palm up. "Like this?"

Milton looked: the tips of her fingers were a little glossy, with no prints.

"Just like that."

"One of Otto's little tricks."

Milton looked up at her face to see whether he could detect any additional work that had been done.

She noticed. "It's hard to spot," she said. "I had my nose and my ears done. The surgeon who does it is very good. He'd cost tens of thousands if he were still practising in Khamovniki."

"You said Otto," Milton said. "Otto Sommer—right?"

"That's right. How much do you know about him?"

"Anna told me a little. East German, ex-Stasi, fled to Russia after the Wall came down."

"Nothing else?"

"Not really."

The breeze tugged at the end of her scarf as she looked away. "He's polite. Quietly spoken—I don't think I've ever heard him raise his voice. He's the most terrifying man I've ever met. His call sign is *Drema*. You speak Russian?"

"A little."

"It means Sandman," she said. "He puts people to sleep. Fuck knows how many times he's killed. Hundreds. I asked you whether you'd been careful coming here—that's why. If he finds out that I've been talking to anyone about what we do..." She made a gun with her fingers and put it to her head. "That'd be that."

She looked away, and Milton could see, beneath her cool insouciance, that she was scared.

He brought the conversation back around. "The hit in Finland—was that him?"

"Yes."

"And did he arrange to have a man broken out of prison in the UK?"

Her eyes narrowed. "Yes. Tristan Huxley."

"Do you know where they took him?"

"To the base."

"In Krasnodar?" Milton asked.

Yevgenia nodded.

"Is he still there?"

"He was this morning."

Milton gripped the rail tightly. He hadn't anticipated good fortune, but it appeared that he had struck lucky twice: his theory about who had attacked Thorsson had been confirmed, and he had found Huxley.

"What do you know about the dead man in Finland?" Yevgenia asked him.

"Not much."

"No name?"

Milton shook his head. "We searched, but nothing came up."

"His name is Alyosha Sommer. Otto's son. Sommer has always been particular about who joins the Unit, but he has a blind spot for his boys. He has three—Alyosha, Lukas and Maxim—and they all joined. Lukas and Maxim are good soldiers, but Alyosha's a drunkard. I worked with him once in Syria—never again. He's unreliable, reckless, unprofessional."

"And dead," Milton said.

"And dead. And that will be a problem. Sommer won't accept that. Your friend would be well advised to disappear. It's not something that'll be forgotten. He's already taken steps to find out where he is."

"How do you mean?"

Yevgenia paused, as if weighing up how much to say. "I was in Finland yesterday. Your friend is a Group Fifteen agent—yes?"

"That's right."

"His boss was in Finland, too. A woman. Her car was ambushed on the road out of the city. She was brought here."

Milton struggled to control his reaction. "How do you know that?"

"Because I was part of the team that took her. I got back last night just before Anna contacted me."

"Describe her for me."

"Middle-aged. Dark hair. Dresses well."

He swallowed on a dry throat. "Where is she now?"

"At the base. Sommer is going to use her to find the man who killed Alyosha."

Milton could barely credit it. The good fortune that had delivered him to within striking distance of Huxley had just become something else. Control was here, too? It sounded very much like it.

He urgently needed to speak to Thorsson.

The ferry's horn boomed out again as the Crimean coast came into view. "Is that enough?" Yevgenia said.

"Not yet. Tell me about the base. How many men?"

"The Unit is small. There are thirty of us, but at least half are in Ukraine. I doubt there's any more than ten there at the moment—and it might be less."

"Security?"

"It's attached to the Tenth Special Mission Brigade of the Spetsnaz. You need to get through their base before you get to ours."

"Is that possible?"

Yevgenia snorted. "It shouldn't be, but it is. We're deep in Russia. The guards take it for granted that no one would be foolish enough to attack them there. Some of the shifts can be on the lax side. Why? You said you just wanted information."

"I need to get inside."

She held up her hands. "Then I'll wish you good luck."

"I'm going to need your help."

"No," Yevgenia said. "That's not what I agreed to."

"The woman you kidnapped last night is the one who can make you disappear. I don't have another way to get it done. If you want to get out, I need to get *her* out first."

She stared at him, then looked down at the churn of water at the prow and muttered something under her breath. "Just get you inside?"

"That's all."

"I'll think about it," she said.

"There's one other thing. I only have your word for what you've just told me. London will want proof before they green-light an operation to get her out. You'll need to get a photograph of her."

She nodded. "That's easy enough. I'm due back at the base tonight."

BRIZE NORTON

40

Lilly and the others were transferred from London to Brize Norton in the back of two SUVs. They travelled light, with no equipment or weapons. Lilly assumed that their kit would be delivered to them when they were in theatre by way of one of the Group quartermasters who were placed in most of the countries in which agents might be expected to work.

Brize Norton was an RAF facility seventy-five miles northwest of London. Lilly had flown out of it before, both during her time in the army and then during her first assignment as a Group Fifteen agent. They were driven into the base and shown through to a large ready room. An officer in a flying suit came over to introduce himself. Lilly could see from the two bars on his rank badge that he was a Flight Lieutenant, equivalent to an Army Captain, and the distinctive wings on his chest said that he was a pilot. He told them that he flew with the Special Forces Flight of Number 47 Squadron and that he would be flying them in one of the flight's C-130Js as soon as their destination was confirmed.

Lilly looked out of the window at the Hercules that was being fuelled on the runway and found that she was anxious. The uncertainty around the operation was beyond anything that she had experienced before, and, judging by the air of nervous tension as they waited, she guessed that it was unusual for everyone else, too.

Four found a remote control and used it to switch on the large television that had been fixed to the wall. He navigated to a rolling news channel and turned up the sound; a reporter was stationed outside Scotland Yard, and, with the familiar sign revolving slowly behind her, the woman provided an update into Tristan Huxley's escape from custody.

"You think this is to do with him?" Ten said.

Four spread his hands. "It'd be a coincidence if it wasn't. He gets out, and then One is attacked, and Control is abducted? I wouldn't bet against it."

"What's he worth?" Eight asked. "Billions? You can hire a lot of muscle with that."

"It'll be him," Four said.

"He's got a private island," Two said. "Maybe we're going there."

"There are worse places," Four said.

There was a table with refreshments in the corner of the room, and Lilly went over to get a cup of coffee and a dough-nut. She was pouring milk into her mug when she noticed that Two had made his way over to the table and was standing behind her. Her skin prickled as he moved in closer than necessary.

"Afternoon."

Lilly put the milk jug back on the table, turned and tried to step around him. He shuffled to the side and blocked her.

"Not now," she muttered under her breath, aware that it would do her no good at all to cause a scene.

"We're stuck here until they tell us where to go. Can't we have a chat?"

"No," she said. "We can't. There's nothing to say. We've said it all before. And do you really want to do this in front of the others?"

He smiled, revealing his perfect white teeth. "Do *what* in front of them? Talk?"

"You're making me uncomfortable."

He ignored her objection. "Have you thought about what I said?"

"How many times are we going to go over this? There's nothing to think about. It doesn't matter what you say—the answer will still be no."

"You're getting divorced."

"That won't change anything. I'm not interested."

"You were interested in Casablanca."

She closed her eyes as she struggled to keep her temper. "That was a mistake. It should never have happened. And it's never going to happen again."

It was funny, Lilly thought, how a moment of weakness could metastasise into something that would have consequences in every part of her life. She often found herself going back to the week the two of them had spent in Morocco six weeks earlier. It had been her first assignment since she had been minted as Number Twelve, the most junior member of the Group. They had been sent to Casablanca. The government had made a post-Brexit manifesto pledge to increase investment into African businesses, and a key strategy focussed on Morocco's burgeoning financial sector. An offer had been made by the London Stock Exchange that would see a partnership agreement signed with its equivalent in Casablanca. The CEO of the Casablancan exchange, a man called Mohammed Bouteflika, had suggested that he would prefer to deal with the French, not least because—the briefing document reported —he had been on the payroll of the French government for years.

Given that billions were at stake, a red-rimmed file had been prepared and handed to Control to action. Two had been chosen as the senior agent, and, given that the assessment suggested that a female operative would be able to get closer to the target, Lilly had been selected, too. She had been nervous as a recent graduate into the field and, as they flew out together, had been relieved to have been paired with the second-most senior agent on the roster.

Their target had previously thwarted an attempt on his life by a Moroccan mafiosi who had tried and failed to launder his money through the purchase of stock options. The experience had fostered a suspicious attitude and had seen the CEO hire a security detail from Manage Risk, the American private military contractor. Lilly's legend saw her as an entrepreneur with an interest in acquiring a tech start-up that was building a solid reputation in the identity verification space. It was Lilly who was said to be the multimillionaire, and, in an inversion of the norms that tickled her at the time, Two was made out to be a diligent partner who was there to offer support. The two of them splashed the cash in a fashion that befitted their putative wealth: they flew first class, took a room at the exclusive Villa Diyafa and dined at all of the best restaurants. They shared a room—it couldn't really be otherwise—but Two slept on the sofa while Lilly had the bed.

Lilly had arranged a meeting with the target where the acquisition of the start-up was discussed, together with an offer for the CEO to join her board and pilot her push into the North African market. The meeting had gone well, and, after an hour of shameless flirting, she had invited him to dinner. He agreed, and, perhaps anticipating an evening that would include more than what was on offer at La Bavaroise, he had left his security detail at home. Lilly had emptied a packet of flunitrazepam into his €100 glass of Le Montrachet Grand Cru, and, seemingly drunk, he had staggered into the taxi that Two had stolen earlier that evening. Lilly had waved him off and left him to his fate.

They had left the city as soon as the deed was done, driving along the coast to Tangier. Their exfiltration plan had them leaving the country by ferry and crossing the Strait of Gibraltar to Algeciras, but, by the time they arrived, it was midnight, and the first ferry didn't depart until eight the following morning. They found a dingy hotel near the docks that couldn't have been more different to the luxury they had left behind and checked in. Lilly was buzzing from the successful conclusion of her first assignment and had not resisted when Two had grabbed her roughly and kissed her.

He told her to ignore his alias and use his real name: Damien. She had said that they didn't need to share personal details, but, lying together in bed afterwards, he had told her his life story, and, feeling that it would be churlish not to reciprocate, she had buckled and told him some of hers. It only occurred to her afterwards that he might not have been honest. He had been more guarded when they woke up the next day, and she was left with the impression that he had fed her the details of another legend that he had used on another job; she had been truthful, and, fresh in the Group, she had cursed herself for her naïveté.

They had returned to London, and, overcome with guilt,

she had confessed to her husband. He had taken it badly and, after a month apart, had demanded a divorce and custody of Lola. She hadn't mentioned her difficulties to anyone, yet Two had somehow known about it. He had invited her to dinner and, when she had politely refused, had tried again and again. She rebuffed him each time, not just because she wasn't interested in him and regretted her error, but because her lawyer had made it plain that Jimmy might have hired a private investigator in an attempt to demonstrate her continued infidelity. Flowers were delivered and sent back. A box of chocolates was thrown in the bin. A bottle of the same Le Montrachet Grand Cru that had sealed the CEO's fate came next. She sent that back, and when Two approached again, she threatened to go to Control.

He had backed away after that, but it had evidently been only a temporary reprieve. He wasn't ready to give up.

"Come on," he said, his eyes gleaming. "Dinner when we get back."

"How many times do I have to tell you? That was a mistake, and it's never—*never*—going to happen again."

His smile faded, and the shine went from his eyes. "Why are you being like this?"

"I don't know how I can be any clearer. It shouldn't have happened. I'm sorry it did."

"I'm not," he said.

"I'm very sorry about that."

"Are you saying that you don't feel anything for me?"

She looked at him and decided that she couldn't say what she wanted to say. She had found him attractive, and she had been excited by the successful outcome to the assignment. Her marriage had been foundering, and she was lonely; she had allowed her resolve to weaken enough for the idea of a night in bed with him to seem like it might be fun. But she had seen something in his eyes that night that terrified her: an absence, a soullessness, a void where his compassion and kindness should have been. She had berated herself that that had surprised her; he was Number Two, after all, and had served in the Group long enough to climb almost all the way to the top. She had no idea how many men and women he might have killed, nor what he had experienced during an army career that he himself had described, as they lay in bed, as "heavy." She had looked at the scars on his sweat-slick skin as he slept and tried to imagine the murders that each one must have commemorated. No wonder he was heartless. No wonder he was immoral. His humanity had been sucked out of him.

"Lilly," he said, "you—"

"Are you fucking *stupid*?" she hissed across him. "Don't use my name."

She took her coffee and moved away, her shoulder bumping against his as she stepped around him. She could feel his eyes on her back as she crossed the room and sat down next to Four, making a show of watching the news while desperately trying not to think of all the ways a vengeful colleague like Two could blight her career and, if he did, what that would mean for her and her daughter.

KRASNODAR

41

M ilton knew that he really ought to have found a secure means of reporting what he had discovered to Thorsson. He knew that there was a chance that someone might intercept the call, either at the point of origin or at the point of receipt, but he also knew that he didn't have the time to find a channel that he could be sure would not be eavesdropped. Instead, he took a bus into Kerch and found a store on Marshala Yereomenka Street where he could buy a phone with a pre-paid SIM. He walked back to the dock, and, while he waited for a ferry to take him back to the other side of the strait, he sat on a bench opposite a deserted amusement park and dialled Thorsson's number.

"It's me," he said once the call had connected.

"John?"

"Call me back from a secure line."

"Hold on."

The line went dead. Milton watched the boats plying the strait as he waited for Thorsson to return his call.

The phone buzzed.

"Are you secure?"

"This is an encrypted line, and I'm in the bubble."

"Just you?"

"Just me."

That was better, Milton thought. It would be difficult for anyone to monitor his line this quickly. Ziggy Penn might have said it was possible—and maybe it was—but it would have to do.

"What is it?" Thorsson asked. "It's pandemonium here."

"Control?"

Thorsson paused. "How do you know about that?"

"I met someone in Krasnodar who was part of the team who took her."

"Shit," he swore. "You were right?"

"Yes. Unit 29155. It was their agents who attacked you, too."

Thorsson paused again before replying, "Are you *sure*?"

"The man you killed is Alyosha Sommer. He's the son of Otto Sommer—he's in charge of the Unit. They were responsible for getting Huxley out of the country, and it looks like they've been put at his disposal in exchange, if you ask me, for him getting the arms deal over the line or because he's blackmailing someone senior or both. But it's definitely them. Huxley sent them after you."

"Why would they do something stupid like taking Control?"

"Maybe Huxley blames her for what happened, too. Or maybe it's for leverage."

"Her for us?"

"Think of how much she knows. The two of us would be easy to give up in exchange. Do you think London would think twice?"

Thorsson swore again.

"What's happening?" Milton asked him.

"The whole of the Group has been put on alert. Everyone who isn't already in the field has been called in, and the others who can be taken off their assignments are on their way back. They've got five agents sitting on the runway at Brize Norton just waiting to be told where she is."

"I can help them with that," Milton said. "She's here, in Krasnodar. The same place they're keeping Huxley."

42

Control was napping when she heard the key in the door to her cell. The guard was probably delivering her dinner, but Control wasn't in the mood to eat, so she stayed where she was on the mattress. The door swung open, but then nothing happened. Confused, Control opened her eyes and saw the woman who had been a part of the team that had taken her in Finland. She was standing in the doorway with a phone held up in front of her. She took a picture.

"What are you doing?"

The woman ignored her, took another picture and then backed out of the cell.

"Hey! Come back!"

The door swung shut, the key turned in the lock, and the woman's footsteps echoed away along the corridor.

~

CONTROL GOT UP AFTER THAT. She sat on the edge of the bed and tried to anticipate what would happen to her. She guessed that she would be taken to Moscow, where she would be interrogated for everything that she knew. She tried to consider how London might react. They wouldn't be able to break her out, but maybe they would try a swap. There were Russian agents who were in custody in the West who could be exchanged for her. But perhaps the Russians wouldn't even acknowledge that they had her; what then? An attempt would be made to ensure that she was silenced. The Firm had assets within the FSB, and Control knew that London would consider that burning one of them would be a price worth paying if it meant that her lips were sealed. The only questions were how it would be done and whether it would happen before the Russian interrogators had broken her resistance.

She heard footsteps approaching again and stood. The key was turned in the lock, and the door opened.

It was the man who had been in charge of the operation to capture her. "You have a visitor."

She retreated, and Tristan Huxley stepped into view.

"Hello, Control." Huxley stepped inside and looked around the room, a smile playing at the edges of his lips. "This is what happens."

"What's that?"

He gestured to the room. "When you cross me. *This* is what happens."

"What happened to you had nothing to do with me."

"Please."

"It really didn't."

"You *didn't* tell Milton and Thorsson to come after me? Come on."

"Milton has developed a conscience in the time that he has been away from the service. It would seem that you fell foul of that."

He snorted and waved a hand dismissively. "I don't believe you."

"It doesn't matter what you believe. And it's all moot. I don't have the slightest problem with what he did. I would have given the order myself if I had known what you'd been doing."

"Spare me the sanctimony. You're all hypocrites—you and everyone else had no problem at all with me when I was working for you. None. You can tell me how offended you are, but we both know it's all just a self-serving sham. You didn't care when I was working for the government. It suited you to turn a blind eye."

Control clenched her jaw, determined not to show her anger in front of him. "What do you want?"

"I just wanted to say hello. I'm leaving soon. We won't see each other again. I wanted you to know that Thorsson and Milton are both going to die for what they did to me."

"Let me guess—India?"

"That's right—New Delhi. I have a deal to close. One of the things that I've learned in business is that you always need to be prepared, and you always need to have an alternative when events make whatever it was you were going to do impossible. I've worked for the British government for years, and it turns out that it all meant nothing. You tossed me aside when it became inconvenient to work with me. Fine. I can adapt. Others are more pragmatic. The Russians and the Indians, for example. They're only interested in what I can deliver for them. So I'm going now, and I'll be out of your reach. I don't need you. I don't need the government. I never did." He backed up to the door. "Goodbye, Control. Enjoy whatever they have planned for you."

He stepped into the corridor, and the door was closed and locked.

Control listened to the sound of his footsteps as he retreated up the corridor. She was overcome with a sense of hopelessness. She was trapped, buried deep within an unfriendly country where, even if those who might have been able to help her had known where she was, there would still have been nothing that they could have done. She thought of her girls and tried to ignore the dread that she would never see them again.

THE BLACK SEA

43

They had been in the air for five hours. Lilly stretched out her legs to try to get the circulation flowing a little better. They had been notified that Control's location had been verified and had scrambled for the Hercules at once. The aircraft had a top speed of six hundred kilometres an hour, and now they were approaching the coordinates in the northern Black Sea that had been selected as their insertion point. The plane had enough range to get there but not enough to make the return trip without refuelling. Lilly hadn't been clued in to the rest of the plan, but assumed that the crew would land at Incirlik in Turkey. The base was operated by NATO, and it ought to be possible to set down quietly and without too many awkward questions about where they had been and what they had been doing.

There was plenty of space for the dispatcher, two other airmen and the five agents even with the twenty-eight-foot-long rigid inflatable that had been loaded into the cargo bay with them. The boat and its launch platform had been slotted onto the runners that ran the length of the bay, with tethers holding everything in place. The additional aircrew were from 47 Air Dispatch Squadron of the Royal Logistics Corps, and, as Lilly watched, one of them spoke with the RAF loadmaster.

Lilly readied herself as the loadmaster signalled that they were approaching the drop zone and that they should form up and attach their static lines. The five agents went to the rear of the bay, safely behind the RIB, and checked that their static lines were securely fixed to their deployment bags. They took the other ends of the lines and hooked them to the cable that ran the length of the fuselage. The loadmaster checked that they were safely attached and then went to lower the ramp.

The warning lights flashed as the ramp descended. Lilly looked out of the back of the Hercules. They were at three thousand feet, and, from up here, all she could see was water. It was a clear night, and the moon painted a silvered line that rippled as gentle waves rolled left to right.

The loadmaster gave the signal that they were ready to deploy. The boat's drogue parachute was deployed and quickly opened in the rush of air behind the Hercules. The tethers were released, and the drogue yanked the boat toward the open door, the platform sliding across the runners and down the ramp and out into the night sky. Lilly watched it as it fell, the static lines opening its four parachutes and slowing its descent. The platform detached from the boat and fell away under its own pair of chutes while the RIB drifted down alone.

The loadmaster gave the signal to jump. *"Go!"*

Two went first. He walked to the ramp, waited for the loadmaster to double check that he was hooked up, and then stepped out. Ten followed, and then it was Lilly's turn. She stepped over the edge, her arms crossed over her chest, and was immediately snatched by the wind. It was tempting to try to maintain stability by extending her arms and legs, but she remembered her training and kept herself symmetrical. The line went tight and yanked the deployment bag from the container on her back. She looked up as the canopy inflated, the canvas snapping and cracking as it opened. The noise of the Hercules's engines grew faint until it was an indistinct hum; Lilly concentrated on the sound of the wind rushing into the canopy.

She steered the chute so that she followed the others down. Two hit the water first, and then Ten. Lilly flared the chute to slow herself down, her boots cutting slices through the spume-topped waves. She took a breath, released the chute and slid under the surface, the sudden shock of the freezing water taking her breath away as surely as a punch in the gut. She kicked up, broke the surface and looked for the boat. It was a hundred yards behind her.

Four got to it first, hauling himself up and over the gunwale. Lilly kicked out, powering through the waves until she was alongside. Ten reached down, slid his fingers beneath her vest and hauled her up. She kicked, hooked a foot over the edge of the gunwale and then clambered onto the deck.

Ten looked down into her face. "You okay?"

She held her thumb and forefinger together to signal that she was, and sat up with her back against the stiff sides of the inflatable hull. Two clambered aboard and then Eight. Ten started the engines, opened the throttle and turned to the north. The boat accelerated away, the twin outboards punching it through and over the waves. Lilly looked up and saw the Hercules in the distance, the captain turning it around and heading south. It would refuel and wait for them, ready to fly them and—they hoped—Control back home.

Ten checked his GPS.

"How far out?" Lilly yelled over the roar of the outboards.

"Forty-seven miles. We're good."

They each had a flask of hot coffee in their packs, and Lilly took hers out. She unscrewed the top, poured out the coffee and drank, grateful for the warmth in her stomach. She looked astern as the winking lights of the Hercules disappeared into the darkness. They were heading toward an unfriendly country, and they were on their own.

KRASNODAR

44

The RIB had two outboard motors and was commanded by Ten from a control console at the stern. It had an inflatable collar built from a neoprene composite tube that was fitted with stowage pouches, lifelines, paddles and a towing eye. There were eight seats, and a machine gun was mounted at the bow.

The sea was a little choppier now that they were in sight of land, and Lilly held onto the grab handles to anchor herself in place. The water stretched around them with darkness in every direction save for dead ahead. The only illumination was to the north. She could see the glow from the settlements on Russia's southern coast: Novorossiysk, she thought.

She looked up and saw that Two was making his way around the edge of the boat. He sat down in the seat next to her, close enough that their shoulders touched.

"Last chance."

"*Please*—not now. Just shut up and do your job."

Lilly looked around anxiously, but none of the others were paying them any attention. The noise of the big outboard motors was loud enough that their conversation would be inaudible.

"You want to think again."

"Or what?"

"You know I have to file the report about Casablanca."

"And? Everything went down like it was supposed to."

"Not how I saw it."

"Fuck off."

"I saw a rookie agent who almost messed it up." He shrugged. "Bouteflika saw through you. He would have gone to the police unless I stopped him."

"That's a lie."

"You know what else I saw? Someone who froze when the time came. Someone who lost her nerve."

"She won't believe you," she said, feeling the blood rushing to her cheeks.

"Really? I'm Number Two—*Two*—and you're Twelve. You need to be realistic. You know what she'll do when I tell her? She'll bounce you out of the Group so fast your feet won't even touch the ground. She doesn't take chances, Lilly. You need that report to be *perfect* or you're done." He reached out and rested his hand on her knee. "It doesn't have to be like that, though. You give me what I want, and I'll put in a good word for you. I'll tell her how good you were."

She tried to stand, but he reached out and grabbed her arm.

"I mean it, Lilly—I will fucking *ruin* you."

She tried to shake his hand off, but he just tightened his grip. "Get *off* me."

He held on for another beat, then let go.

She stood, then turned back and leaned in so that her lips were right up against his ear. "Touch me like that again and it'll be the last thing you do."

He grinned and gave her a wink.

Ten pulled back on the throttle, and, the speed bleeding away, the prow dipped down into the water. Lilly went and sat in a spare seat in the first row; Two stayed where he was, just behind, and she felt his eyes on her like a prickle on the skin. She had to hold onto the grab handles to stop her hands from shaking. She was full of anger that he would blackmail her like this and full of fear that, unless she did what he wanted, she would suffer. She couldn't afford to lose her position, not now, not when she was desperate for money she didn't have to pay for the lawyers. She was caught, compromised by a moment of stupidity and now made to pay for it. She tried to clear her mind. It would have to wait. She needed to get back home in one piece. She would be no good at all to Lola if she ended up dead or lost somewhere in Russia.

45

Milton was on the outskirts of Adygeysk, a small hamlet on the banks of the vast fifteen-mile-long lake formed by the Kuban River. He had followed the instructions that Yevgenia had provided him, driving to the Gazprom petrol station that served drivers on the north-south road that ran out of Krasnodar and following the track opposite it toward the water. He hadn't been sure that she would agree to provide them with additional assistance beyond the intelligence that she had already supplied, but Thorsson had relayed a guarantee from Whitehall that she would be given everything she had asked for on the condition that she helped secure Control's release. That had been enough, and she had confirmed to Milton that she would help them get inside the base; everything else would be down to them.

Milton drove on. The lake was enormous, and the silver of the moon glittered against the mirror-smooth surface. He saw a derelict building on the other side of the pebbled track and pulled over. The building looked as if it was deserted, but, as Milton eyed it, the door opened, and Yevgenia stepped outside.

"Are they still there?" he asked.

"Yes."

"Both of them?"

She nodded. "But not for long. Huxley is being moved."

"Do you know where?"

"No. But Otto's jet is being prepared, and they say Huxley is going to be on it."

"When?"

"I don't know. You're going to have to keep your fingers crossed."

Milton knew that he had an advantage over Huxley: he could not have imagined that anyone knew where he was, nor that he could possibly be vulnerable here. But if he was allowed to move? It might prove difficult to locate him again, and, even if Milton *could* do that, tonight offered all sorts of advantages that were unlikely to be repeated.

Milton gestured to the building. "What is this?"

"A boathouse. It hasn't been used for years. And it'll be quiet. Perfect for what we need."

Milton looked at the surrounding area. It was isolated, and the bundles of silage wrapped in polythene bags that had been stacked opposite the boathouse were the only obstacles that obscured the otherwise open sight lines. They would have plenty of notice should anyone try to approach. The location had been well chosen.

Yevgenia had provided coordinates earlier that day, and Milton had encrypted them and sent them to the consulate-general in Saint Petersburg. They were taking a chance in trusting her, but Milton had considered the risks and concluded that it was one that was worth taking. Anna had vouched for her, and Yevgenia was clearly invested in securing a life away from the Unit. There was a chance that she might decide that she could do better for herself by betraying Milton and the inbound team, but, even if she did that, she would have to explain to Moscow how she had found herself in a position where she had been introduced to them in the first place. Anna had explained how she had been selling them out for years; Milton doubted that she would be ready to take the risk that her sins would be absolved. He wasn't thrilled with the leap of faith that they would have to take, but, given the stakes, it was unavoidable.

Yevgenia pushed open the door to the boathouse and led the way inside. Milton peered into the gloomy interior. One end was open to the lake, and an interior dock had been built; the remains of a rotted hull were tied up there. The water was still, and the boat barely moved, occasionally bumping the dock as the gentle breeze raised the smallest ripples. Barrels with iron straps had been stacked to one side, coils of rope hung from hooks, and an iron track led out of the water and up into the rear of the building where boats could be hauled out for repair. The structure was falling down in places, and a wide hole in the roof revealed a patch of sky that sparkled with stars.

Yevgenia went to the door and looked out. "When are they coming?"

Milton looked at his watch: it was one in the morning. Thorsson had explained that the team would be coming in by boat and that the drive from the coast was around a hundred kilometres.

"A couple of hours," he said.

46

The boat continued on for another ten minutes, the prow slicing through the swell. The only noise was the rumble of the engines, the slap of the waves against the hull and the call of seabirds high above. The coast drew nearer, a stony beach that led up to gentle hills. The terrain beyond the beach was thickly wooded with larch and fir. The hills formed a small cove that would offer a useful spot to leave the boat without fear that it would be seen.

Lilly was searching for signs of their rendezvous when she saw a torch flicking on and off. Ten saw it, too, and changed course slightly so that he could beach nearby, driving them up onto the sand. It was sloped, enabling him to nose up so that they could disembark without getting wet. Lilly jumped down first, her feet slapping on the damp sand as she hurried to the fringe of vegetation and the spot where she had seen the torch.

The trees were packed in tightly, with dense undergrowth filling the spaces between the trunks. She saw a big man waiting there, his blond hair particularly visible in the gloom.

"Who are you?" he said.

"Twelve."

"I'm One," he said, stepping away from the tree. He was enormous, a good eight inches taller than Lilly.

Two stepped around Lilly.

One turned to him. "Status?"

"All to plan," he said.

"Good. There's a parking space a mile to the north. We need to get a move on."

The team removed their lightweight tactical immersion suits, stowed them on the RIB and then followed One through the undergrowth. A track had been cut through the trees, and they made much swifter progress once they had reached it. The path climbed the gentle slope of the hill, reached the summit and then continued down the other side to an unpaved road. One followed it to a small parking area that had been cleared, with the trunks of felled trees used to mark its boundaries. A large UAZ-2206 had been parked there, a seven-seat minibus with enough space for a decent amount of luggage as well.

He opened the rear doors to reveal four large bags that had been stacked there.

"Equipment," he said, gesturing to the bags. "We'll equip once we get to the RV. Get in—we need to get on the road."

Lilly went around to the side of the minibus and opened the sliding door. She climbed inside, grateful that it was Ten and not Two who slid onto the seat next to her. One went around to the front and got into the driver's seat, starting the engine and waiting for them all to embark. The doors were slid shut, and One put the minibus into gear, bumping over the rough track as they set off. They followed it through the trees for five minutes before they came to a junction with a four-lane highway that hugged the coast. One turned right, heading east, and brought the minibus up to eighty kilometres an hour.

"It'll be ninety minutes from here," he called back to them.

47

They arrived at just before three in the morning. Milton heard the squeak and bounce of the minibus's suspension as it negotiated the uneven surface of the road. It approached with its headlights off; Milton and Yevgenia stayed inside the boathouse, watching as it slowed to a halt. Yevgenia pulled a pistol from her jacket and held it down low, against her leg. Milton was painfully aware that he was unarmed and knew that he would have difficulties if she had sold him out to the Russians. He looked over to a metal bar that had been used to jam open the gears of the small crane that would once have been used to lift boats into and out of the water, but that was it. Yevgenia and an armed Spetsnaz team from the base just a mile to the south would have made short work of him, iron bar or not.

But it wasn't a Spetsnaz team. The driver's door opened, and Björn Thorsson stepped out.

"Know him?" Yevgenia said.

"Yes—wait here."

Milton held position for another moment to be as sure

as he could be that Thorsson hadn't been followed, and then stepped out of the boathouse. Thorsson saw him, raised a hand in acknowledgement and opened the side door. Three men and two women disembarked. They were wearing black combat trousers, black tactical jackets and boots. Milton thought that he recognised one of the trio of men from the time he had worked with the Group to protect Huxley, but didn't think he had seen the others before.

The newcomers drew closer. The men wore their hair short and had the physiques of special forces soldiers, not overly large, but obviously fit and strong and with bearings that suggested confidence. The women had the same confident demeanour.

Thorsson approached Milton. "All good?"

"It's fine. Did you meet the quartermaster?"

Thorsson nodded. "They left the vehicle where they said they would with the gear inside." He went to the back and pointed to the bags. "Let's move it and unpack."

He took out a large bag and hauled it over the track to the boathouse.

"How's the Russian?" he said.

"She's done what she said she'd do," Milton said, hefting a second bag out of the van.

"Trust her?"

"Would it make any difference? We don't get anywhere without her."

Thorsson sucked his teeth and then nodded. He deposited the bag inside the boathouse and waited for Milton to do the same. The remaining bags were brought inside by two of the agents.

Thorsson closed the door. "Let's get the introductions out of the way first."

"I'm Ten," said one of the men.

"Twelve," the woman next to him said.

"Two," said a man with a cruel turn to his lips.

"Four."

"Eight," said the second woman.

Two turned to Milton. "You?"

"John Smith," Milton said, wary of introducing himself by his real name in front of Yevgenia.

Two turned to the Russian. "And her?"

"She's our Russian contact," Milton said. "She's going to help us to get in."

Yevgenia pointed to the bags. "Equipment?"

Thorsson nodded. He unzipped the first bag and started to take out the items that had been stowed inside. He took out seven M4 rifles with barrel-mounted lights, then a dozen additional magazines with 5.56mm ammunition. Milton opened a bag and withdrew seven M9 pistols with drop holsters, additional 9mm magazines, and two Mossberg shotguns with pouches of 12-gauge rounds. Two opened a bag and took out the first of several ballistic vests. Twelve arranged two dozen flashbangs and fragmentation grenades, flex-cuffs and pistol belts with knives, compasses, IR chem-stick spinners and red-light LEDs. By the time they had finished, the boathouse contained a small armoury that was more than sufficient to equip them all.

Yevgenia watched as the gear was arranged and then nodded in appreciation. "That'll do."

Milton strapped on one of the holsters and put the M9 inside, taking an additional magazine and shoving it into the pocket of his jeans. "Shall we get started?"

48

Yevgenia took out a map and spread it across the floor. She dropped to her knees, fished a pencil from her pocket and drew a circle around the terrain to the west of the north-south E592 road that Milton had taken to arrive at the boathouse.

"The base is here," she said, tapping the pencil against the area that she had just encircled. "Two bases, really: one for the Spetsnaz and one for the Unit." She took out a printout from Google Earth that showed the view from a satellite overhead. "The Spetsnaz base is the larger one—here." She tapped the map against a large built-up area that Milton estimated to be perhaps a mile and a half from top to bottom and a mile from side to side. "The Unit is here." She moved the tip of the pencil and drew a circle over the collection of buildings to the north.

Milton leaned down so that he could examine the satellite photo. The base was the shape of a large rectangle, widest on its east-west axis. There were three large buildings that looked like warehouses on the outside, forming a barrier to a collection of smaller buildings that were arranged around a large courtyard.

"It's around six acres," Yevgenia said. "The outer perimeter is behind a ten-foot-tall fence with razor wire. There's another perimeter inside that one that's electrified. There are cameras and regular patrols."

"How good are the guards?" Thorsson asked.

"Poor. They use locals. They take it for granted that the base is secure. They're lazy."

"How many soldiers at the base?"

"Five hundred at the main facility. Most likely ten with the Unit."

Two cocked an eyebrow. "Why so few?"

"There are only thirty in total. The others are on assignment."

"So who's left?"

"Enough of us to break Huxley out and then to go into Finland and get the woman you're so concerned about."

Milton looked down at the map. "How would you get inside?"

"There's forest to the north of the facility," she said, tapping her pencil against an area of dense green. "They've cleared a margin between it and the fence, but you'll still be able to get close without being seen. The patrols are lax— once every half hour, less often if you're lucky. You ought to be able to cut through the fence and get inside without anyone raising the alarm."

"And then?"

"The cameras."

"Could you switch them off?"

"I think so."

"How would we know?"

"We'll synchronise watches and agree on a time. I'll make sure they're off when they need to be."

Thorsson laid his finger on the map. "Good. We get through the fence, avoid the guards—then what?"

"The second fence is electrified. I'll deal with that at the same time as the cameras."

Thorsson turned his attention back to the map. "Assume we get through the second fence. What next?"

Yevgenia tapped the pencil against the three larger buildings on the satellite map. "Warehouses here and here and here. The steam plant is here, and the garage and maintenance facility is here. The buildings in the centre, around the courtyard, are for accommodation. That's where she's being held."

"Which one?"

She laid the pencil on the building at the northeast corner of the courtyard. "Here, but I heard they were going to move her to one of the other blocks. Not sure which one."

"Doesn't matter," Thorsson said. "We'll sweep the buildings and eliminate anyone we see. I don't want any pursuit." He gestured to the door. "Could you wait outside for a moment, please?"

Yevgenia didn't object. She left the map and the printout on the floor of the boathouse, took out a pack of cigarettes and a lighter and went outside.

"We've got to go in soon," Thorsson said. "They won't want to leave her here for long. They'll move her to Moscow, and that'll be the last anyone ever sees of her."

"Agreed," Four said. "It's got to be now."

Two held up a hand. "Hold on." He pointed to Milton. "I know who you are—we all know who you are—but no one has explained why you're here. What does Control have to do with you?"

"It's not because of—"

"He owes her." Thorsson spoke over him. "He owes Control, and he owes me. There was a file on him, and I refused to action it. And then, when I brought him in instead, she rescinded it. That's why."

"You feel obliged?" Two said, not ready to stand down.

"Something like that," Milton said.

Two wasn't convinced. "Doesn't sound like what I know about you."

"Leave it," Thorsson said.

Two looked as if he was going to say something else but, as he looked at Thorsson's glower, thought better of it.

"We leave in ten minutes," Thorsson said. "Get equipped."

Thorsson went outside and indicated that Milton should follow. Yevgenia was smoking next to the minibus and out of earshot.

Milton gestured back to the boathouse. "They don't know about Huxley, do they?"

"No. Just Control. Huxley isn't the objective—she is."

"There's something you need to know," Milton said. "He's being moved. Yevgenia told me."

"When?"

"Tonight," Milton said. "He might already have gone."

Thorsson swore.

"Leave him to me," Milton said. "You and the others get Control. I'll search the other buildings for him. If he's still there, I'll take him out."

"But not Sommer," Thorsson said. "If he's there, he's mine."

49

They drove to the coordinates that Yevgenia had
supplied and then turned off the main road,
following a short track to a clearing where they
would be able to leave the minibus without fear that it
would be spotted. Ten killed the engine, and they all got out,
each of them with carbines cradled and ready, holstered
pistols worn on belts or shoulder rigs, and grenades and
other equipment fitted into the pouches that were arranged
on the fronts of their ballistic vests. Milton had one of the
M4s now in addition to the holstered M9. He had checked
both weapons before they had left the boathouse and was
satisfied that they were clean, oiled, and in full working
order and that he had sufficient ammunition in the event
that things didn't go quite as they had planned. The intention was to get in, get Control and get out again without
attracting the attention of the guards or the agents stationed
at the base, but they all knew that the chances of doing that
without firing a shot were slight.

They each had night-vision goggles, and Milton pulled
his down and settled the strap so that the goggles sat

comfortably, the rubber eyepieces pressing against his forehead and the tops of his cheekbones. He reached up and
switched them on, waiting for a moment before the familiar
green wash descended.

"Comms check," Thorsson said.

Each member of the team checked in, confirming that
they were both transmitting and receiving satisfactorily.
Milton went last, making sure that the throat mic was
clipped to the front of his jacket and adjusting the earpiece
so that it was a little more comfortable.

They had all synchronised their watches before leaving,
with Yevgenia also confirming that she had the same time.
Milton checked his watch now: it was just after zero five
hundred hours. Yevgenia said that they had around an hour
before sunrise, darkness might help them going in, but it
was unlikely to be relevant when they were on their way out.

Thorsson signalled that they should move, and they
set out.

MILTON FOLLOWED Thorsson down the slope that led from
the parking area. They formed up in three pairs. Thorsson
and Two moved forwards first while those behind waited.
They found cover, and the second pair moved out, then the
third. The movements of the six agents were smooth and
natural, like a reflex, and Milton—bringing up the rear—
found himself adapting easily to their rhythm. The sky was
clear, with more moonlight than Milton would have liked,
but the grasses were long, and they were all dressed in black,
shadows that passed through the vegetation with barely a
whisper.

The slope ended at a stream; they waded through it and

continued through a meadow of long grass that delivered them to the start of the tree line. It had been years since Milton had been involved in this kind of mission with other Group agents, but he had had dealings with them in the years since he had left service and knew that standards had been kept as high as when he had been Number One. Thorsson was very good, and Milton could see from the way that the others moved that they were just as competent. There was an almost unconscious understanding between them that he recognised from before; they each knew their roles so completely that they fitted together as a seamless whole.

Thorsson stopped just inside the tree line. He waited for Milton to reach them and then set off again. Milton remembered Yevgenia's map and knew that they had just over a kilometre to cover before they reached the first fence. They moved more quickly now that they were under the cover of the branches, and then Thorsson found an animal track that carved a path between the trunks of the conifers and birch that reached up all around them. The track was treacherous, with patches of slippery moss and lichens; the undergrowth was composed of rhododendron and gooseberries and blueberries that pressed in against them as they moved. Thorns snagged against the fabric of Milton's sleeves and scraped across the chest plate of his vest. The agents moved with speed and stealth, and Milton found that he was breathing hard at the pace that they had set. He reflected ruefully, and not for the first time, that he was not as young as he used to be. He would have matched their pace easily if this had been fifteen years earlier, but it wasn't. He could keep up, but he was working harder than they were. The pace was necessary; Yevgenia had agreed to cut the power to the second fence at zero-five-forty hours, meaning that they had less than thirty minutes to get to it.

Thorsson raised his closed fist, and they stopped, each of them dropping to one knee. Milton rested his finger against the carbine's trigger guard and scanned his arc of responsibility. He breathed in and out, annoyed with how hard he was having to work, and looked down the barrel of the gun as a large roe deer burst between the trunks of two spruce, paused for a moment to look in their direction and then, scenting their spoor, bolted away in the direction from which it had arrived.

Thorsson signalled that they should advance and then set off, each pair proceeding once more with the same margins between them. The terrain dipped down into a valley that was bisected by another stream. They forded it by way of a series of natural stepping stones and then climbed the opposite slope. The trees became less dense at the top, and then, as the ground levelled out, Thorsson stopped and signalled that they should gather once more.

Milton reached the others and wiped the sweat from his brow. They had covered the ground quickly, and, as he looked at his watch, he saw that they had sixteen minutes before the power would be cut. But before they could think about that, they had the matter of the first fence to attend to. The obstacle in front of them was as tall as Yevgenia had suggested, and topped with a nasty coil of razor wire that would be impossible to scale without it cutting them to shreds.

Thorsson put his finger to his lips to order silence, and gestured to indicate that he had seen motion. They waited in the cover of the undergrowth until they saw the shaft of white from the torch of the guard who was making his rounds. It was just a single man, and it was evident from his ambling gait that Yevgenia had been correct about the lack-adaisical attitude to security. The guard stopped, reached into his jacket and took something out; the glow of red gave away the cigarette that he lit and clamped between his lips. Milton looked at his watch; they couldn't afford to wait for him for too much longer if they wanted to get to the second fence in time to coincide with it being switched off. Milton was considering whether they might have to shoot the guard when, after a protracted pause, he flicked away what was left of the cigarette and carried on his rounds.

Thorsson indicated that he would cut the fence. The others stayed in cover as he scurried ahead. He pulled a pair of cutters from one of the pouches on his vest and set to work, starting at the bottom of the fence and working up.

Milton kept watch, and, as Thorsson snipped through the final wires and began to open a hole that would be big enough for them to slide through, Milton saw movement from the direction in which the guard had disappeared.

He pressed the transmit button and whispered into the microphone, "He's coming back!"

50

Thorsson was caught in no man's land; he would have to cross the cleared ground before he was able to get back into cover, and—assuming that the guard was awake enough to notice him—he would be easy to spot. He lay flat and still as Milton and Four, who were the closest members of the group to him, laid themselves prone and shuffled ahead so that they could aim through the undergrowth. Milton pushed his goggles up and put his eye to the optical sight on his rifle, centring the reticule so that it was over the guard's body. He slipped his finger through the guard and squeezed back until he felt the give of the trigger between his joints.

Four did the same. "I have the shot," he said, his voice hushed and tight with the tension.

The guard reached the spot where he had dropped his cigarette and bent down.

"Wait," Milton said.

"Do I take the shot?" Four said, ignoring him.

"Don't shoot," Milton hissed. "Repeat: do not shoot."

The guard picked something up, turned around and continued on his rounds again.

"He dropped his lighter," Thorsson reported, his voice a little tighter than usual. "Let him go."

Thorsson waited until the guard was out of sight before rising to his knees and continuing to open the fence. He slid through. There was no cover on the other side, so he quickly scurried ahead, staying low.

The others followed, one by one, with Milton coming last of all. The sharp edges of the wires snagged at his jacket and the straps of his vest, but he worked his way through them and sprinted across the open ground, reaching the second fence where the others were waiting. Two and Ten were lying prone in firing positions, their weapons aimed so that they could cover the approaches in both directions should the patrolling guard return before they were able to get inside.

Milton checked his watch. "It should be off."

He reached forward and, taking a breath, held the back of his hand against the fence. If there was voltage, the muscles in his hand would spasm, and, if he had used his palm, there was a chance that he would grip the fence and wouldn't be able to let go.

Nothing happened.

"It's off."

Thorsson took the cutters, shuffled up closer to the fence and cut through the first wire. It snapped with a metallic twang, and he moved onto the second.

Milton recce'd their immediate surroundings and compared it to what he remembered from Yevgenia's maps. The base was arranged in a rectangular shape, bordered by the forest to the east, south and west and a road to the north.

They had breached the two fences in the northeastern corner and were now facing one of the long buildings that Yevgenia had identified as warehousing. It was around a hundred feet long, with a gap between it and the next identical building. Milton recalled the map: the warehouses surrounded a courtyard within which the smaller buildings that comprised the administrative headquarters and accommodation for the Unit could be found. The road to the north was the route that would be taken to get into and out of the base; it led back to the larger facility to the south, so they would retrace their steps once Control had been located and secured.

Thorsson held up three fingers and, on cue, the seven of them split into three separate groups: Milton, Thorsson and Eight went left, following the warehouse in the direction of the gap between the buildings; Four and Ten went around the edge to the right; Two and Twelve waited a moment and followed, with the intention of making their way around the third warehouse so that they could approach the courtyard from the south.

Milton and the others stayed close to the wall, hurrying from cover to cover: a wooden crate that looked as if it had been used to transport ammunition; an SUV with mud-splattered wheels. Milton swung the rifle around so that he could carry it on the strap without using his hands and drew the M9. It was fitted with a suppressor that, while it wouldn't eliminate the sound of a shot, would muffle it enough so that the odds of detection were reduced, if only by a little.

The three of them reached the corner and looked out at the buildings that made up the headquarters. They were much smaller than the warehouses, single-storey brick-built structures that looked as if they had been erected sometime in the last few years. Milton could see wide parking spaces that were used, he guessed, to accommodate the private vehicles of the soldiers as they made their way to and from the facility. There were a handful of cars parked in the bays, together with military vehicles. Milton was surprised to see a TELAR vehicle, one component of the BUK-M3 medium-range surface-to-air missile system, the tracked launch vehicle mounted with the system's standard six-tube missile launcher array at the rear and the fire control radar at the front.

There was no sign of anyone: no soldiers, no guards, no civilians. The base was quiet. Milton scanned the buildings until he found the door of the one they had been assigned. There was a single lightbulb above it that cast a warm glow out onto the hard ground. There was a series of windows on either side of the door, but they were covered, and no light was visible from within. It could have been a barracks, but it was difficult to be sure from this distance.

Thorsson reached for the transmit button and pressed it. "Group, this is Ghost One. We're in position. Over."

Milton saw movement from one of the other buildings and swept the binoculars around. It was the building in the middle of the row—the one that Two and Twelve had been allotted—and, as Milton watched, three men stepped out. He focussed the binoculars. Two of the men were facing in his direction, blocking the third man behind them. It was difficult to make out any detail in the pre-dawn gloom, save that the man to the left of the trio was older than his companions and wearing a suit. The younger man to his right, his face turned away now, was wearing army fatigues.

"Group, this is Ghost Two. Are you seeing this? Ghost One, acknowledge. Over."

"Ghost Two, Ghost One, acknowledged. Continue to observe. Take no action unless engaged or on my orders. Out."

Milton recognised the old man, too. Yevgenia had shown them a picture, and the man in the suit was definitely him. He had a better view of the second man now, but didn't recognise him. The two men at the front of the trio parted to reveal the man behind them, and Milton cursed under his breath.

Huxley.

Sommer said something, and Huxley acknowledged it with a nod; Sommer pointed to one of the other buildings, and the three of them set off in that direction.

Milton edged over to Thorsson. "I can't let him leave."

Thorsson put the binoculars down. "If we take him out now, we'll never be able to get to Control."

"I'll follow. If you can find her and get clear, *then* I'll take him out."

"If not?"

"I'll stay on him for as long as I can."

"All right." Thorsson opened the channel. "Group, this is Ghost One. Wait for the tangos to move out; then we breach on my mark. Acknowledge. Over."

The others radioed back that they understood their orders. Milton watched as Sommer, Huxley and the third man stepped away from the building. There was a decent distance between them—Milton thought around a hundred yards—but he could still hear the braying of Huxley's laughter. He looked relaxed and without a care; the thought of his nonchalance infuriated him, and, for a moment, he doubted himself. He wanted to slot him there and then, but he knew that he would be putting the others at risk and dooming Control. It was selfish; he had to wait, much as it stuck in his craw.

The three men disappeared into the next building along.

Thorsson turned to look at Milton. "Go."

Milton nodded and set off. There was a better vantage point on the other side of the courtyard, and, if he hurried, he would be able to get there without anyone seeing him.

He was fifty yards away when he heard Thorsson's voice in his ear.

"Group, this is Ghost One. DAGGER in fifteen seconds. Out."

DAGGER was the agreed codeword for a silent, unopposed entry.

Milton started to count down from fifteen.

"Group, Ghost One, DAGGER now. Out."

51

L illy had tried to avoid being paired with Two, but he had indicated that he would go in with her, and that was that. He went first, scurrying across the courtyard while Lilly covered him. They had been given the building at the northwestern corner of the courtyard, identified by the Russian mole as an accommodation block. Thorsson had taken the block that Yevgenia said was where Control had been kept when she had taken her photograph, but, given that the base was not heavily manned and that they had surprise on their side, it had been decided that they would take steps to minimise the possibility that they might be pursued once Control had been located. It was left unsaid, but there was another motive for taking out anyone they found on the base: the Unit had crossed a line with their campaign against the Group, and they would make sure that a heavy price was exacted.

Two reached the building, pressed himself up against the door and signalled that Lilly should follow. She took a breath, checked that she couldn't see anyone in the pre-dawn gloaming, and, satisfied, she ran out to join him. She reached the building and took up position on the other side of the door. Number One had made his way to the building where they believed Control was being held, and now his partner, Eight, crossed as he covered her. Lilly saw movement as John Milton, on the other side of the courtyard, took up a spot where he could observe the building into which the three men that they had seen earlier had entered. Lilly didn't know his orders, nor how they intersected with what the rest of them were there to do, but it made no difference to her. She knew what she had been told to do: clear the building and eliminate anyone they found inside.

Two pointed to himself to signify that he would be the breacher, Twelve nodded that she understood, and then Two raised five fingers, indicating that he would go in on five. Twelve slung her rifle on its strap, moved it around so that it was across her back and drew her M9. Two took a breath and then stepped in front of the door, gently trying the handle. Finding it unlocked, he opened the door and slowly pushed it back.

They went in, both with their guns up and ready, but there was no one there. The corridor ahead of them had three doors on either side; they were identical and provided —Lilly guessed—accommodation for agents who were required to stay on base. They split, Two going to the doors on the left and Twelve to the doors on the right, and started to clear them. Lilly tried the first door; it was unlocked. She opened it and stepped inside. She was right: the room beyond had a bed, a wardrobe and a desk. The lights were off, and, from what she could see, it was empty.

"Clear," she whispered.

Two was in the doorway of the adjacent room. He stepped inside and, after a moment, reported that it was also clear. They met in the corridor again, and, for a moment, their eyes locked. She saw something there—a hunger, a gleam of self-satisfaction—and she fumbled the tethers that were anchoring her in the moment.

Two started along the corridor to the next door; she froze.

He noticed and turned back. "Come on," he muttered.

Lilly had been clinging on, clearing her mind so that she could focus on navigating the danger that they were in, but now it felt as if she were floating free. It had taken only that one look into his eyes, and she had known that he would never stop.

"Twelve," he said, "we need to move."

She saw the smugness in his face, the confidence that he had snared her in a dilemma that had reduced her options until there were only two choices left: submit to him or quit. Except that it wasn't a choice, not really, because without her place in the Group, she wouldn't be able to afford her lawyers, and, without them, she would lose Lola, and, without her, what would be the point of anything? Two knew her vulnerabilities and would leverage them to force her to do what he wanted. Lilly started to panic, and then, when she remembered where she was, her panic deepened until it became dread. She was buffeted by a sudden swell of dizziness so powerful that she reached out a hand to steady herself against the wall.

She felt a hand on her shoulder—Two's hand—and, without thinking about what she was doing, she jerked her hand up and struck him, the butt of her pistol cracking into his face. He staggered back, his nose bleeding onto his lip, his eyes burning with fierce anger. Lilly's panic became something closer to hysteria, and, even as she saw her future contracting into a single hopeless point of failure and despair, she saw her last desperate option and took it without thinking.

She raised her arm and aimed the pistol at him, the barrel quivering with the trembling of her hand.

He saw it and shook his head. "Don't be so fucking stupid—"

She pulled the trigger.

There was no distance between them; she couldn't miss. He was wearing a flak jacket, so she put the bullet into his forehead.

He fell.

Lilly stepped over him and fired again.

52

Milton had found a spot behind a giant 2S7 Malka 203mm self-propelled howitzer. He was surprised to see a gun like that in the camp, but was glad of the cover and was able to observe the door that Huxley, Sommer and the third man had used to get inside the building. It was impossible to say whether there was another way out, but Milton couldn't easily go around the back and check. He reassured himself that there was no real prospect that they knew the base had been infiltrated, and no reason for them to try to leave without being seen. He had his M4 and was confident that he would have been able to hit them from his firing position, but couldn't engage them until Thorsson and the others—hopefully with Control—had made their escape. And, he admitted, a kill at range would be unsatisfactory. He wanted to get up close so that Huxley knew it was him.

He had decided to wait where he was until they emerged when the door opened, and the light from the interior was cast over the slabs of the yard. Huxley, Sommer and the third man stepped outside and started walking in the direction of the parked cars to the south. Milton stiffened. There was cover between here and there that he could use, but not without risking exposure while negotiating the spaces in between.

He gave them a head start and then pursued, striking a balance between speed and caution: he was wary of losing them yet concerned that he might give himself away were they, or anyone else, to look in his direction. They reached the parking area. Milton hurried behind a large crate of artillery shells and looked around it; Sommer was standing beside an Audi A6 that looked out of place between a Ural-4320 six-wheeled truck and a UAZ-469 light utility vehicle. Milton shouldered his rifle and put the scope to his eye. This wasn't an ideal firing position, but there was only a hundred yards between him and Huxley, and he would have backed himself to make the shot.

Milton pressed the push-to-talk button. "Ghost One, this is Ghost One-Four. What's your status? Over."

The third man came around and opened the rear door for Huxley.

"Ghost One-Four, Ghost One," Thorsson replied. "Nothing yet. Out."

Huxley got into the rear of the car. Milton nudged the barrel down and sighted through the windscreen. He would be able to take him; the 5.56mm round would punch straight through the glass and then through him. He put his finger to the trigger and took up the first pressure. A squeeze to apply just a little more pressure would fire the round, but he couldn't. Not yet; not until they were clear.

Sommer leaned into the back, said something to Huxley, shut the door and slapped his palm against the roof.

"Ghost One-Four this is Ghost One. SITREP? Over."

"Ghost One, no change. Out."

Milton looked through the sight as the lights of the Audi flicked on. Sommer returned to the courtyard on foot while the car rolled through a puddle of mud and turned so that it could make its way through the compound to the access road.

Milton's mind raced. He could go north and try to intercept them on the road, but he would have to negotiate the two fences; it wouldn't be possible in time. He still had a shot, but that wasn't an option, either, not without putting Thorsson and the others at risk.

He watched the car negotiate the courtyard and knew that he couldn't just let Huxley go.

He slung the rifle over his shoulder, checked that the way ahead was clear and unobserved, and sprinted for the nearest car. It was a VW Tiguan, and, to Milton's relief, the door had been left unlocked. He opened it, passed his rifle into the cabin and rested it on the passenger seat with the barrel in the footwell, and looked for the key fob. It appeared that the owner was not concerned that the vehicle might be taken; Milton found the fob in the cupholder. He pressed the ignition, closed the door and, leaving the lights off, he dabbed the accelerator and turned the wheel.

"Ghost One, this is Ghost One-Four. Huxley is leaving— I'm going to follow. Good luck. Out."

The Audi was a distance away from him; Milton pressed down on the accelerator and picked up speed.

53

Thorsson reached for the handle. The door was unlocked, and he was able to push it open. He checked that Eight was ready to follow, raised his M4 and went inside. A corridor reached back from the main door, with a series of internal doors to the left and right. The decor was ascetic, with walls painted in beige and the doors made from unfinished wood. Thorsson checked the door to his left and right and found an empty office, with computers on simple metal desks and filing cabinets that, when he opened them to check, contained reams of documents in Russian that he couldn't read. Eight cleared the room to the right, signalling that it was empty, and Thorsson moved along the corridor. The second room he checked looked to be used as a gym: there was a rack of dumbbells against one of the walls, and a static bike that looked as if it had seen better days.

Thorsson pressed the push-to-talk button. "Group, this is Ghost One. SITREP? Over."

"Ghost One, this is Ghost Four. Nothing. Over."

Thorsson waited for Two or Twelve to report, but there was nothing.

"Ghost Two, this is Ghost One," he said. "SITREP. Over."

He waited, but there was no response. He was about to try again when he heard Twelve's voice.

"Ghost One, this is Ghost Twelve. Nothing yet. Out."

Thorsson allowed himself to wonder: What if the intelligence they had been given was wrong? What if she wasn't here? Or what if she *had* been here but had been moved somewhere else? What would they do then?

What if Milton's Russian source wasn't playing straight?

What if she was still working for the Unit?

Could they have blundered into a trap?

They didn't know Yevgenia; Milton didn't, either. She had been persuasive with the intelligence that she had provided, and her details had checked out when the analysts in Group Six had verified them, but they were still taking a leap of faith.

He chastised himself for the distraction of dwelling upon his doubts and continued. Eight continued in the lead, and they cleared two rooms that were used for accommodation. There were beds—made up but unused—with wardrobes and televisions. The first room looked as if it was vacant, but the second had clothes in the wardrobe and a large rucksack propped up against the wall.

Thorsson backed out of the bedroom, closed the door and led the way along the corridor to the end. It led to a T junction, with branches running left and right. Thorsson turned to the right and almost bumped into the soldier who was coming in the opposite direction. He was dressed in boxer shorts, had a towel around his shoulders, and his hair was wet. He had a packet of cigarettes in one hand, a lighter in the other and a cigarette between his lips. He was trying

—without success—to strike flame from the lighter. His attention was distracted, and, by the time he noticed Thorsson, it was too late. Thorsson stepped into him and crunched the butt of his pistol flush against his jaw. The blow had been hasty, prioritising speed over power, and, rather than knocking the man down, it sent him staggering back into the wall. Eight raised her pistol and fired. The bullet struck him in the forehead, and he fell forward, face first, bouncing once and then lying still on the floor.

Thorsson held his pistol in a two-handed grip and waited to see whether the noise had aroused any additional attention. He could hear nothing. It was obvious what had happened: the man was using the bedroom with the clothes in the wardrobe and had gone to a communal bathroom for his ablutions. Thorsson reached down and slipped his hands beneath the man's shoulders. He dragged him back along the corridor to the bedroom and dumped him inside.

He shut the door and went to join Eight at the junction. He turned right, passed the open door of the bathroom and continued to a final door before the corridor came to an end. This one was identical save for a viewing hatch that had been inserted at eye level. Thorsson moved the slat to the side and looked into the room. It was a bedroom, just like the ones that he had just seen, but this one was occupied. The light was on, and a woman was sitting on the edge of the bed.

Control.

54

L illy felt the warmth on her face and reached up with her free hand, wiping her palm across her forehead and eyes. The skin was stained red with Two's blood.

The earpiece buzzed. "Group, this is Ghost One. SITREP? Over."

Lilly looked down at Two's body. The second bullet had punched a hole straight through his head, going in just beneath his right eye and then out again somewhere on the other side. He had toppled over and landed on his back; his limbs had spasmed, but not for long. He was still now, quite dead.

"Ghost Two, this is Ghost One. SITREP. Over."

Lilly's pulse was racing, and her breath, despite her best efforts, was coming in ragged gulps. She needed to work out what to do next, but, to do that, she needed to bring herself back under control.

Come on, she told herself. *Think of Lola.*

She closed her eyes and counted to ten. She breathed: in and out, in and out, in and out. It helped. Her hands trembled from the adrenaline, but she no longer felt as if she was going to faint. She bit down on her lip and concentrated on Lola until she could picture her face: the way she nibbled her nails, the freckles that were scattered across her cheeks and the bridge of her nose, the strand of errant hair that always ended up in her mouth. What would happen to her if she didn't get home again? Jimmy didn't want her—not really; the attempt to get custody was about scoring points.

She tasted blood in her mouth and realised that she had bitten into her lip.

She opened the channel. "Ghost One, this is Ghost Twelve. Nothing yet. Out."

Footsteps.

She opened her eyes and froze.

Footsteps in the corridor.

"Yuri?"

It was a male voice. The block was occupied after all. There were at least two men inside: the speaker and Yuri, whoever that was. Lilly knew that her choices, already limited, had now narrowed even more so that there was only one thing left to do.

She raised her hands as the speaker came around the corner of the corridor. He was half naked, wearing the boxer shorts that he must have been wearing to bed, and unarmed.

He swore as he saw her.

"My name is Lilly," she said in Russian. "I'm a British agent. I'm going to put my pistol on the floor."

She knelt down, the pistol pointing up at the ceiling, until she was able to reach to the side and lay it down. She left the rifle where it was, out of reach on its strap behind her.

"See," Lilly said, spreading the fingers of both hands. "No weapon."

"Step away from it," he said.

She straightened, took five paces back and kept her hands high as the man retrieved the pistol and aimed it at her.

He gestured at her. "The rifle."

She slowly and deliberately lifted the strap over her head, crouched down again and laid the M4 on the floor.

"Turn around."

She placed her palms against the wall and hung her head. The man came up behind her and told her to get to her knees.

"I need to speak to Otto Sommer."

The man muttered something under his breath. "Him— on the floor. Who is he?"

"A British agent—like me."

"Who shot him?"

"I did."

The man frisked her with his free hand.

"Stop wasting time," she told him. "Your base is being attacked. You need to tell Sommer. They're here to get the woman who was taken in Finland."

"Why are you telling me that?"

"Because I want to defect," she said.

55

The door to the cell was locked, but the key had been left there. Thorsson turned it and opened the door. Control turned at the sound, and, as she saw him, the look of resignation on her face changed to surprise.

"Number One?"

"Yes, ma'am. With five others. Are you all right?"

"Fine," she said. "How did you find me?"

"It was Milton. We can explain later, once we're away. But we need to leave now."

She nodded. Thorsson had no idea about her background—he didn't even know her real name—but she had always impressed him with her sangfroid. She displayed it now, rising from the bed and crossing the room to the door.

"Just tell me what I need to do."

"Do you know how many men are stationed here at the moment?"

"No."

"Have you seen many?"

"No—I did think it was rather quiet. You know the man in charge?"

"Otto Sommer."

She nodded. "I've spoken to him. And Huxley is here, too, but they're moving him somewhere."

"They're moving him now. Milton is waiting until we're clear, and then he'll do what needs to be done."

Thorsson led the way out of the cell and back along the corridor. He opened a channel and reported that he had secured Control, and that the others should make preparations for immediate exfiltration. They each acknowledged receipt of the order.

Thorsson opened the channel again. "Ghost One to Ghost One-Four. Please acknowledge. Over."

Thorsson could hear the sound of a car's engine when Milton replied, "Ghost One-Four, go ahead Ghost One. Over."

"Ghost One-Four, send SITREP. Over."

"Ghost One, he's on the move. I still have eyes on. Over."

"Ghost One to Ghost One-Four, give us ten minutes to get clear and then take the shot. Read back. Over."

"Ghost One, I read back: take the shot in ten minutes. Out."

56

C ontrol followed Thorsson out of the cell and along the corridor. Eight was waiting at the junction, pressed up against the wall so that she was hidden from the main corridor that ended in the door to the courtyard. Both she and Thorsson were carrying carbines and pistols, and, as they passed the open doorway to one of the rooms, she saw that they had had reason to use them. A man was lying just inside the door, sprawled out on the floor with a pool of blood next to his body. Control had heard a bang and realised now that it must have been a muffled gunshot.

"How are we getting out?" she asked him.

"We have a vehicle in the woods north of the base," he said. "It'll be thirty minutes or so across tricky ground—are you fit enough to make it?"

"I'll be fine," she said. "You don't need to worry about me."

They reached the door. Thorsson waited and spoke into the microphone that was taped against his throat. He requested a status update, and, although Control couldn't hear the responses from the rest of the team, she could see that Thorsson was bothered by something.

"What is it?"

"Two and Twelve aren't responding," he said. He thumbed the push-to-talk button. "Ghost One to Ghost Two and Ghost Twelve. Send SITREP. Out."

Control watched his face for a reaction: his concern deepened before he gave a little nod of relief.

"They're okay?"

"Twelve just said they are," Eight said. "They've cleared their building, and they're on their way out."

Thorsson appeared to be satisfied that it was safe to continue. "This first part is going to be the most dangerous. We need to get through the base, then the perimeter fences, before we get into cover. It was quiet when we came in, but that was earlier—the sun will be up soon. We'll have to move quickly."

Control was wearing the pair of kitten heels and suit that she had chosen for her dinner with Teemu Koskinen. She was hardly dressed for a run across awkward terrain, but there was no point in complaining. She would do as best she could and hope that she didn't slow the others down.

Thorsson spoke into the microphone again. "Ghost One to Group. Weapons free. Repeat: we are weapons free. Out."

Eight replaced her pistol in its holster and took a two-handed grip of the M4. Control had been responsible for her recruitment into the Group and knew that something like this wouldn't faze her; she had seen action in some of the world's most dangerous places—both before and after joining the Group—and Control knew she wouldn't hesitate to use the rifle if the occasion demanded it. Thorsson, too, was extremely competent. He had joined the Group while Pope had been Control, but she had sent him out on most of his assignments. She couldn't think of anyone she would rather have in her corner for a situation like this.

Thorsson turned back to Eight. "Ready?"

She nodded.

He put his hand on the handle. "Ma'am? Ready?"

Control nodded, too.

"Ghost One to Group. Let's go. Out."

Thorsson opened the door and, with his carbine up and ready to fire, stepped out into the courtyard beyond. Eight followed, holding up a hand to warn Control to stay back, and then, when she was happy that the way ahead was clear, beckoned for her to follow. Control stepped out into the courtyard. Four and Ten were emerging from the building adjacent to theirs, but there was no sign of Two or Twelve.

Thorsson noticed that, too; he reached up for the push-to-talk button but never had the chance to use it. Control saw movement from all around the courtyard: armed men and women appeared from between the buildings and behind the vehicles that had been left there.

"Put your weapons down!"

Control saw eight, then ten, then more. They were all around them, all armed, all toting pistols and rifles and all aiming them at the five of them.

"Weapons down—*now!*"

The command was underlined by a single shot that was fired into the air. They were surrounded, and Control could see that they would be cut to shreds if the order to fire was given.

"Do what they say," she said.

57

The man pressed the barrel of the gun into the middle of Lilly's back.

"Outside."

She pushed the door and went out into the courtyard. The others—and Control—were kneeling in a line, their hands on their heads. They were surrounded by a dozen soldiers, all of them armed. The man behind Lilly shoved her in the back, and she stumbled ahead.

"On your knees."

She kept her hands above her head and lowered herself down to the ground. The soldiers drew closer until they were just yards away from them.

One looked at Lilly and then behind her. "Where's Two?"

The man behind him reversed his rifle and jabbed the stock into his head. One grunted in pain and put down his hand to maintain his balance.

"No talking."

The man who had led Lilly out of the building stood

behind her. "There's another one inside. Dead. She says she shot him."

"What?" One muttered.

The rifle butt jammed down against the back of his head for a second time. "Quiet."

Lilly stared down at the ground.

Control angled her head so that she could look at her. "What are you doing, Lilly?"

She steeled herself, the die was cast now, and there was no other choice but to continue. "I want to speak to Otto Sommer."

"*Stop*," Control hissed.

A dark-haired woman crouched down in front of Lilly. "Who are you?"

"Group Fifteen agents."

"Twelve," Control warned.

The man standing behind Control pressed the barrel of his gun against her head. "Don't give me an excuse."

The woman shook her head. "Not her. There's a plan for her." She turned back to Lilly. "Why do you want to speak to Sommer?"

"I want to defect."

The woman took a moment to consider that, then turned away and consulted with one of the other soldiers. Their discussion, though, was moot. The cordon parted to allow Otto Sommer to pass through. Lilly lifted her head so that she could look at him: she recognised him from the photographs she had been given while they waited to depart, but they didn't convey his impression of quiet menace. He wasn't tall or physically imposing, and the clothes he wore were neat and tidy without being ostenta-tious. It was the calmness with which he regarded the scene —the six of them lined up at gunpoint—that was so disconcerting. He looked utterly unperturbed, as if it were the most normal thing in the world.

"That one," the woman said, pointing to Lilly.

Sommer turned to her. "You want to speak to me?"

"I want to defect."

"Easy to say that with a gun to your head."

"You want proof? There's an agent in the building behind me. I shot him. Go and look."

"True?" Sommer asked the others.

"Yes," said the soldier behind Lilly. "He's dead."

Sommer drew nearer and crouched before her. "Why should I listen to you?"

"I'll give you something valuable. You had Tristan Huxley here. He just left."

"How is that relevant?"

"There's a man who came here to kill him. His name is Milton. He took a car and went after Huxley. Call him. Ask him if he's being followed."

Sommer stared at her as he weighed up what she had just told him. Lilly knew that her life depended on what he decided to do. If he humoured her, perhaps her gambit stood a chance of success. If he didn't, she was finished. He would shoot her just as quickly as the rest of them.

She held her breath.

He narrowed his eyes and, after another pause, stood up and turned to one of the other men. "Call Maxim. Tell him to check that they are not being followed."

58

H uxley sat in the back of the car and looked out through the window as dawn broke over the wide, open landscape.

Sommer's son Maxim was driving, and there was another man—Maxim had introduced him as Dovlatov—in the passenger seat.

"How long to the airport?" Huxley asked.

"Thirty minutes," Maxim said.

"And the plane is ready?"

"It is. We'll be on our way as soon as we get there. You'll be in Delhi this afternoon."

Huxley was reassured that Sommer was taking his security seriously. Maxim was clearly extremely competent, and Dovlatov had a similar air of confidence about him. There was no reason to think that there was any threat to him at the moment, but Huxley had still been pleased when Sommer had said that the two men would be accompanying him to India. The Indians would assign additional security when he landed, but, even though he had no reason to think that the Russians were acting out of anything other than a purely commercial motive, he had been impressed and felt comfortable with them. He wondered whether he might be able to poach Maxim to head up his personal security detail. Cronje had betrayed him, and, anyway, Milton had killed him. That had created a vacancy, and Huxley wondered how much he would have to offer Sommer to have his son fill it. He suspected that he might be reluctant, but, in Huxley's experience, there was always a number that could get things done. Money talked. It always had.

A phone rang in the front of the car. Sommer took his cell from his pocket and put the call on speaker. The conversation took place in Russian, and Huxley was only able to understand a little of it. He could see Maxim's reflection in the glass of the windscreen and felt an emptiness in his stomach as he frowned in obvious concern. The conversation continued, and Huxley waited with growing anxiety until he heard a word that crystallised it into panic.

Milton.

"What is it?" he said. "He said Milton."

Maxim ended the call. "That was my father. The base has been attacked."

"By Milton?"

"By Group Fifteen."

Huxley panicked. "Shit. *Shit.*"

"Another car was seen leaving the base just after us. It belongs to one of the men, but he wasn't in it. Someone stole it."

"Milton?"

Huxley turned around. There was a car behind them. It wasn't close—maybe a quarter of a mile away—and too distant for him to be able to see anything behind the glare of its lights.

"That one? Is it following us?"

"It's impossible to say."

"It's five thirty in the morning. This can't be a busy road."

"It's the main road into Krasnodar," Maxim said. "We can check, though."

There was a turning ahead, just before a Rosneft gas station. Maxim turned the wheel and took it.

59

Milton squinted into the gloom ahead of him and watched as the car turned onto the slip road and took the exit. He didn't have a map or anything that would give him an idea of where they might be going, but it was unexpected; he had guessed that they were going to Krasnodar, the nearest and most obvious place where Huxley could be put on a plane to get him out of the country. But now? He couldn't be sure.

He had no option but to follow. He turned onto the slip road and followed them around. The road made a sharp right-hand turn and then bent to the right again. He went over a bridge that spanned the road to Krasnodar that he had just left and then continued, eschewing a turn onto an unpaved road that looked as if it offered access to an area of cheap housing and bending back around to the right.

Milton saw the car parked on the left-hand side of the road. It had come to a stop next to a gate in a tall concrete barrier that looked as if it might offer access to some sort of industrial facility. The car's lights were off, and the passenger-side door was open. Milton saw the man standing in front of the vehicle with a weapon to his shoulder aimed in his direction. It was a compact assault rifle—it looked like an AK-12 or an A-545 KORD—and Milton knew that he was in trouble. He hammered the brake and swerved the car to the right, bouncing over an area of rough land and scrub. The rifle fired, and bullets cracked against the bodywork of the car; one round punched through the side window, crossed through the cabin and punched out through the windscreen; another went through the same window and sliced out through the roof.

The car slewed to the right. Milton wrestled the wheel, but couldn't control the car as it slid around, swinging through a complete circle. Milton saw the wooden telephone pole coming and knew that there was no way that he was going to be able to avoid it; the car slammed into it, the impact crushing the driver's-side door and setting off the airbags.

Milton knew he had to move quickly. The door had crumpled around the pole, and there was no way that he was going to be able to open it; he unclipped his belt, struggled to negotiate the airbag and wriggled across the cabin. He reached for the handle of the passenger-side door, then saw muzzle flash, ducking down as another fusillade peppered the car from front to back. He slid his rifle into the back and then followed it, squeezing between the seats and praying that he had enough time to get out before the shooter or shooters fired again.

The rear door had been damaged by the impact, but not as badly as the one in front, and he was able to kick it open. He dropped down onto the ground and reached for the rifle. He had seen three people get into the car: Huxley and two others. He doubted that Huxley would have been given a weapon and suspected that, even if he had, he wouldn't have had the first clue as to how to use it effectively. The other two were another matter and had already outsmarted him once. Milton was outnumbered and outgunned, but there was one thing that was in his favour: he doubted that they would put Huxley at risk.

He took a breath and then swivelled around the side of the car, bringing the rifle up, taking aim at the car and firing. There were fifty yards between him and his target, and, even with an unstable firing position and a quick aim, he still heard the shots as they punched through the bodywork. The soldiers returned fire, and Milton swung back into cover just as the incoming fire cracked into the opposite side of the car. He had two spare magazines for the M9 slotted into the pouches on his vest, together with the M4 and two spare magazines for that. He ignored those for now and took out a fragmentation grenade.

"Huxley!" he called out, using the pause so that he could better understand the tactical situation. "There's no point in running."

There was no reply.

"You know me," he shouted again. "I'm not going to stop."

Another fusillade rang out against the car, pinning him in place. He put his finger through the ring and was readying himself to stand so that he could throw it when he heard the sound of an engine whining, then the churn of tyres against loose scree. He stood, pulled the pin and tossed the grenade as hard as he could. The car was moving away, and the grenade landed short. It bounced, once and then twice, and exploded in a shower of shrapnel. The car was too far away by then to have been caught in the blast; he watched in frustration as the driver reached the end of the track and turned right to join the main road that they had been on before. They were heading away from Krasnodar now, but Milton had seen a gap in the central reservation not far to the south where they would be able to cross onto the northbound carriageway and continue into the city.

Milton left the rifle behind and ran, pounding across the loose dirt of the track, through the dust and smoke that had been thrown up by the grenade, and, finally, reached the main road. The car had just completed the U-turn from one side of the road to the other and was now heading north again, quickly picking up speed.

Milton took his pistol, held it in both hands and prepared to shoot. He held position, bracing himself for the impact of the recoil, and took aim into the driver's side of the cabin. He was about to squeeze the trigger when he saw the starburst from the passenger-side window in the corner of his eye. The volley was unaimed, yet still whistled by close enough for Milton to abandon his shot and drop to the ground.

He came up again as the car raced by on the other side of the road. He aimed and fired, emptying the magazine in the vain hope that he might get lucky. It wasn't clear that any of his desperate fusillade hit; the car was still accelerating as it disappeared away to the north.

Milton watched it go, cursing himself for losing Huxley. It would have been easy to wallow in frustration and self-pity, but Milton knew he didn't have that luxury. He was without transport, in a hostile country and still dangerously close to the base.

He was considering the best course of action when he saw the lights of a car approaching from the south. He drew the pistol and stood in the road, facing the car as it approached him. He raised the gun and aimed it at the driver, raising his free hand to indicate that he needed to stop. The car slowed down and came to a halt. Milton, the gun still trained on the driver, went around to the door and opened it. He indicated that the man should get out, and, as he put his feet on the asphalt, Milton knotted his fist in the lapels of his jacket and yanked him all the way out.

He lowered himself into the driver's seat and stamped on the gas.

The second man took out a phone and made a call. Lilly waited and wondered what would happen if the call was not answered.

"I'm serious about what I said. I want to defect. I work for British intelligence. I can—"

"Be quiet," Sommer said.

The others were still on their knees with their hands clasped on top of their heads.

She could feel their disgust at what she was doing.

"You're making a big mistake," One said.

"*Quiet.*"

One raised his head and stared up at Sommer. "Or what?"

"Thorsson," Control warned.

Sommer frowned. "What did you say his name was?"

Control hung her head and looked down at the ground.

"Thorsson? That's what you said, isn't it?" He looked down at One. "Björn Thorsson?"

One raised his chin. "That's right. Björn Thorsson. You sent your son to Finland."

"And you killed him."

"He murdered my girlfriend."

"I don't care."

"Sommer," Control said. "*Don't—*"

The sound of the gunshot, from close range, was ear-splittingly loud. Thorsson fell forward and splashed, face first, in the puddle of water that had gathered on the ground. Lilly squeezed her eyes tightly shut and waited for the second shot; it came, and then a third and fourth, but none of them were for her. She opened her eyes and saw that Four and Eight were face down, too. Ten must have tried to scramble clear; he was on his back, his hand reaching up.

Control cried out. "What have you *done*?"

Sommer raised the still smoking gun and aimed it at Lilly.

"Please," she begged. "*Please*. I'm telling the truth."

She closed her eyes, certain that her gambit had failed and the next bullet would be for her. She saw Lola's face again and wished that she could hold her one final time before it all came to an end.

A phone rang.

"Wait," said the man who had called Maxim.

The man answered the call, but listened rather than speaking; his expression was blank, too, and Lilly couldn't work out what he was being told.

The call ended.

"Well?" Sommer said.

"She's right," the man reported. "They *were* being followed."

"They're sure?"

"They took a detour, and the car followed. There was a firefight. They were able to get away."

"It's John Milton," Lilly said. "Look him up. The rest of us came here to get her, but he wants Huxley."

Sommer kept the gun on her. "What's your name?"

"Lilly Moon."

"You are a part of Group Fifteen?"

"Yes. Number Twelve."

"And you are willing to work for the Russian government?"

"*Lilly*," Control warned.

Sommer gestured to Control with an irritated flick of his fingers. "Get her inside."

Lilly looked up as Control was manhandled to her feet and marched back into the building where she had been kept.

"You're making a mistake," she called over her shoulder before she was dragged away.

Sommer stepped forward and rested the barrel of the gun against Lilly's head. "Answer the question. You will work for the Russian government?"

The barrel was hot against her scalp. "I will."

"And why do you think we would be interested in what you have to say?"

"You just killed four Group Fifteen agents. Do you know what that means? It means that I just became more senior and more valuable to you. I was Number Twelve before this. Five of the agents who were more senior than me died tonight—I move up in seniority because of that. *Think*. Think what that's worth."

Sommer kept the gun on her; she had no idea what he was thinking.

"No one knows what happened here. All the witnesses are dead, and Control's not going back, is she? I go back home and tell London that it all went wrong, and I was the only one to get away. Who could dispute that? You'd have a senior asset in one of the most sensitive intelligence bodies in the whole of the British system."

"Why would you do that?"

"I don't want to die."

"That's it?"

"And I need money. I've already proven myself once, right? Just now, with Huxley. I'll do it again when I get back —I'll give you something valuable as a thank you. As a getting-to-know-you present. But, after that, if the Kremlin wants me to betray my country, I'll need to be bought."

Sommer didn't reply, but he pulled back on the gun a little.

"You need to decide quickly," she said. "I'll need to get to the extraction point if we're going to make them believe me."

"Where is it?"

"We came in by fast boat. The plan was to follow the coast east and rendezvous with an extraction team in Gagra."

"Georgia?"

She nodded.

"Thank you. What is your name again?"

"Lilly Moon."

"What's your *real* name?"

"That's it. That's my real name."

The gun was removed. "Get up and come with me."

Lilly got to her feet. The dead agents were sprawled around her, and she had to step over a slick of blood that was slowly spreading from the wound in One's head. His blond hair, so light that it had almost been white, was now stained with a red that was darkening as it dried. Lilly tried not to think about what she had done. She had not pulled the trigger, at least not literally. One had brought it upon himself and the others; he could have chosen to stay silent, but he had provoked Sommer with his defiance. Perhaps they would have otherwise been spared? Lilly knew that she could easily lose herself in guilt, but she reminded herself that it had not been her fault, and, even more to the point, she had no other choice. Her daughter needed her, and she would sacrifice anything to be able to go home and have her at her side.

Sommer took Lilly into one of the buildings and led the way to a room that she guessed was used as a mess. He pointed to a table and chairs and gestured that she should sit. One of the soldiers from outside had followed them, and, as Lilly pulled out a chair and lowered herself down onto it, he stood at the door with his arms folded across his chest.

"Please," Sommer said. "You will wait here."

"Wait for what?"

"I need to speak to Moscow. They will want to make enquiries. They will be thorough. If there is anything you haven't told me, now would be the time. There will be no second chances if you have not been honest with me."

"I've told you the truth."

"Then I'm sure you have nothing to be concerned about." He smiled at her, his lips parting just enough to show a mouthful of perfect teeth. "I will be back as soon as I can. Fyodor will wait with you."

61

Huxley clung onto the door handle as Maxim floored the pedal and the car raced away. The speedometer hit a hundred and ninety kilometres an hour before he took his foot off and allowed the car to drift back down to a hundred and twenty. He couldn't believe it had been Milton. Maxim had taken Huxley around to the other side of the car before they opened fire, and he had been able to hear the threats that Milton had made. They had driven away only to find that Milton had made it to the road; Dovlatov had sprayed bullets in his direction, forcing him to hit the ground, and they had been able to make their escape.

Maxim still had his pistol, but now, with a mile between them and Milton, he put it back into its holster and took the wheel in both hands. He muttered something in Russian to Dovlatov that Huxley couldn't catch, and then exhaled.

"Did you get him?" Huxley said.

"No," he said. "I don't think so."

Huxley banged his palm against the back of the seat. *"Shit!"*

"That was John Milton? The man you want us to kill?"

"Yes. And that was the best chance you'll ever have."

"I doubt it," Maxim said.

"You had the jump on him. There are two of you."

"And he had a grenade."

Huxley clenched his fists so hard his joints ached. "He's insane."

"We can use that to our advantage. Tonight was *his* best chance, not ours. We had no reason to think that he would be here. We weren't prepared. But we will be next time."

"*Next* time? You saw him—he's a *maniac*. I don't *want* there to be a next time."

"But you do want him dead?"

"Of course."

"Then you need to trust us. There will be a next time, but it'll be on our terms. And it'll be the last time you ever have to worry about him again."

62

Abbas Kader loitered on the street over the road from the house that he had been watching. It was a busy throughfare, and there was a kiosk on the corner that sold *panipuri* and *chole bhature*. There was always a motley collection of locals who gathered next to the kiosk to eat and smoke and moan about whatever it was that was vexing them, and it was busy enough that Kader, with a cigarette dangling from his lip and a deep-fried crisp bread in his hand, didn't feel as if he would stand out enough to be noticed.

He had left for New Delhi as soon as he had finished his meeting with Khan and Nazimuddin at the ISI compound in Islamabad. The intelligence was that Huxley would be heading to the city to conclude the deal with the Russians, and Kader wanted to be in place and ready to move when that happened. He had been staying in an ISI safe house in Rohini, where he had been able to communicate with the agency by way of an encrypted satellite phone. A source within the Indian government had confirmed that Huxley would be on his way shortly, together with details on where he would be staying.

That had been his signal to move.

Kader drew down on his cigarette, dropping the butt and grinding it underfoot. He took the packet and was about to tap out another cigarette when he noticed Shashi Chopra emerging from the gate of the house. The intelligence agency had researched the members of staff at the hotel and had selected Chopra as most suitable for what Kader required. He was a bellhop and employed by an agency instead of by the hotel. He had been on the door for three weeks as cover for an employee who had been signed off on long-term sickness.

Kader put one of the straps of his rucksack over his shoulder, crossed the road and made his way to the gate. It had closed, and, at eight feet tall and facing the road, there was no prospect of being able to scale it without being seen. It didn't matter; there was a gap between the stucco walls of the house and its neighbour, just wide enough for Kader to slip inside. He turned sideways and shuffled along until he reached the rear of the property. The passage had kinked to the right enough so that he wasn't visible from the road. He jumped up and grabbed the top of the wall, wedging himself with one foot on either side as he scrambled up, swinging one leg over and then the other. He lowered the rucksack to the ground on the other side and dropped down after it.

The property had a small garden that, despite the lack of space, was well stocked with plants and flowers and kept trimmed and tidy. Kader crossed the lawn to the rear door and, with the use of one of his lock picks, was quickly able to open the door and step into the kitchen. He waited quietly for a minute until he was certain that the house was unoccupied and then searched it to be sure. The property had two bedrooms, a bathroom, a sitting room and kitchen. It was empty.

He put his rucksack on the kitchen table, unzipped it and took out the items that had been delivered to the safe house: two fragmentation grenades, a 9mm pistol and ammunition. He had given thought to the best tools to complete his assignment and had settled on these. Five pounds of C-4 fixed to the bottom of a car would be no good at all; Kader wanted to see the whites of Huxley's eyes.

Chopra wasn't due back until the end of his shift this evening. Kader left the gun and the grenades on the table and went over to the kitchen counter. He filled the kettle and put it on the stove to boil.

63

Huxley had gone north, and Milton followed. He pressed down on the accelerator, squeezing out as much speed as he could. The display read one hundred and thirty and then one hundred and forty. It was a two-lane highway and it was almost completely empty. There was a truck hauling a trailer full of lumber up ahead; Milton devoured the distance between them and raced by, the driver signalling his displeasure with a long blast of the horn.

The road passed through Kazazov and continued north, the wide body of water formed by the Kuban River passing on the right-hand side. Milton reached the northern bank of the lake and saw the lights of another car up in the distance. It was too far away for him to be confident that it was Huxley's car, but, seeing as there was so little traffic on the road, it had to be possible. He closed the distance between them to about half a mile and watched as the car ahead passed into the suburbs of Krasnodar and ran beneath a line of streetlights. It was still a long way off, but Milton could see that it was black and of the right shape; he was confident that it was them. He peeled back on his pace, dropping down to ninety so that he could continue to close the distance between them without making it obvious that he was in pursuit. He knew that he would be outnumbered and outgunned when he forced another confrontation, but that was not going to stop him. He was resigned to the likelihood that he wouldn't start the new day in one piece, but that was just the way it would have to be. If he lost Huxley now, he might never see him again, and that was unacceptable.

They were in the city proper now, with industrial buildings on either side. Milton narrowed the distance a little more and then swore in irritation as a police car pulled out of a side road and merged ahead of him. He slowed down to the speed limit as the convoy continued to the north, then looked down at the satnav in the dash and zoomed out, trying to see where they might be going. A large residential area was to his left, with factories and warehouses to his right; the road bent to the northeast and headed straight for the airport.

Milton banged his fist against the wheel in frustration. He was stymied. The odds would have been against him before, but now they had become impossible. He didn't have a choice: he would follow Huxley for as long as he could, and then, unless the police car turned off and he was presented with an attempt that had a reasonable chance of success, he would regroup and try again.

They reached the junction for the airport, and both cars in front of Milton turned off. It would have been obvious now that Milton was following them, and, deciding that it made no sense to prompt a confrontation, he slowed down and allowed them to pull ahead. Ulitsa Aeroportovskaya continued by showrooms for Ford, Renault and Lexus, passed through an unmanned security checkpoint and then terminated in a wide parking lot. The lot was not busy; Milton found a space next to a SUV and killed the lights. He watched as the police car slowed, turned around and set off back along the road in the opposite direction; Huxley's car waited for a gate to be wheeled back and then drove into the terminal. There would be a private jet inside waiting to whisk him away.

He opened the door and got out, jogging across the lot to the gate. He slowed his pace to a walk as he assessed the security: there were cameras high overhead, and the gate was topped with coils of razor wire. It wasn't going to be easy to get inside without being seen. He turned and jogged south to where another gate offered access to the terminal. A garbage truck was slowly backing out, and Milton was able to hide behind it and slip inside.

The terminal buildings were to his left, with the wide-open space of the runway ahead of him. Milton saw the tail-lights of Huxley's car as it drove alongside a row of parked commercial jets. The brake lights glowed red as the car came to a halt next to a smaller jet with its running lights switched on. There must have been half a mile between it and Milton, and, even if he ran, he doubted that he would be able to get to it in time. He watched as the doors to the car opened, and the occupants—he counted three men—stepped out. It was too far for Milton to be able to say that Huxley was definitely in their number, but he didn't need to see him to be sure; he was there.

He took out his phone and called London.

"Global Logistics. How can I place your call?"

"Fifth floor, please."

"Which department?"

"Travel."

"And who should I say is calling?"

"John Smith."

"Hold the line, please."

Milton had provided a coded instruction indicating that he wanted to speak to an analyst in Group Three, the division responsible for communications interception, reconnaissance and surveillance. He waited for the call to be transferred, watching as the three men climbed the steps and boarded the jet.

"How can I help you, Mr. Smith?"

"I need details on a private jet that is just about to leave Krasnodar airport in Russia."

"I should be able to help with that. Any other details?"

"It looks like a Gulfstream—might be a 550."

"Registration?"

Milton squinted. "RR-345... or it might be 346."

"Hold the line."

Milton gritted his teeth and watched helplessly as the steps were retracted and the fuselage door closed. He heard the sound of the engines as the pilot increased thrust, and the jet navigated a lazy turn and started to roll toward the runway.

"Mr. Smith?"

"I'm here."

"I've found the flight log for a Gulfstream 550 with the registration RR-345. It's registered to a company that we believe to be a front for the GRU."

The jet reached the end of the runway, and, with no other planes ahead of it, the pilot opened the throttles all the way so that the roar of the engine echoed off the terminal buildings.

"Where is it going?"

The jet accelerated, the nose lifted, and, a moment later, it was aloft. The pilot sent it streaking away from the airport, and then, when he had enough altitude, he started a slow turn to the south.

"New Delhi. The flight plan has it due to land in four and half hours. Do you need anything else?"

"Yes," Milton said. "Can you arrange for someone to meet the jet when it lands? I need to know where the passengers are going."

"Of course."

"And get me on a flight to Delhi, please. The fastest route possible."

L illy took a seat at one of the tables and waited for any indication of what might come next. She didn't know what else she could do. She had made her offer, and now it was up to Sommer and whoever it was with whom he was speaking to decide whether or not to accept it. It seemed to her that she had made a compelling case. The prospect of a double agent working within Group Fifteen was, surely, a tantalising one. She would be at the heart of the establishment and, given the events of the evening, at a more senior level than she had been at the beginning of the operation. She had taken an enormous gamble, but, despite the spontaneity of her decision, she would have made the same choice again. It made her a traitor, but she didn't care. Some things were more important than that.

Loyalty to her daughter trumped loyalty to her country.

Fyodor took a call on his phone and then motioned that she should get up.

"What's happening?"

"Come with me."

The soldier led her out into the courtyard again. The sun

had come up while she had been in the mess, and the grisly tableau that was revealed in the gentle light was difficult to look at. The bodies had been left where they had fallen, with the blood that had spilled from their wounds now congealed and a rust-coloured red.

"This way," Fyodor said, pointing to the parking area.

They headed to a Mercedes GLS that was waiting with its engine running. Fyodor opened the door for her, and she saw that Sommer was waiting inside. She stepped in, settling into the generously upholstered seat next to him. Fyodor got into the passenger seat, and the driver pulled away and followed the track that led into the main base.

Lilly turned to Sommer. "Where are we going?"

"You will take us to where you left your boat."

"You spoke to Moscow?"

"I did."

"And they'll work with me?"

"I have been given the authority to make that decision. You and I will have a conversation. You must persuade me that you can be trusted. If you can do that, then we will see."

The driver followed the perimeter and, after negotiating a checkpoint, joined a main road and headed south toward the coast.

"And if I can't?"

Sommer took off his jacket. "I doubt I need to spell that out for you."

"You'll shoot me like you did the others? Leave me at the side of the road?"

He hung the jacket from the hook above the window. "Let's hope that isn't necessary."

"You don't need to try to frighten me. I'm already frightened. I'm not going to betray you."

"But not because you agree with our way of thinking about things?"

"Because I know what will happen if I don't. And because I need the money you're going to give me."

"The legal case over custody of your daughter." He smiled. "Yes—we know about that. Your husband is a rich man, and you are worried that you won't be able to compete with him. Again—I am not trying to threaten you, Lilly. I just want you to know that we have done our research."

"Really? It sounds like a threat."

"A reminder of the consequences, then. You must see it from our perspective. You are frightened now—yes. But it is easy to forget that fear when you are safely back at home. We might reach an agreement to work together this morning, and you might decide that you do not want to honour it. I would counsel you against such foolishness. You know that we have a very long reach. The fact that you are at home will mean nothing. We will reach out for your daughter and your mother and anyone else you care about, and then we will come for you."

He let that hang for a moment.

"But," he said at last, "please. Let's just talk."

"What do you want to know?"

"I have some of your history, but I would like to know more. Tell me about yourself. Tell me about your career. What led you to work for Group Fifteen?"

She explained that she had served in the Special Reconnaissance Regiment, that she had seen action in a number of hostile environments and that she had been recruited to join the Group after distinguishing herself during a successful deployment to Afghanistan. He listened intently, prompting her with additional questions about the recruitment process, her training and her assignments. He asked about how the Group operated, what she knew about Control and the other senior men and women who worked for the Firm.

Lilly knew that the time for circumspection was over, and answered truthfully and in as much detail as possible. She suspected that he knew the answers to some of the questions and that he was laying traps for her. She knew that her future depended upon his endorsement and that, if she failed to win it, she would not be going home. The thought of never seeing her daughter again was all the encouragement that she needed, so she spoke with complete honesty and candour.

"What about the agent who pursued Huxley?" he asked.

"Milton?"

"Yes—Milton. What can you tell me about him?"

"Is he still alive?"

Sommer nodded. "He is very resourceful."

"I don't know very much about him at all," she admitted. "The first time I met him was when we arrived in Krasnodar. I'm not sure I even spoke to him."

"But you must have heard of him?"

"I always thought he was more of a myth. He left the Group years before I joined. I heard that he and Control —*his* Control, not mine—had a disagreement, and he went on the run. He was a ghost until he was found and brought back when Huxley insisted on working with him. Beyond that, though?" She shrugged. "That's it."

Sommer leaned back in his seat and steepled his fingers. "I think perhaps I know more about Comrade Milton than you. He is an impressive man, but there is something about the way he is behaving now that strikes me as *impulsive*. Our files are of someone who was cold and calculating—he would have made an excellent KGB agent. But now? Acting on his conscience? Chasing a man like Huxley into a place like this, knowing that success could only ever be the toss of a coin?" He shook his head. "That is very different to the man I read about. I was hoping you might be able to shed a little light on what has happened to him, but perhaps I was hoping for too much. Perhaps that could be the demonstration of value that we spoke about. Find his file and send it to me. Could you do that?"

"I don't know," she said. "I could try."

"It seems that he will continue his vendetta against Huxley, and I've been charged with keeping him safe. Anything that you could deliver that would help me to do that would be a very good start to our working relationship."

65

C ontrol paced the room, backwards and forwards and backwards and forwards again and again. She had no idea how the Group had found her location as quickly as they had, and had certainly not expected them to mount an operation to release her. It might very well have succeeded were it not for Number Twelve's betrayal.

She couldn't understand what had possessed her to do something so calamitously stupid. Control had been deeply involved in her recruitment, reviewing her file after she had been recommended for a transfer to the Group. There was nothing that suggested she was susceptible to being turned. Her father had been a decorated Coldstream Guards officer, and her mother had worked in the Houses of Parliament as a researcher. Her upbringing had been normal and happy, and her military career had been every bit as successful as her father's. Her record was exemplary; she had shone during her interviews and had impressed her trainers at the Group's facility in Wiltshire. Control had been looking to

bring additional women to the roster and had been confident that Lilly Moon would be an excellent addition.

What had she *missed*?

Control knew that Moon was embroiled in a court case
with her estranged husband, but there had been nothing to
suggest that it was anything other than a domestic dispute.
She had asked for her to be vetted once again and had
discovered, after the crackers of Group Two had hacked the
servers of the solicitors acting for both parties, that the
breakup was acrimonious. There was a child involved, and it
seemed that custody of the girl would be the focus of the
divorce.

Control wondered: could it have been something to do
with that?

She thought that she had been thorough, but there *had*
to have been something that she'd missed, and the consequences had been catastrophic. Four of her agents were
dead. Number One—*Thorsson*—was dead. Twelve had
offered to defect, and Control knew that the Russians would
send her back to London to work for them from the inside.

She had done incalculable damage already, but that
might just be the start of it.

A Russian spy in the Group didn't bear thinking about.

She heard approaching footsteps and stepped back from
the door as it was unlocked and opened by a guard.

"Where's Sommer? I want to speak to him."

"He is not here." He was holding a pair of handcuffs, and
he held them out for Control to take. "Put these on, please."

"Why?"

"You are being moved."

"No," she said.

"Perhaps, if you cooperate, you will be released. I don't
know. But I *do* know that you are going, one way or another."

66

L illy and Sommer spoke for an hour, and they were still talking when the driver brought the car to a stop in the parking area where Lilly and the others had met Number One. That had been just twelve hours earlier, but so much had happened since then that it seemed like much longer. The driver switched off the engine.

"Well?" Lilly said to Sommer. "Do you trust me now?"

"Trust is earned, Lilly. You'll need to demonstrate your value."

She allowed herself a little hope. "Does that mean you'll let me leave?"

"Yes," he said. "Find the boat and take it out to the rendezvous. You will need to persuade the crew that you were betrayed. They will take you to London, and you will need to persuade them again—I would expect their questions to be just as difficult as mine. The consequences for failure will be the same, too."

"How will you be in touch with me?"

"You will be appointed a handler. You will start to take walks along the Thames at lunchtime. Walk up to the bus stop at Salamanca Street. Your handler will tape a thumb drive beneath the right-hand side of the bench. You will find instructions on that drive that explain how we will communicate with each other. Read it, memorise it, then destroy the drive. Understood?"

"Yes."

"Good. You mentioned the need to earn our trust. That is correct. We will expect you to deliver something valuable as a demonstration of your potential worth. Milton's file would be a good start. If you are able to do that, then we will be able to discuss a future commercial relationship. You have been granted a reprieve and an opportunity to make yourself rich. You will need to deliver on what you have promised."

"You don't have to threaten me. I know. And I'll do what I said I'd do."

67

M ilton knew that he was taking a chance by flying out of Krasnodar, but he decided that he would probably be fine provided he moved quickly. Taking longer to exfiltrate would increase the advantage that Huxley had already won. It was worth the risk. The first flight that morning was to Tbilisi, and, after buying a ticket with cash, he crossed his fingers and made his way to security.

He put his valuables into a box, placed them on the belt and waited for his turn to pass through the scanner. The attendant said something in Russian and pointed down at his feet. Milton took off his shoes and put them in the box, too. He rejoined the queue and managed to look sheepish as he passed through the arch. The scanner was silent; the guard gave him a nod that managed to mix permission with unfriendliness, and he stepped forward, collecting his shoes and valuables and taking them over to a bench where he could sort himself out without holding anyone else up. He put his shoes back on, fed his belt through the loops of his trousers and put his phone and his loose change into his pockets.

He looked at his watch: twenty minutes until boarding closed. There were several connecting flights from Tbilisi to New Delhi, and, provided that there were no delays, he should be there later that afternoon. He would get to India and find somewhere unobtrusive to serve as a base, and then he would make an appointment with the local quarter-master. In the meantime, he would ask Groups Two and Three to locate Huxley.

He reached the gate, bought a coffee and pastry and took them to an empty seat. He took out his phone, woke it and wondered whether he should contact Thorsson. The agents and Control should have been well on their way by now—probably on the boat and likely having made good progress toward the rendezvous on the Georgian coast. They had just under two hundred kilometres to cover before they reached safety. It wouldn't be long until they landed and the extraction specialists from Group Five brought them back to London.

Milton put the phone back in his pocket. He doubted that he would be able to reach the Icelander now, and, anyway, the last thing he would have wanted was to be distracted as he made his way out of the country to safety.

It could wait.

68

L illy had hammered the engines as soon as she was three miles out to sea and had covered the hundred and fifty miles to Gagra in four hours, including a stop to refuel from the cans of diesel that had been lashed beneath the seats. She had seen evidence of shipping farther out to sea, but nothing came close enough to give her any reason to think that she had given cause for suspicion.

She spent much of the voyage going over the story that she was going to tell. She knew that she would need to keep things as simple as she could to avoid tripping over a lie when she was questioned in London. She was going to deliver cataclysmic news that would echo through White-hall and was sure that she would be interrogated. She decided to concentrate on the basics of her story, and no more; elaboration would lead to confusion, and that would, in turn, lead to suspicion. She would say that she had made her escape once Number One had ordered it, and that she hadn't been there to see what had ultimately happened. She could only speak for herself. Ignorance would be her best policy.

Lilly checked the satnav and saw that she had reached her destination. Gagra was a small town on the northeast coast of the Black Sea with the Caucasus Mountains looming behind it. The rendezvous had been set for an isolated cove to the north of the town, an inlet that crept inland between two wooded promontories. She cut the power and allowed the RIB to drift in toward the beach. It was early afternoon now, and, as the vessel bobbed on the swells, she saw a man waiting on the shingle. She opened the throttle and edged forwards again, the bow scraping up against the sandy bottom when she was twenty metres back from the water's edge.

The man was joined by two others. She didn't recognise the newcomers, but she did recognise him: it was Number Five. He had been involved in her training and the two of them had always got along. Five saw her and waded out into the surf up to his waist, grabbing the tripping line and anchor that she tossed down, and then taking it up the beach so that the RIB could be secured.

Lilly slid over the side, dropped down and waded through the water until she was alongside him.

"Where are the others?" he asked her.

She shook her head.

His face fell. "What happened?"

"There was an ambush. One ordered the retreat, but I was the only one who made it to the boat."

"They're dead?"

She nodded. "It was John Milton. We need to tell London. He sold us out to the Russians."

NEW DELHI

69

Milton stepped out of the air-conditioned oasis of the Arrivals lounge and into the sticky heat of the New Delhi evening. The air was so thick that he felt as if he could chew it. It was eight o'clock, but the humidity in the air was still like a wet slap to the face. The heat was just one thing; the stench was something else altogether. It smelled as if the city were on fire. Milton could pick out diesel fuel, sun-baked dust, the fumes of a million cars, the fires that the slumdwellers lit to cook their food, and the waste products from the factories and chemical plants that surrounded the city. He breathed in and felt it in his lungs.

He needed to start making preparations. He found a payphone, paid for a call and dialled Thorsson's number.

The call rang out and then went to voicemail.

That was strange.

He checked his watch. Thorsson and the others should have exfiltrated by now and been on their way back to London. Perhaps that was it: Thorsson was in the air without coverage. Milton would leave it until he was in his hotel and then try again.

He dialled the number for Global Logistics and asked to be connected to the analyst from Group Three who had helped him track Huxley's jet.

"Mr. Smith, I—"

"Please tell me you know where he is."

"I'm afraid I don't have the best news for you. He arrived this afternoon and transferred by helicopter. We obviously couldn't follow. We don't know where he is now."

"But you're still looking?"

"Yes, we are, and we'll find him. Do you have a number I can call you on?"

"I'll call you."

"Can I help with anything else? A safe house, perhaps? There's one in Old Delhi that you could use."

The analyst read out the address, and Milton committed it to memory.

"One more thing," Milton said. "There was a job in Russia, and I haven't been able to speak to the colleagues who were out there. What happened?"

"They're on the way back to London now."

"It was a success?"

"I believe so."

Milton ended the call and followed the signs for the taxi rank. There was a queue, and, as Milton waited, he glanced over at a kiosk selling newspapers. There was a wide variety on offer, including several in English. His eye was caught by the front page of the *Times of India*: 'Massive Arms Deal Highlights India's Continuing Reliance on Russia.'

Milton left the queue and bought a copy of the newspaper, then rejoined the queue and read:

India and Russia announced an expanding defence relation-

ship on Monday during a visit by Russian foreign minister Nikolay Timofeyevich to New Delhi, including the details of a $5 billion missile defence system sale to India. The missile defence system deal, first agreed upon in 2018, will go ahead despite threats of an escalating arms race with Pakistan and concerns that it could affect India's relations with the United States. It is understood that the deal will be signed during a ceremony at the Majestic Hotel tomorrow, during which nuclear energy, space exploration and economics are also due to be discussed.

Finally, Milton thought, *a little good fortune.*

He knew Huxley well enough to know that he wouldn't be able to stay away when the deal he had worked so long to put together was finally consummated. The Firm might have lost him when he arrived in Delhi, but at least Milton knew where he would be tomorrow.

A taxi captain in a bright blue tabard indicated that he should take the next car to approach, and he did, sliding into the back and telling the cabbie to drive him into the city. The man grunted, put the car into gear and drove off. The radio was tuned to a station playing Bollywood music, and the driver seemed more intent on that than on starting a conversation.

"Where in the city?" he asked gruffly.

"Meena Bazar," Milton said, using the address that he had been given.

He found he was anxious to get to the safe house so that he could begin the preparations for tomorrow.

He had a lot of work to do.

70

The driver dropped Milton in Chandni Chowk, the chaotic market in the centre of Old Delhi. Milton paid and opened the door, immediately letting in a waft of hot air that had him sweating in moments. This was one of the busiest parts of the city, with thousands of locals and tourists scratching for room in a space that had long since ceased being large enough for them. Buildings had been built almost on top of each other, and cars muscled along streets with just inches between them. Impatient drivers sounded their horns as mercurial scooter riders slipped through gaps that quickly closed after them. Milton smelled sweat, exhaust fumes, boiling grease and the deeper, primal funk of sewage from drains that had been pushed beyond their capacity.

He stopped at the corner of two streets and tried to regain his bearings. The analyst had given him directions in addition to the address, and he looked now for an alleyway with fast-food shacks on both sides. There were no pavements, and he had to step into the traffic to navigate the cars that had been parked up against the walls of the buildings.

Rubbish had been dumped around the roots of a neem tree, while a tiny temple had been arranged beneath the downward-dropping roots of a banyan. The analyst had mentioned the tree, and, pausing, Milton saw an alleyway with an open fast-food shack to the left and a shuttered one on the right.

He crossed over and followed the alley, his confidence dwindling as he turned right and then left. There were mopeds and motorbikes parked on both sides, and balconies bulged out from the walls with damp washing draped from the balustrades to dry in the humid air. A nest of telephone and electricity cables stretched overhead, and ancient air-conditioning units dripped moisture that gathered in puddles below. There was only just enough space for Milton to walk along the alley, turning again until the noise of the main road was muffled. Milton approached an elderly man and stepped to the side to allow him a path through; the man's flip-flops slapped against the damp concrete as he went by.

It was with surprise and relief that he saw the red-painted door on the left. He reached up to the lintel, his fingers probing for the loose brick, finding it and then working it free. He reached into the void that was left, felt the key against the rough edges of the bricks, and took it out.

He unlocked the door, opened it and went inside.

The place was a Group Fifteen safe house. There were dozens of them all around the world, places where agents could go when they needed to stay out of sight, prepare for an assignment or equip. This one was similar to the others that he had used over the years: three small rooms, furnished as if the occupier had just popped out and would soon be returning.

He went into the kitchen and, remembering what the

analyst had told him, grabbed the fridge and pulled it out enough so that he could slide between it and the wall. The plasterboard behind it was dusty and festooned with cobwebs, but, as he reached in with his fingertips, he felt the subtle give of the panel that had been fashioned there. He pressed it, heard the click as it was released from its fixings, and allowed it to fall forwards so he could lower it to the floor. A compartment had been crafted there, a recess that had been dug out of the course of thick blocks that formed the exterior wall. Hooks and brackets had been fitted to what remained of the block and, from those hung a collection of weapons: a C8 carbine reached from the top to the bottom of the recess, with an MP5 compact submachine gun hung next to it; there were also a selection of handguns and a variety of grenades. Milton was going to struggle to conceal either of the larger weapons, so he made do with a Glock 17 and two magazines that would each take seventeen 9x19mm Parabellum rounds.

There was a plastic box in the recess; Milton took it over to the kitchen table and flipped the lid open. There was a standard-issue disguise kit inside, with two wigs, a selection of spectacles, a fake moustache and beard and pots of make-up. He tapped a finger against his chin as he contemplated what he might do, then closed the lid and left the box on the table. A simple change of appearance would be a good idea —not extravagant, simply a disguise to help him to become invisible on the street—but he would take care of it tomorrow.

Milton put the pistol and the magazines on the kitchen table, replaced the panel until it clicked back into position, and then shouldered the fridge back so that the cache was hidden once again. He took a cloth and wiped away the scuff marks that the feet of the fridge had left on the floor.

He looked at his watch: it was coming up to nine, and he was tired. Tomorrow would be a challenging day. Getting to Huxley was not going to be a simple task, and there was a chance that it would come at the price of his own life. Milton was resigned to that. The longer he waited, the more difficult it would be to find him and deliver justice. Huxley had enough money to disappear or, if he preferred not to do that, buy enough security to make himself impossible to reach. Milton had an opportunity now, it wasn't ideal, and it would be dangerous, but it was likely to be the best chance that he would have. He had no choice but to take it.

He would stand a better chance of success if he was fresh. The dwelling had a bedroom with a mattress on the floor, and he decided to sleep here rather than checking into a hotel. He was hungry, too, so he locked up and made his way back to the road in search of a meal.

TBILISI

71

L illy waited as Five passed through the scanner. The machine was silent, and the attendant gestured for Lilly to follow. She did, grateful that the machine was quiet for her, too. She collected her valuables from the belt and joined Five outside the entrance to duty-free.

He gestured to the shelves. "Do you want anything for the flight?"

"Sleep would be nice."

"Get some on the plane," he said. "It'll probably be the only chance we'll get until this is done."

Lilly checked the screen with the details of the departing flights and saw that they had been called to the gate. They set off together.

It had been a trying day. The amount of concentration required for Lilly to keep her story straight had been almost dizzying. The effort had started as soon as Five had driven her to Tbilisi, with constant questions about what had happened in Krasnodar. It had become more serious at the safe house. Five had established a secure connection to London, and she had briefed a conference room of intelligence mandarins on what had happened. She explained that Milton had sold them out and that she was the only member of the team who had arrived at the fast boat and exfiltrated in line with the plan. There had been a battery of questions; Lilly had answered them as best she could, claiming ignorance whenever she could rather than gild her story with lies that she might forget.

Once she had finished, Lilly and Five had been briefed on Milton's movements. He had followed Tristan Huxley to the airport in Krasnodar but had been unable to stop him flying out of the country. He had called Group Three for assistance and had been told that Huxley was headed to New Delhi. A check of the passenger manifests revealed that Milton, under an alias, had purchased a last-minute ticket on a flight to Tbilisi and had then taken a connecting flight to the Indian capital.

Their orders had followed, and they were clear and unambiguous: they were to follow Milton and take him into custody. Lilly was happy that she was involved but had no interest in detaining him. Milton and Control were the only witnesses to her betrayal; she doubted that Control would ever be returned to London, and that meant that Milton was her only threat.

His death would insulate her from discovery.

Her audacity would pay off.

They reached the gate that had been assigned to their flight.

"I need to go to the bathroom," Lilly said.

"Don't be long. We're boarding in five minutes."

Lilly turned into the doorway of the restroom, but, rather than continuing inside, she waited there for ten seconds before retracing her steps. She paused at the door and looked around it; Five was at the window, looking out onto the runway as a jet readied for take-off. She stepped out of the doorway and retraced her steps to the payphone that she had noticed earlier.

It would have been easy for Five to see her if he came back in this direction, but Lilly didn't see that she had a choice. This was a chance to demonstrate that she was going to be a valuable asset. She picked up the receiver, and, feeling exposed, she dialled the number that Sommer had given her.

The call connected, and, after a brief message in Russian and a beep, Lilly found herself pausing, the words caught in her throat. Her reluctance was foolish, she was already committed and compromised, and hesitation now was just weakness.

She left a short message, put the receiver back in the cradle, turned around and returned to the gate.

NEW DELHI

72

A bbas Kader stayed inside the house all day. He had nothing that he needed to do, and, more importantly, he didn't want to take the chance that he would be spotted leaving or returning to the property.

It had just gone eleven o'clock when he heard the sound of footsteps approaching the front door from outside. Chopra worked the day shift, leaving his house at six so that he was able to clock in at eight. Kader had surveilled him for two days: he was an active member of his temple and had gone to worship straight from the hotel on both prior evenings. Kader had expected the same tonight.

He took a knife from the block on the worktop and waited behind the kitchen door. Chopra turned his key in the lock and came inside, whistling a tune as he closed the door behind him. Kader had seen a handful of letters that had been left on the small table next to the hatstand, and he waited patiently as Chopra undid them one by one, a muttered complaint about bills only briefly interrupting his cheerful tune.

He came into the kitchen, switched on the light and, still whistling the same jaunty tune, crossed the room to the sink. Kader came out from behind the door and followed him, silently closing the distance between them until he could reach his left hand around to secure him while bringing his right hand—the one with the knife—around in the opposite direction. He stabbed the blade into the side of Chopra's neck all the way up to the hilt, then pushed it forward and out so that the edge sliced through the jugular and the windpipe. Kader anchored Chopra against the countertop as he bled out.

It took him a minute to die, choking on the blood that ran back down his throat. Kader lowered him to the floor. He would normally have disposed of the body and cleaned up, but that wasn't going to be necessary this time. Kader knew that the mission would likely be his last, but if he died —*when* he died—it would be with his reputation restored and his need for vengeance sated.

He went up to the bathroom to shower, standing under the jet until the water, initially stained red from Chopra's blood, ran clear. He dried himself and went into the bedroom. He shut his eyes and drifted off to sleep, his dreams busy with thoughts of redemption and revenge.

73

L illy was exhausted. She had grabbed a couple of hours of sleep on the plane, but it was never going to be enough. It had been a long two days since she had left Lola with her mother, with little rest ever since they had boarded the Hercules at Brize Norton. She had been powering through on adrenaline, but that could only go so far; she felt wrung out and needed sleep.

But that would have to wait.

It was three in the morning, and it had taken longer than they had hoped to get from Tbilisi to New Delhi. Their flight had been delayed for thirty minutes, and then there had been another delay in the air as they waited for a slot to land. At least the airport was quiet enough that they had passed through it with minimal delay.

Five had gone to make a call to London and had asked Lilly to find their transport. The Indians had been told that they were coming and had agreed to provide assistance, starting with the car that was waiting in the car park. The key had been balanced on top of the left rear wheel, and Lilly used it to pop the boot. She looked inside to see a lime-green Samsonite case that was secured with two bright red straps. The car was at the back of the lot, and there was no one else who might have been able to observe her, so Lilly decided to check the contents. She removed the straps and opened the lid to look down on two Beretta Px4 Storms, the pistol used by Indian special forces, plus ammunition.

Lilly closed the case and got into the car. The Indians would provide assistance as they needed it. Lilly didn't try to unscramble the political equations that must have been challenging the brass in London, save that she knew the Firm had been protecting Tristan Huxley before his fall from grace and that the deal he was negotiating must have been valued more highly than bringing him to trial for his crimes. The government had made all the right noises about justice for his victims, but she knew there was a good chance that they were behind the plan to spring him from custody, or that they had supplied assistance—or turned a blind eye —to whoever had. The Indians and Russians both wanted to close the deal, and London had evidently decided to continue to offer its support. Those considerations were above her pay grade, however, and she put them to one side. The Indians had been told that Milton was here and that he was here for Huxley; it was in their interests to help Lilly and Five stop him.

Lilly drove to the pickup zone where Five was waiting. She corrected herself, *not* Five, not any longer, but Two. The deaths in Krasnodar had shuffled the pack, most likely in as radical a fashion as had ever happened in the Group's history. There were, of course, no official records of such things that agents could access, but Lilly couldn't imagine that there had ever been an incident where this many agents had been killed at the same time. Now, Number Three had been promoted to Number One, Five was Number Two, and

Lilly had moved from Twelve to Seven. She wondered how long it would take to backfill behind her.

Two got into the car. "Is the gear in the back?"

"Two Berettas and spare magazines. What about Milton?"

"Arrived five hours ago. The Indians messed up—the message to stop him wasn't delivered in time."

"So we don't know where he is?"

"Not necessarily. Milton doesn't know you got out, and he doesn't know he's been exposed. He called Group Five, and they gave him the address of a safe house he can use. He needs somewhere he can equip and stay out of sight while he plans what's next. That'll be as good a place as any. London preferred not to pass the location on to India, for obvious reasons."

"Where is it?"

"Old Delhi. This might be easier than we thought."

74

M ilton's sleep was fitful and beset by nightmares. He found himself back in the desert, watching the madrassa at the foot of the valley as the Warthog they had summoned lined up on its bombing run. He saw the munitions as they fell through a slow arc that ended with a blinding white flash, the detonation picking him up and throwing him aside. He stood and found that he wasn't in the desert but in the Alps, looking down the barrel of his pistol at the child cowering in the back of the car. The boy's parents were dead, spread-eagled in the gravel, and his father's blood had sprayed across his face in a swipe that might have been mistaken for paint.

Milton jerked upright, drenched in sweat. It was stiflingly hot, there was no AC in the apartment, and his sheets had soaked through. His heart was thumping in his chest, and it took him a moment to remember where he was. He reached for his watch and saw that it was four in the morning. He lay back and closed his eyes, but it was no good. Adrenaline was in his blood now, and there was no prospect of a return to sleep. He got up. The apartment didn't have a shower or a bath, so he found a bucket in the kitchen, filled it with water and used that to wash, finishing by splashing double handfuls onto his face. Even the water was tepid, but at least he felt cleaner and more awake.

He went back into the kitchen and sat down at the kitchen table. He opened the disguise kit and removed a black wig, setting it on his head and checking it in the mirror that was fixed to the inside of the box. He took a pot of dye and carefully applied it to his face, darkening the tone a shade or two. He took a moustache and whiskers that matched the wig, found the pot of glue and applied it to his skin and then the back of the fake hair. He pressed the moustache onto his top lip and the beard on his chin. He added a pair of thick-rimmed glasses with clear lenses to draw attention away from his face and looked down at the mirror again to check his work. He was certainly not in the same league as the experts in Group Five—he had seen them change a male agent into an elderly woman before— but he was happy enough with what he had done. Anyone who was really looking for him would probably see through the disguise, but those who were working off a photograph might look past him, especially if he was in a crowd. That would have to do.

He replaced the make-up kit in the secret compartment behind the fridge and put the panel back into position. Straightening, he pushed the Glock into the waistband of his jeans and pulled out his shirt to cover it, then put the spare magazines into his pockets. He left the apartment, locking the door behind him and stepping out into the cloying humidity that was ever present, regardless of the hour.

The alleyway was empty. Milton took out his phone, opened the map and plotted a route from Old Delhi to the Majestic Hotel. It was five kilometres, but, since it was early, and he wanted to get a better idea of the beat and rhythm of the city, Milton decided that he would walk.

75

L illy drove as quickly as she dared. She looked out of the window as they headed west, marvelling at how busy it was despite the fact that it was still early in the morning. The roads were heavy with traffic, and she was forced to divert several times in an attempt to make the journey as fast as possible. There were rickshaws and carts drawn by donkeys, with cows and goats loitering in the road, the animals ignoring the blares of angry horns and in no hurry to move. The car had aircon, but Lilly still had the window down to try to encourage the breeze, letting in a riot of smells: incense, dust, hot grease and dung.

They reached Old Delhi and parked.

"Too much traffic," Lilly said.

"We'll walk the rest of the way."

Two had taken the Berettas out of the case and handed one to her with two magazines. She took it and hid it in the waistband of her jeans, adjusting it so that the frame was snug against her back.

Two said that he had used the safe house before, so he led the way, taking a route into the heart of the walled city in the direction of the Red Fort. Dawn was breaking, but the light struggled to filter down between the tall buildings that formed the nest of alleys and passageways that made up the area. The tiny stores in the by-lanes were beginning to open up, and the shopkeepers were arranging the fresh vegetables and fruit that they had sourced from the wholesalers. Lilly looked through dusty windows and saw clothes, perfumes, cheap jewellery and idols of deities.

Two reached a junction where a narrow alleyway was framed by two stores, one offering street food while the other had been boarded up. A man had just emerged from the alleyway and turned away from them, heading south. He was deeply tanned and had shoulder-length black hair. Lilly paused; there was something about the way he walked that held her attention.

Two noticed. "What is it?"

She watched the man for a moment and then looked away. "Nothing. Which way?"

He pointed. "Down the alley and around the corner."

The alleyway was particularly narrow, with mopeds and bicycles pressed up against the walls so that there was only the slenderest gap through which they could pass. Two led the way left and then right and then left again, the walls above them blocking out the light so that they traced a path through gloom.

They reached a red-painted door, and Two raised his hand and stopped, then reached around for the pistol. He tried the handle and shook his head: it was locked. He took a set of picks from his pocket and knelt down to address the lock while Lilly watched the alley. Two gave a low whistle that he was done. He put a finger to his lips and indicated that they should both form up on either side of the door. They drew their weapons, Lilly drawing a deep breath to try to bring her pulse back under control. She had been trained to breach houses and had put that training to good use many times, but there was something about what they were doing now that made her inordinately nervous. She knew what it was: Milton's reputation and the knowledge that with his death there was little chance that her deceit would be revealed.

She slid her finger through the guard and felt the trigger.

Two counted down from three, and, as he reached one, he turned the handle and stepped inside.

Lilly followed.

The apartment inside was tiny: a bathroom, bedroom and kitchen. They checked the rooms quickly, arriving at the bedroom and finding it empty.

"Look," Lilly said.

The bed was unmade, and, when she rested her palm against the sheets, she felt that they were damp.

Two banged his fist against the wall. "Shit!"

They found more evidence that Milton had been in the flat as they looked around: a bucket of filmy water sat on the floor, and there were greasy papers from takeout street food left in the trash. Two went to the refrigerator, grabbed it on both sides and then heaved it away from the wall. He pulled it back enough so that he could slip behind it and remove the false panel that had been hidden there.

He cursed again.

Lilly glanced over his shoulder and looked into the recess that he had revealed. She saw a rifle and a compact submachine gun and also the empty bracket where a smaller handgun would have been hung.

"Does it have to have been him?" she asked. "Could somebody else have been here?"

"The quartermaster would have replenished everything. No. It's him. We were unlucky. We just missed him."

Lilly saw a plastic box at the foot of the recess, took it out and opened the lid. She took out a wig and bottles of make-up. She remembered something that she had seen earlier and shook her head in disbelief.

"What is it?"

"We passed him."

"When... where?"

"There was a guy on the street. I only saw him from behind, but there was something about him that looked familiar. The way he walked."

"Sure?"

"Not sure, not a hundred per cent, but... I think so."

"Did he see you?"

"Don't think so. He was walking away from us."

Two put the pistol back into the waistband of his jeans. "Maybe we can catch him up."

76

Kader woke early. He went downstairs, picked up the phone and dialled the number for the personnel department at the hotel. He introduced himself as a member of staff at the agency who helped the hotel when they needed cover and said that, with apologies, Mr. Chopra was sick and would not be able to work. He said that a replacement had been found and that the man—Arjun Dass—would report at the usual time. There was little to which the woman from the hotel could object; she said that it was important that the replacement had excellent experience on the basis that there was an important event scheduled for the afternoon, but Kader—who had anticipated her concern—assured her that Dass had an excellent resumé and that he was more than qualified to cover until Mr. Chopra came back. That was good enough for her; she said that she would be waiting for him at seven thirty so that she could show him around prior to the start of his shift.

KADER TOOK the bus to the hotel and followed the path that he had seen during his reconnaissance to the staff entrance at the side of the building. The woman was waiting for him just as she had promised.

"Mr. Dass?"

"Yes. Good morning."

"You're on time—that's a good start. We need to get you sorted out with a uniform. This way, please."

She led the way along a utilitarian corridor until they reached a room where the staff uniforms were cleaned and stored. The man who worked behind the desk looked at Kader and sized him up, then disappeared into the back and returned with a *jama*, the traditional jacket that was worn by male members of staff. It was long, falling down to the knees, and loose. Kader had seen the staff wearing them and knew that it would be perfectly suited to his needs.

"Get changed," she said. "Your shift starts in fifteen minutes."

The changing room was empty, with lockers on one wall and a bench against the other. Kader took out the *jama* and undressed, leaving his clothes in a spare locker. He folded them neatly, out of habit, even though he knew he would not return to retrieve them. He unzipped the rucksack and took out the shoulder holster, putting it on and then slotting the pistol in place. He put on the *jama* over that, then took the grenades and dropped them in opposite pockets. He arranged the jacket so that the fabric fell in such a way as to obscure the holster and the bumps of the grenades. He checked his reflection in the mirror; none of his armaments was obvious.

He went back outside and followed the woman to the front door.

77

Otto Sommer arranged for a driver to meet him at the airport so that he could be taken straight to the Majestic. Changing his plans at short notice was not something that he liked to do, but, following the message that he received from Lilly Moon, he had known that he had no choice. His own Gulfstream had still to return from delivering Huxley and Maxim to New Delhi, so he had to call in a favour from a contact at the FSB. A government G650 had been sent to Krasnodar, where it had been fuelled and prepared for the six-hour flight to the south.

Sommer got out of the car and looked up at the hotel. It was big and grand and garish and, to his jaundiced eye, had negligible security. He could see two armed officers in the lobby, but neither of them was paying attention to the job at hand. It was early—a little after six—but that was no excuse. Neither man paid him any attention as he crossed the lobby and summoned an elevator to take him up to the penthouse suite. He had hoped to see more observant guards when he disembarked, but, instead, he was dismayed to find that there were none. Sommer knew which suite had been allotted to Huxley and followed the corridor until he reached the door, his irritation at the lack of security increasing with every step.

He knocked on the door and then waited, assuming that Maxim would at least use the spyhole before letting him in.

He heard the turn of the lock and the rattle as the security chain was fed out of its bracket.

"Father?" Maxim said.

"You don't seem pleased to see me."

"No, not that. I'm confused. This wasn't planned."

Sommer came inside. "The man who came after Huxley —John Milton. He's here."

"How do you know that?"

"Because the source I'm developing is here, too. She's been sent to find him."

"Just him? Alone?" Maxim shook his head. "Then you've had a wasted trip. I don't need your help for one man."

Sommer took a breath. All of his sons were headstrong, but he had hoped that Maxim, at least, had curbed the foolishness of youth with a little common sense. Perhaps he was wrong. "Do you know anything about him?"

"I know that he's lucky he's still alive."

"It's not *luck*. He was in Group Fifteen for a decade. You know as well as I do that you don't last as long as that because you're *lucky*." He shook his head. "I asked for his file so I could read it on the flight here. Do you know how many targets the FSB think he killed during his career? More than a hundred and fifty. He tried to quit, and they sent agents after him. There was a confrontation in Russia, and they all died. There are only a handful of men alive who would give me cause for concern—Milton is one of them."

Maxim frowned but didn't object.

Sommer went on. "And it's just as well that I came. Do you know how easy it was for me to get up here? Do you know how many times I was stopped?"

"I'm here all the time. I haven't—"

"I wasn't stopped *once*, Maxim. Not once. The men in the lobby might as well not have been there for all the good they did. There's no one outside the elevator. There's no one in the corridor or on the door. And if *I* can walk straight inside, someone like Milton could, too. And if he can—if he can get up to the suite without being stopped—it won't matter how vigilant you are. You would already be dead."

"I've been here all the time," Maxim protested. "No one gets inside the suite unless I let them inside."

Sommer could see that Maxim would be stubborn about that. His sons were all proud men, but Maxim—at least most of the time—was able to back it up. There would be a time to correct the errors that he had made, but it wasn't now.

"There's another reason we need Milton out of the way. The source I am developing has the potential to be very valuable. *Very* valuable. She offers us access into Group Fifteen at the same time as being simple to control because of a lie she has told. There are two people who know that she is lying: one of them is on her way to Moscow and a cell in Lefortovo, and the other one is John Milton. Finding him would normally be difficult. But we *know* that he is here now. He's *right* here. That is why I thought I should come."

"I understand, Father."

Sommer smiled. "Where is Huxley?"

"Asleep."

"Good."

Sommer went over to the French doors and slid them open, stepping out onto the terrace. Maxim followed.

"Tell me about his itinerary."

"He will be having breakfast with the Indians and the Russians."

"Where? Here? At the hotel?"

"Hyderabad House. It's where the negotiations will be held afterwards. I visited it last night—it is secure."

"Sure?"

"It's a government building. It's inside a walled compound, and armed diplomatic protection officers are providing security. Milton would have to get inside, and that wouldn't be easy."

"But not impossible?"

"You want to change the plan for the day?"

"That's the last thing I want. Huxley is the reason Milton has come here, and we can use that to our advantage. Everything continues with no changes. Huxley follows the itinerary to the letter."

"He's the bait?"

He smiled. "We watch and wait, and if Milton shows his hand—*when* he does..." He clicked his fingers. "We do what needs to be done."

"What about Huxley? We're putting him at risk."

"The goals are not mutually exclusive. We can protect Huxley while disposing of Milton. But if something was to happen to Huxley?" He shrugged. "Would it really be the end of the world? My new source is more important in the long run. She could be irreplaceable. Men like Huxley are common—there will always be another one like him coming around the corner."

"What do you want to do?"

"What time is he going to the breakfast meeting?"

"Eight."

"Good. I'll wait downstairs and watch."

78

Milton took his time, allowing himself to acclimatise to the feel of the city as it awoke for the day ahead. His route took him through a spice market where, even at six in the morning, the merchants had prepared their pitches for the trade they hoped to do. They sat in small, tiled alcoves with their spices and chillies overflowing from open hessian sacks. Other men heaved produce from stall to stall, muscling them onto outsized scales so that they could be weighed. A cloud of tobacco smoke mixed with the tang of the spice, and Milton had to fight the urge to sneeze.

The market ended and opened into a warren of alleyways that cut baffling routes between apartment buildings. Milton saw more men leaning in the tiled alcoves and others who slept, using wooden carts as makeshift beds. He continued south until he broke through into neater, more regimented streets. The road followed the path of the Yamuna River, skirting India Gate and then cutting through the green, open spaces of the parkland on either side of the water.

Milton scouted the area as thoroughly as he could, circling the block within which the Majestic was accommodated. It was close by the cramped streets of Old Delhi, almost as if there was a line drawn between them: on the one side, crowds of people and cheap buildings that looked ready to collapse; on the other, open spaces, green grass, and a striking building that looked like money. There was a wide area for vehicles to park with a fountain in the centre, and then, a short walk away, the conference centre that was attached to the hotel.

There was a payphone on a post at a nearby junction. Milton had saved the number of the hotel and dialled it, then waited for someone on the desk to pick up.

"This is the Majestic. Good morning. How can I help you?"

"Could I speak to one of your guests, please?"

"Of course. Who would you like to speak to?"

"Tristan Huxley. He checked in last night."

"Do you have a room number?"

"I'm afraid not. I left him before he checked in and said I'd call him when I got up."

Milton heard the sound of typing.

"Please hold the line, sir. Allow me to check."

Milton replaced the handset in the cradle. He didn't need to speak to Huxley; the operator had checked the hotel's guestlist and had confirmed that Huxley was there, and now she was asking whether he would take the call.

There was a car parked against the kerb next to him, and Milton used the windscreen to check his reflection. He adjusted his disguise and, satisfied that he would not immediately be identified, decided that the time was right to take a chance. He walked toward the hotel, turned onto the drive and approached the entrance. There was a café next to the lobby with a dozen tables arranged outside on a wide terrace. He took a seat at one of the empty tables at the back, partially hidden by a fern in an outsized terracotta pot. He turned the chair around so that he was able to watch the door without drawing attention to himself.

A waitress came over to ask what he would like, Milton asked her for a cappuccino, and, as she departed to deliver the order to the barista, Milton picked up a copy of a newspaper that had been left on the table, settled in and waited.

79

They went back to the road where Lilly thought she might have seen Milton and went south; in the same direction he had gone. Lilly could quickly see that it was hopeless. The streets had been busy then, and they were even busier now, and, beyond that, the layout of the passages and alleyways was so confusing as to quickly become incomprehensible. They stayed on the main road rather than straying onto one of its tributaries, but she knew that someone with Milton's tradecraft would be wary and just as likely to take a more circuitous—and hard to follow —route to his destination. And they didn't know *that*, either. Where was he going? They didn't know very much at all other than the fact that he had been in the safe house and now he wasn't.

"We're wasting time," Two said. "We can't just leave it to luck. We should go to the hotel."

"How would Milton know Huxley's there?"

"He's here for the arms deal. It's being signed today—it was in the papers. It wouldn't be hard to join the dots from that."

Lilly opened the map on her phone. "It's five kilometres away."

"We'll need the car. We'll need to warn the Indians, too. They said they'll hold him for us until we can take him. We'll call them on the way."

They retraced their steps. Children appeared at Lilly's side, offering her bottles of water that they said were fresh and chilled, but she knew had probably just been filled from the standpipe they had passed earlier. She shooed them away and watched as they latched onto another Westerner, trying the same shtick with her.

Lilly took stock. There was certainly no reason for complacency, but events were proceeding in a way that would have delighted her as she skimmed the fast boat over the waves of the Black Sea with Sommer's silken threats fresh in her mind. London had bought her story of Milton's betrayal, and, when they found him, there would be no one left to counter her lies. She would return to London and start to earn; life would be different. Life would be *better*.

80

Huxley had slept well. The hotel was not quite as *exclusive* as he would have liked, but it was certainly comfortable, and the suite that they had been given was well appointed. There were two bedrooms, and Maxim had taken the smaller of the two so that he could remain at Huxley's side. Rami Sant, the Defence Minister, said that the Indians were taking security seriously, too, and had posted a team of armed guards in the lobby.

There was a knock on the door. "Who is it?"

Maxim checked through the eyeglass. "It's Sant."

"Let him in."

Rami Sant came inside, beaming a wide smile. "Mr. Huxley, how did you sleep?"

"Fine."

"I'm glad to hear it."

Huxley felt like showing him the listening devices that Maxim had found during his search of the suite and telling him that he would have slept a lot better knowing that his hosts were not trying to eavesdrop on him—even when he was taking a *shit*—but he decided to let it go. There was no sense in martyring himself over something that he would also have done in Sant's position, and, anyway, pragmatism was better when so much money was at stake.

Sant was wearing ceremonial dress: a full-sleeved khaki-coloured *kurta*, with white *churidar* trousers and a beige-toned shawl. It was a sign that the Indians were taking the signing of the contract very seriously. They were desperate for the armaments and were going to make a song and dance so that the rest of the world—especially Pakistan—knew about it.

"The Russians will be leaving shortly," Sant said.

"What's the schedule?"

"We'll have breakfast together first. Vikkas Khanna is preparing it now."

"Am I supposed to know who that is?"

Sant smiled indulgently. "The best chef in India. He does the most wonderful flatbreads. You'll have to trust me—it'll be delicious."

"And then?"

"Then we will need you to work your magic. The final points of the contract need to be agreed before it is signed. We've invited the press for the ceremony this afternoon."

"Mr. Huxley won't be there for that," Maxim said.

"Yes," Huxley said. "No pictures."

"Of course not. We'll be discreet—you have my word."

Maxim grunted, his concern evidently unassuaged.

"When do we go?" Huxley said.

"We're expected there at eight," he said. "Why don't you make your way over there now?"

81

Two drove as fast as the traffic allowed, taking the most direct route to the hotel. Lilly was impatient; every minute made her more and more certain that she had indeed seen Milton, and that he was headed this way to end his vendetta with Tristan Huxley. Two seemed confident, too, and they shared barely a word as he negotiated the busy streets.

The traffic slowed as a lorry reversed up ahead.

"You clear on the rules of engagement?" he asked her.

"I'm clear."

He waved his hand for her to elaborate.

"Jesus," she muttered. "Fine. We get him off the street and into the car and then away. *Please*. You think I haven't done this before? I have. You don't need to patronise me."

He ignored her irritation. "I've got the lead here. What I say goes."

He turned off the main road in an attempt to navigate around the jam. She hadn't had to manufacture her disdain for his talk of the rules of engagement and his concern about her experience; chauvinism was something that she had become accustomed to over the years, and, while it still irritated her—how could it not?—she didn't let the annoyance linger.

It appeared that plenty of drivers had the same idea as Two had; the next road along was blocked, too.

"What about the Indians?" she said.

"They have officers at the hotel," Two replied tersely. "They've been warned that Huxley might be in danger, but there's not much more we can do until this *fucking* road clears."

He slammed the heel of his palm against the wheel, and the horn sounded, joining the cacophony of irritation from the other drivers caught in the jam.

She looked over at Two and thought that, in this context, his chauvinism was funny. He had no idea what she had done and, perhaps more to the point, what she *would* do to protect herself and her daughter. She knew what their orders were, but she had no intention of following them. She couldn't take the risk that he might say something that revealed her lies. She would shoot him, the first chance that she got, and deal with the consequences later.

"Fuck it."

Two turned the wheel and drove up onto the pavement. He accelerated, cutting around the cause of the jam— another roaming cow—and bounced back onto the road. The way ahead was clear now that they had passed the obstruction, and Lilly could see that the hotel was on the next block.

"Another minute and we'll be there," she said.

82

S ommer saw Huxley as he and Maxim stepped out of the lift. He folded up his newspaper and stood up, abandoning his vantage point at the side of the lobby. He had been able to observe the comings and goings of the staff and guests, the rhythm of the hotel as momentum gathered for the rest of the day. He had seen nothing that gave him any cause for alarm: no one else appeared to be surveilling, and no one looked out of place. There was certainly no sign of John Milton. Despite that, Sommer wouldn't allow himself the luxury of lowering his guard. That would come later, when Huxley's business in the city was done and they had been discharged as his protectors. A man like Milton was dangerous beyond measure, and Sommer knew that they would need to focus.

He cut them off before they could reach the exit.

Huxley stopped, his mouth falling open. "What are you doing here?"

"Keeping you safe."

"I've already got Maxim doing that. And the Indians—"

"The Indians are fools," Sommer cut over him. "Their

men are lazy and feckless. They've barely looked up since I got here."

Huxley looked ready to reply, but Maxim held up a hand to hush him. "I'm taking Mr. Huxley to the breakfast meeting."

"Wait here," Sommer said. "I'll look outside first."

83

The first half hour of Kader's shift had passed without too much incident. He had been shown around the front of the hotel and introduced to the other members of staff—the concierge, the other bell-hops—with whom he would be working. He had no experience of the work and knew that, eventually, his bluff would be called; that wouldn't matter, though. All he had to do was stay where he was until Huxley emerged to be taken to the venue where the contract would be signed. The intelligence that he had received from Islamabad had suggested that there was a breakfast meeting; he looked at his watch, saw that it was eight, and knew that he couldn't have too much longer to wait.

A taxi pulled up, and a young couple stepped out. Kader went over to them, greeted them and went around to the boot to unload their luggage. He loaded the trolley, took their names for the ticket and then opened the hotel's door and showed them the way to the check-in desk.

"Thank you," the man said, offering his hand and then palming him a tip.

"Thank you, sir. Have a wonderful stay."

Kader was filling out the ticket with their details when he saw activity from the elevator lobby. The police officers whom he had noticed had been stationed downstairs moved in that direction, disappearing around the corner before returning with a man with close-cropped hair and Tristan Huxley.

Kader swallowed, his throat suddenly a little dry.

Huxley started walking, but before he could manage more than a handful of paces, he was intercepted by an older, well-dressed man. Kader didn't recognise him but thought he could see a resemblance between him and the man with the close-cropped hair. They looked similar. Father and son, perhaps?

The lift chimed, and another group disembarked: three large men in suits, certainly ex-military and most likely working as close protection. They glanced around the lobby as they waited to be joined by their charges, a delegation including a man whom Kader recognised as Nikolay Timofeyevich, the foreign minister of Russia. Huxley nodded in recognition but stayed where he was while Timofeyevich and his guards crossed the lobby.

Kader knew that Huxley might recognise him, so he turned his back, pushed through the revolving doors and went to stand behind the lectern that the bellboys used. He glanced around the drop-off zone and saw that a police van had parked in it. Six armed officers were in the process of disembarking.

One of the other bellhops on the shift with Kader gestured to the officers. "What's *that* all about?"

"I have no idea," he said as he reached into the right-hand pocket of his jacket and let his fingertip dab against the grenade he had hidden there.

Patience, he told himself. *Not long now.*

84

M ilton saw activity across the courtyard at the entrance to the lobby. A police van pulled up, disgorging six officers, who fanned out beneath the awning and waited. The van moved away just as three long sedans with blacked-out windows drew up, each of them with miniature flags of the Russian Federation attached to their bonnets above the headlights. Burly men in suits stepped out and stood guard while a smartly-dressed delegation emerged through the revolving doors and headed toward the cars. Milton recognised Nikolay Timo-feyevich. He and Thorsson had seen him on Huxley's island during the negotiations for the deal. The drivers waited for their passengers to get inside, then shut the doors of the cars and pulled out.

Milton saw more movement from the doorway. An older man, short in stature and dressed in a neat suit, stepped outside and looked left and right.

Otto Sommer.

A second man, younger and with tightly cropped blond hair, came next. Milton recognised him, too: one of the bodyguards from the Unit who had driven Huxley away from the base in Krasnodar, the man who had set an ambush for Milton and hosed his car with 5.45mm rounds. There was a clear familial resemblance between the two, and Milton guessed that he was looking at one of Sommer's sons.

He unconsciously reached around and touched his fingers against the butt of the pistol, confident that he was about to be presented with the opportunity to do what he had come here to do. He doubted that he would be able to get away afterwards, but he wasn't concerned about that. He'd had a good run—much longer than he had expected, and more than he deserved—and if he was to go out, he would do so while adding, one final time, a credit to his ledger. It wouldn't balance things out—Milton would never have been able to do that, not even if he lived to be a hundred—but it was the right thing to do, and it would help.

There was more activity: another car approached, moving steadily along the drive before swinging around the fountain and stopping behind the police van. Two of the officers, their hands on the butts of their weapons, made their way to the vehicle as the occupants stepped out. There were two of them, a man and a woman, but they were blocked by the police van, and Milton wasn't able to get a good look.

Sommer recce'd the drop-off zone and then turned and gestured that someone waiting inside the lobby should come out.

The revolving door spun again and disgorged Tristan Huxley. He looked haughty and gestured vaguely into the air—complaining about the heat, perhaps—with the expression of someone who has been inconvenienced into doing something that he has no desire to do.

Milton got up.

Huxley looked over, and, for a moment, their eyes locked.

He stopped, halfway between the door and the car that was waiting for him.

Milton reached for the pistol.

"*Gun!*"

The shout wasn't aimed at him.

It was from one of the bellboys, and in the direction of the couple who had just stepped out of the car.

Milton aimed.

Huxley froze.

Milton saw movement in the corner of his eye. A woman —one of the couple from the car, he thought—was pointing a pistol at him.

Milton ducked.

Someone screamed.

Milton winced. It felt as if he had been punched in the shoulder.

85

Lilly cursed. Milton had seen her and had moved, just enough, right at the last. The bullet had tagged him somewhere on the left shoulder when it should—and *would*, had his attention remained on Huxley —have run him right through the throat.

Two reached for her arm. "What are you doing? *Alive.* We take him *alive.*"

Fuck.

She'd blown it. She was only going to get one shot; she'd taken it and missed.

Milton's table had overturned when he had fallen, and now he was sheltering behind it. Two approached the table, his pistol pointed down and ready to fire.

Lilly didn't know what to do next. She couldn't very well shoot Milton now; the moment when she could say that she had seen him pull his weapon and had fired in self-defence had passed. She could shoot Two, then shoot Milton, but no, that was impossible, not with witnesses everywhere. She was going to have to be inventive. There would be a moment when she could deal with Two, then Milton, and she would say that Milton had tricked them, that *he* had killed Two before Lilly had taken him down.

Two was edging around one side of the table. Lilly grasped her pistol in both hands and aimed down, making her way around the table in the opposite direction.

"You're hit," Two called out to Milton. "And there are two of us. It's over. Let me see your hands, or I'm going to empty a magazine through the table."

86

Milton knew the pain was coming, but it still caused him to grunt when it did.

"You're hit," a male voice called out.

He looked down at his shoulder and saw that the top of the jacket had been scorched, the fabric separated into a neat furrow by the bullet that had only just missed his throat. It had sliced through the muscle atop his clavicle, a flesh wound that, while it hurt, was not going to be a serious problem. It was his left side, too, and he had full movement in his right as he scooped up the pistol from where it had fallen to the ground.

"And there are two of us. It's over. Let me see your hands, or I'm going to empty a magazine through the table."

Milton saw movement to his left and right, two people, a man and a woman, both aiming pistols dead square at him. He reached up, ignoring the snarl of pain from his shoulder, and raised his hands to the level of his head.

"Put the gun down."

The speaker was male. Milton hadn't seen him before, but he spoke in English with a northern accent.

Milton lowered the gun.

"*Slowly.*"

He placed it on the ground and then raised his hand again.

He turned to look at the woman and recognised her at once: it was Twelve, one of the agents who had gone into Krasnodar to get Control.

"What is this?" Milton said.

"Shut up," the man said.

"You're from the Group?"

"Face down on the ground."

"Tell me what's happening."

"Face down, hands behind your back—*now*."

87

K ader had no idea what was happening save that the gunshot stirred up panic: at first everyone had frozen, but, now that the sudden shock was gone, pandemonium had rushed in. Three people had pulled guns: the two Westerners who had stepped out of a car and the man with the black hair and the beard who had been sitting at a table in the café. The man with the beard looked to have been shot, and now he was out of sight behind his upturned table as the other two covered him.

Huxley was in the doorway, and Kader knew that he had to act now, before his protection hustled him back inside. *It has to be now.* He had come here knowing that he had no future in the agency, that his career was over with the botched assignment in the grounds of Huxley's mansion. They would never trust him with anything again; they might have had him shot but had chosen to give him the opportunity to erase his shame, to record a final success that might draw a veil over his failure so that his many successes might shine.

Kader was grateful for that.

He reached into his pocket for the first grenade. He found it and clasped his hand around the hard, ridged body.

Huxley had been backed into the open wings of the revolving door.

Kader took out the grenade, pulled the pin, and rolled it underhand. It bounced once, then again, before rebounding off the central shaft of the door and coming to rest.

And then it detonated.

88

Sommer saw the bellhop toss the grenade, but there was nothing that he could do about it. It bounced into the same compartment as Huxley and settled at his feet. Sommer yelled for Maxim to get down and flung himself to the ground.

The grenade exploded with a loud crack, followed immediately by the sound of shattered glass and the *thwip-thwip-thwip* as shrapnel perforated anything and everything in its way.

Sommer rolled onto his back so that he could draw his pistol. He raised his head and took it all in: a wreck of debris and broken glass where the door had been; patrons from the café, some scattering, others on the ground; Maxim, slowly getting to his feet. Sommer was disorientated by the blast and swept his gun left and right, looking for the bellhop. He found him: he was supporting himself against the wall, blood running from a gash in his scalp. Sommer had blood in his eyes; he wiped it away with his left hand as he aimed, clasping the pistol in both hands and squeezing back on the trigger as the bellhop pulled the pin on a second grenade.

He yelled to Maxim to get down as he pulled the trigger —once, twice, three times—and then brought his forearms up to bracket his head.

All three shots found their mark.

The grenade dropped out of the bellhop's hand and rolled away from him.

89

L illy heard the banshee shriek of an alarm from somewhere in the building and then answering screams from all around. She probed herself for injury, finding nothing more than scrapes and bruises, then realised she had to move. There were threats everywhere: Milton, most notably, and the man who had thrown the grenade.

She pushed herself to her hands and knees and looked up. Two was unsteady on his feet, his right hand clutched to his chest. She put her hand down to steady herself, her palm prickling against the fragments of glass that glistened in the morning sun. She raised her weapon. The surface of the upturned table was studded with fragments of metal and shards of glass, but Milton wasn't there.

She turned again, saw the bellhop, and saw that he had another grenade. There came a gunshot, then two more; the man fell to his side, and the second grenade rolled out of his hands.

Lilly launched herself over the table and covered her head.

The second explosion was louder without being muffled by the door. Lilly cringed at the barrage of shrapnel that crashed against the wood. The echo faded away, and there was a silence that lasted for several seconds before it was interrupted by a bloodcurdling scream and the wail of another alarm.

It was dark; Lilly panicked until she remembered that she had squeezed her eyes shut.

"Get up."

She opened her eyes and looked into the barrel of a pistol.

"Get *up!*"

She blinked the fuzz out of her eyes, focussed beyond the gun and saw that Milton was standing over her. The wig had fallen off, leaving streaks of glue that gummed up his dark hair into messy tufts. Half of the moustache was gone, too, but his eyes—glacial, burning blue—stared down at her with such pitilessness that she knew he would pull the trigger without even thinking about it. She looked over at her gun, close enough to reach with a lunge, but he saw, too, and flicked it away with the toe of his shoe.

"Last chance."

She got to her hands and knees. Milton switched the gun to his left hand and dragged her up with his right. Now that she was above the top of the table's edge, she could see the damage that had been caused by the two explosions. The first grenade must have been almost directly underneath Huxley when it detonated; his legs had been blown off and almost all of the glass in the door was gone, the only panels that survived smeared with his blood. The second grenade had exploded near to the bellboy; his body was slumped against the wall of the hotel, three bullet holes in his chest leaking blood. She looked for Sommer and saw him flat on his face, his body weighed down beneath the bodies of another man and a woman.

She looked for Two. The bellboys' lectern had been upset and so had the wheeled brass cage that was used to ferry luggage into and out of the lobby. That was where she saw him: he was beneath the cage, lying still. She couldn't see how badly injured he was, but she knew that he would have been close to the grenade when it exploded.

There was movement to her left, and she turned to see the man with the cropped hair who had come outside with Huxley. He was clambering to his feet, a pistol in hand. He aimed the gun at Milton, but his reactions were slow, as if trying to move his arm through treacle. Milton saw him, aimed the pistol and fired. The gun was close to Lilly's head, and the report was loud enough to make her ears ring. The man with the short hair took the round in the head and fell, his back jackknifing across an upturned chair.

Milton yanked her to the left, turned her away from the hotel and shoved her in the direction of their car.

"You're driving," he said.

Lilly knew that he still had the gun and that he would use it if she didn't do as he told her. She opened the door, lowered herself into the driver's seat, and, feeling his weight as he got into the back, she started the engine.

"Drive," he said.

90

M ilton pushed the pistol between the seat and the headrest so that the woman knew it was there. He recognised her from Krasnodar— Number Twelve—and assumed that her partner was from the Group, too.

"Please. I have a daughter."

"Should've thought of that before."

"She's eight."

"And I don't care. Drive."

They left the hotel grounds and turned onto one of the main thoroughfares that cut through the city. Milton had been worried that the traffic would be too dense and that he would have to abandon the car, but, to his surprise, the flow was moving easily. He knew he was going to have to disappear, but not before he understood what had just happened. There was one thing about which he was absolutely sure: Huxley was dead. He hadn't recognised the man in the bell-hop's uniform at first, but now he did; it was Abbas Kader, the ISI agent who had tried—and failed—to get to Huxley in the grounds of his mansion. He had succeeded now, but

at the cost of his life. The second grenade had torn him to
pieces.

Twelve glanced up into the mirror. "What happened to
my partner?"

"What number was he?"

"Two. What do you mean 'was'? He's dead?"

"He was too close to the grenade."

She didn't react.

"Where are we going?"

"Away from here."

Milton looked behind them, worried that the police
would give pursuit. He knew that he didn't have long; there
were witnesses who had seen what had happened, and who
would have been able to give a description of the car. And,
as valid as all of that was the fact that the car had been
damaged by the two grenades: the bodywork had been
peppered with shrapnel, and there were holes in the glass,
spiderwebbed fault lines radiating out from them.

"Turn off up here," Milton said.

She flicked the indicator and turned left, following
Milton's directions until they were on a quieter road.

"I'm going to ask you some questions," he said. "You're
going to answer them, and you don't want me to think you're
not being truthful."

She clenched her jaw, her hands tight on the wheel. "Go
on, then."

"Why were you here?"

She paused. "What?"

"The two of you—you were here for me."

"What did you expect?"

"Why?"

"Seriously? After what you did?"

"After what *I* did?"

She laughed without humour. "I was *there*, Milton. In Krasnodar. I saw it—I saw all of it. You sold us out."

"No," he said.

"They were waiting for us. How'd they know we were coming?"

He jabbed the gun forward, pushing the barrel right into the nape of her neck. "*What happened?*"

"They ambushed us. They're dead because of you. All of them."

Milton shook his head. "What about Control?"

"*Seriously?* You're going to play dumb? Fuck you, Milton. Fuck *you*. She's dead or in a gulag somewhere—you tell me."

He tried to put it all together. Something had happened after Milton had left the base in pursuit of Huxley. That would explain why he had been unable to reach Thorsson. But Milton knew that *he* hadn't betrayed anyone.

"They're not *all* dead. You—"

Twelve yanked the wheel to the left, and the car swerved across the central reservation, struck a lamppost and spun out of control. Milton's injured shoulder slammed against the window; he let go of the pistol, reaching up with both hands to press against the roof as he locked his feet beneath the seat and tried to hold himself in place. The car spun and spun again before the wheels caught the edge of the kerb, and the car flipped onto its side and then onto its roof. Milton grimaced with the effort, but it was impossible; he tried to anchor himself and failed, dropping headfirst against the roof of the car as it spun through one full circle and then a second. The car's slide was finally arrested as it came off the road and bumped into the trunk of a tree.

The rear windows had smashed, and the roof had crumpled a little beneath the weight of the chassis. Milton rolled to his side and righted himself. He heard a grunt of effort, a curse, two heavy blows and then the crack of splintering glass. Milton turned and saw Twelve slithering out of the car, sliding through the space where the windscreen had been. He looked for the gun, saw it was still jammed beneath the headrest and yanked it free. Twelve was all the way out of the car now, scrabbling backwards until she was out from beneath the bonnet and able to get to her feet. Milton aimed, but she saw him and ran, darting sharp right so that the driver's seat was between them.

Milton cursed. He shuffled around, kicked the rest of the glass out of the side window and began worming his way out, the shards that were still stuck in the frame digging into his legs and back.

The passing cars had stopped, and a handful of pedestrians had hurried over to see if there was anything they could do to help. Milton staggered toward them, someone saw the gun in his hand, and the group parted. There was a line of trees and then, beyond them, streets of densely packed buildings.

Milton ignored the pain in his shoulder and ran.

EPILOGUE

The headquarters of the Firm were found in a ten-storey office building that was reached by way of an alley off Horse Guards Parade. The building was typical for those in the area: it was a hundred years old and, thanks to a parsimonious approach to maintaining the Crown Estate, starting to look its age. Lilly Moon pushed open the doors and went inside. She signed in at the desk, waiting as the concierge checked her details on the screen that sat on his desk. The man did not look like the type who would usually be found behind a desk, and Lilly knew that he would very likely have been drawn from the military and would almost certainly be wearing a shoulder holster with a pistol beneath his jacket.

"Thank you," he said. "Conference room on the fifth floor. They're waiting for you."

Lilly thanked him, made her way to the lobby and pressed the button to summon one of the two lifts. The exterior of the building was grandiose, but that impression was not maintained beyond the foyer. The corridors were painted in the same neutral magnolia as would be found in any normal municipal office, with patches of damp where moisture had gradually seeped through the brick and into the plaster. Lilly rode the lift to the fifth floor and followed the corridor to the conference room. There was a panel of glass in the door, and she could see that the man on the desk had been right; two people were sat around the table.

She knocked.

"Come in."

She opened the door. The conference room, like the corridors, had not been decorated for years. It was panelled in oak that, in places, had been affected by the damp. The windows were dusty and, outside, a fat pigeon perched on the windowsill and regarded them with indignation at being disturbed. The cast iron radiators gurgled as hot water slowly circulated through ancient pipes. The table was too large for the space, and the chairs could barely be pulled back without bumping into the wall.

The man and woman sitting at the table were representatives of the Intelligence Steering Committee, the body responsible for overseeing the work of the fifteen Groups that, together, comprised the Firm. It was staffed by mandarins from the main Whitehall departments and members of Cabinet. Lilly recognised only the man at the head of the table. It was Sir Benjamin Stone, the chief of the Secret Intelligence Service, who had briefed them before they embarked on the assignment in Russia.

"Sir," she said.

"Number Six," he said. "Thank you for coming. Please— shut the door and sit down."

Lilly did as she was told.

Stone pointed to the woman to his right. "This is Elizabeth Cheetham."

Cheetham was the director general of the Secret Service. She put out her hand. "I don't believe we've met."

"No, ma'am. We haven't."

"How are you feeling?" Cheetham asked her.

"I'm fine, ma'am."

"No injuries?"

"I was lucky. Just cuts and bruises."

"That's good to hear."

"We wanted to take the chance to speak to you personally," Stone said. "We've read your report, and we wanted to ask a couple of questions."

Lilly ignored the empty feeling in her gut and gave a nod. "Of course. What do you want to know?"

"We'd like to hear you explain what happened in New Delhi."

"It's in my—"

"We've read it," Stone cut across her. "We'd like you to tell us again."

"Of course, sir."

Lilly had rehearsed the story so many times now that it was difficult to tell where the truth ended and her dissembling began. She explained how she and Two had travelled to India and how they had missed their chance at quietly taking Milton when they arrived minutes too late at the safe house. She told them how they had followed him to the hotel, and how their attempt to make an arrest had been thwarted by the murder of Huxley and the chaos that had ensued.

"We've read an eyewitness account that said you took a shot at Milton."

"I did," she said, knowing the question was likely to come and ready with an answer. "He pulled a weapon."

"He had you drive him away," Cheetham said.

"Yes, ma'am. At gunpoint."

"And you crashed the car?"

"I was concerned he would shoot me."

"Before that, though—what did he say to you?"

"Nothing—just that I had to drive."

"He didn't mention what happened to Huxley?"

"No, ma'am."

"Nothing at all?"

"No. Why?"

"It's been suggested that he might have been working with the man who killed him."

"Has he been identified?"

"We believe his name was Abbas Kader. He worked for the ISI."

"And tried to kill Huxley before, but Milton stopped him. Why would they work together now?"

"We don't know," Cheetham said. "But there's a lot we don't know."

Stone looked at Lilly for a moment and then nodded. "Thank you, Number Six. There will be a briefing of the surviving Group Fifteen agents this evening. You are all being stood down from existing commitments and redeployed to two critical objectives. The entire apparatus of British intelligence has been tasked with finding Control."

"And Milton?"

"Do you really need to ask?" Cheetham said. "John Milton has been a liability for the last time. If we find him —*when* we find him—you will be sent to put an end to him once and for all."

THEY DIDN'T SAY where they had taken her, but Control knew: it had to be Lefortovo Prison in Moscow, the same place the FSB took the prisoners it wanted to break. They had drugged her again for the transfer from Krasnodar, and she had woken up in her windowless cell in the basement of the building on the left bank of the Yauzy River. A female guard had visited at some point during the first few hours to provide a set of prison fatigues that were stiff with starch and stinking of insecticide. The woman waited while she changed, then explained that she would be fed three times a day, that she would have access to a shower once a week and that there would be only cold water in the cell. She took Control's clothes and left and had not returned since. Her meals and insulin had been slid through the hatch at the bottom of the door, and although Control had tried to use the deliveries as a way of judging the passing of time, she had lost count and now wouldn't even have hazarded a guess. A day? A week? She couldn't say.

Control sat on her thin mattress with her legs drawn up to her chin. Everything she had thought about this mess of a situation had been wrong. She had told herself that she would be released, but that hadn't happened. Indeed, it had quickly become worse; she had been moved from Finland to Krasnodar to the most notorious prison in Moscow with an alacrity that was hard to credit. She knew that London would try to find her again, but she knew, too, that if the Russians didn't want her to be found, then she wouldn't be.

She heard the sound of footsteps outside and then the sound of the key turning in the lock. The door opened, and she was too late in looking away; the artificial light was blindingly bright given that she had been in darkness for who knew how long. She squeezed her eyes shut and then slowly opened them, millimetre by millimetre, until they had adjusted.

A man was standing in the doorway. She blinked, trying to focus, and saw Otto Sommer.

"Control," he said, "are you well?"

She couldn't help a smirk of disdain. "Please, Otto. Let's not pretend to be civil. You killed my agents, and now you're holding me against my will. I know this isn't your call, so how's this—you piss off now and get whichever of Putin's cronies is in charge. I'd rather speak to the organ grinder than to the monkey."

He stared at her, and, for a moment, she saw the coldness in his eyes. "Civility should be welcomed by a woman in your situation. You have value at the moment, but that might not always be the case. And there is the matter of your family." He clicked his fingers. "They could be killed as easily as that."

"That's your idea of civility? Threats?"

Her eyes had adjusted enough by now that she was able to get a better look at him. He was wearing a tailored grey suit with a pink shirt and black tie, a pocket square adding a flamboyant splash of colour. She was struck, once again, by how much younger and fitter than his age he looked.

He stayed where he was in the corridor. "Do you want to know what happened to Tristan Huxley? The Pakistanis sent an agent to kill him."

"I hope they succeeded."

"They did. He's dead."

"What does that have to do with me?"

"John Milton was there to finish his vendetta with Huxley. Two of your agents were sent to stop him, and they failed. One of them died."

"The other one?"

"She works for me now. "

Sommer stepped into the light, and, for the first time, Control was able to see him properly. There had been a whimsy to his expression before, but it was absent now; his lips were pursed, and his cheeks were pinched, and his eyes burned with anger. Control saw it and wondered if she had underestimated the danger that she was in.

"Two of my sons are dead," Sommer said. "Thorsson killed Alyosha, and Milton killed Maxim. You asked what I want. It is very simple. I want *him*."

"And you think I can help with that? Look around."

He smiled one of his thin-lipped smiles. "I'm here to offer you a little hope, Control. You will be released provided that Milton is delivered to me. It would be in your interests to help me with that."

"What about my agent? You let me out and she's burned."

"Miss Moon?" He shrugged. "There's no question she has great value, and it would be a shame to set that aside— but I would. I want Milton, Control. He's the only thing I want."

"Did he see the agents?"

"He did."

"Then you're wasting your time. He'll know what's happened, and he's already disappeared. You know he did that before, don't you? For years? We only found him because we got lucky."

Sommer adjusted a button on his suit jacket. "Come," he said, gesturing to the open door. "I want to show something."

Control was fearful, but she was curious, too, so she rose from the bed and followed on stiff legs as Sommer led the way along the corridor. Control looked around, confused; it wasn't what she was expecting at all. She knew what Lefortovo was like from reading the accounts of people who had been held there: the floors of the hallways were carpeted, and the prisoners were kept behind thick iron doors. This place was different. The walls were made of wood, with shafts of bright light piercing the gaps in the planks. There was a sense of space about it, and then Control realised: it was silent. There was no traffic, no voices, none of the hum and buzz and fizz of the city.

"This isn't Lefortovo."

He laughed. "Moscow? No, Control, this is not Moscow. Please—this way."

Sommer turned at the end of the corridor and then opened a pair of double doors that led outside. He descended a flight of stone steps and waited for Control at the bottom. She paused at the threshold, looking out onto a breathtaking landscape. The building had been built on higher ground that overlooked thousands of acres of forest that stretched from horizon to horizon. A track serpentined down into the forest and then vanished into the green. An area of trees had been cleared, and a military helicopter—a Kazan Ansat-U multipurpose chopper—sat there, its rotors drooping down over the fuselage. The wheeled vehicles that had been parked near to the buildings were unusual: Trekols with huge balloon tyres that would be able to negotiate heavy terrain.

Sommer took in the wilderness with an expansive sweep of his arm. "Welcome to Salekhard."

"What was this?" she said. "A gulag?"

"Very good," he said. "Stalin was concerned about Nazi submarines in the Arctic. He wanted a railroad to connect the northeastern coast with the network in the west. It would allow supplies to reach the naval port that he wished to build and allow local nickel to be sent to the factories in the west. But it was never built. This place was too harsh, and the prisoners all died. What you see here is all that remains."

"The government gave you this?"

"They did, and why not? They have no other use for it. We have our base at Krasnodar, as you know, but I wanted something with more privacy. This, out here?" He gestured again. "The snow is ten feet deep in winter, and the bogs are impenetrable in summer. The camp was sinking into the forest with the weight of each year's snow. We have revived it and given it another life."

Control looked out over the treetops again and realised that there was no sign of habitation anywhere. The Russian tundra was vast and could take weeks to traverse. And the solitude… At least if she had been in Moscow, there was a good chance that an asset embedded within the FSB would have seen her and passed word back to London. But here? There was no one.

"The government doesn't know that I'm here, do they?"

"No," he said. "You were taken so that I could get to Thorsson. And now I will swap you for Milton."

"London won't cooperate with you."

"Really? With everything that you know? I disagree. There's something else I want you to see. Please—this way."

Sommer picked a way down a path that was marked out by piles of stone. They reached a plateau that held the rotting remains of a building that looked as if it might once have been used for accommodation. A stack of railway sleepers was off to the side, together with a length of rail that had been stamped with a sentence in Russian. The door to the building opened, and a woman stumbled out, followed by a man toting an assault rifle. The woman's face was bruised; she had a split lip and dried blood in her nostrils and scalp. The man with the rifle shoved her again, and she tripped and fell, landing flat on her face in the muck.

"This is Vera Romanova," Sommer said. "Do you remember her?"

"One of your team who killed my driver and abducted me."

"That's right. She was a valuable member of the Unit until she was tempted by the money she could make selling stories about us to credulous journalists. And then she told Milton about you and Krasnodar and... well, she is responsible for a lot of what has happened since."

The woman looked up, but there was resignation in her face. She knew what was going to happen to her and that any appeal to Sommer would be a waste of breath.

"Vera had a contact," Sommer said. "A journalist. She was given a warning years ago, and she would have been wise to take it. She didn't. And because of that, and because she has continued to make trouble for us, she was found floating in the harbour at Riga this morning."

Sommer gestured that the man should hand him the rifle. He did, and Sommer took a pace back and lowered the barrel.

Romanova let her head hang down.

Control looked away.

The gun fired once, the shot echoing back at them from the trees. Control heard a thud, and, when she glanced back, Romanova was on the ground with blood running from a wound in her head.

Control watched as Sommer handed the gun back to the guard, flicked his fingers in the direction of the woman's body and told him to get rid of it. He looked down at the cuff of his suit jacket and saw a speck of red. He tutted, reached for the pocket square, moistened a corner of it with his tongue and then used it to gently dab the stain away.

"I'm not frightened of you," she said.

He shrugged, looked at the pocket square and, with an upturned lip, tossed it onto the woman's body. "That's unwise."

"You want to know what's unwise? Picking a fight with someone like John Milton."

The guard took Romanova by the ankles and started to drag her body away. Sommer walked away a few steps and looked down onto the forest.

"This is a place of death. Everything here is built on bones. The railway that Stalin couldn't build—do you know what the prisoners called it? The Dead Road. One way or another, I will bring Milton here and make him pay for what he has done. Not like Romanova—she was a traitor, yet I was gentle with her. His treatment will be less merciful. And you will remain here until he takes your place."

MILTON TOOK off his shirt and angled himself so that he could see his shoulder in the mirror. He reached up and peeled away the dressing, the adhesive plucking at his skin as he tugged it off. He had been lucky: the wound to his shoulder had been superficial. The bullet had sliced through skin and muscle, missing the blood vessels and bone that, if struck, would have caused more serious problems. It had still needed treatment, though, and Milton had broken into a veterinary practice in the suburbs of the city and taken the supplies that he needed: tweezers so that he could remove the bits of fabric from his clothes that had lodged in the wound, antibiotic ointment, petroleum jelly to keep the wound moist and a selection of dressings. He leaned closer to the mirror and examined the wound more carefully, reaching around to dab his fingers against it where it had started to heal. It was nothing, really. It had been painful, but that was about the extent of it. The flesh had already started to knit back together, and he had no doubt that all he would be left with in a week or two was another scar to add to his collection.

The roadside hotel was near Katra, a town in the foothills of the Trikuta Mountains, nearly five hundred kilometres northwest of New Delhi. Milton had taken his time on the journey, concerned that what had happened at the hotel would be blamed on him and that the police would be seeking his arrest. He had taken a bus to the outskirts of the city and then bought a second-class ticket on the overnight train toward Kashmir. There were four berths in his compartment, each provided with a semblance of privacy by way of a curtain. Milton had the top bunk. He had closed the curtain and allowed himself to sleep; when he woke up, the train was chugging through the flat alluvial plains of the Punjab.

This hotel was close to the railway station, and Milton had booked a room for a week while he assessed his situation and the best way to proceed. He had purchased a burner phone from a kiosk in town and had made contact with the only person possessing both the access to the information he needed and Milton's trust. Ziggy Penn had reacted with his usual weary acceptance of yet *another* task, but Milton knew that—as ever—it was feigned. Ziggy loved to show off to Milton, and anything that allowed him the opportunity to do that—including hacking into the information architecture of the Firm—was like catnip to him.

Milton took a clean dressing and pressed it over the wound, took his phone from the nightstand and went outside. It was a bright day, and the forecast was for temperatures in the high thirties. Milton walked to the town square, bought a plastic cup of *lassi* garnished with pieces of dry fruit and sat down on a bench where he could watch the comings and goings around the market. He took out his phone and dialled the number that Ziggy had given him.

Ziggy answered on the third ring. "*Jesus*, Milton. What have you *done*?"

"How long have you got?"

"I thought you'd been taken off their shit list."

"I was," Milton said. "Things might have changed."

"They've *definitely* changed. They're coming for you again. I couldn't dig deep enough to find out why, but it looks like it's going to be worse than before. I've seen the file: shoot on sight, no hesitation, no excuses. They want you dead. What did you do?"

"I've been set up," he said. "It doesn't matter. What about Control?"

"That's the weirdest thing of all. I can't find anything about her. There was a meeting of the steering committee yesterday—I've had a way to get at the agendas of those ever since I left—and she's never missed one until now. I can't find anything that might explain where she is."

"Keep looking."

"I'm going to need a steer. You have anything else that'll help?"

"Try Russia," Milton said.

"What? She's defected?"

"No. But I was told something that made me think she might be there."

"Context, Milton?"

"I can't give you anything else yet. Just do what you can."

"That's it?"

"One more thing. One of the agents in the Group—Number Twelve: I need everything you can get on her. Background, military history, family, friends."

"That won't be easy."

"That's what you always say, and yet, every time..."

"I'll do my best, but it's different now. There's heat on you now like there never was before. I'll have to tread very carefully."

"I'm confident you'll manage."

"Well, that makes me feel all warm and fuzzy. How do you want me to get it to you?"

"I'm going dark," Milton said. "I'll call you next week."

Milton ended the call, took the SIM out of the phone and dropped it in his empty cup. There was a bin next to the fast-food stall, and he dropped the cup inside. He stood there for a moment, looking at the activity around him, the hustle and bustle of life. He knew that he could probably stay here for a month, maybe two, but that, eventually, he would be found. He had managed to stay ahead of his pursuers before, but it had come at a heavy price: this time, as before, there would be no roots, no patterns that could be traced, no relationships that could lead to betrayal or put others in danger. He didn't mind any of that, not really, and was happy in his own company. But perhaps he had allowed his guard to slip over the last year or two; that would have to change.

The fast-food vendor was selling soft drinks that he was trying—and failing—to keep cold in a dustbin of water. Milton bought a can of Diet Coke and popped the tab. He knew he was putting Ziggy in danger by contacting him, but it was necessary. He needed to know what had happened in

London that had changed things so drastically that he had become a hunted man once more. And, he consoled himself, Ziggy knew how to look after himself.

There really was no point in waiting. Kashmir would be an interesting place to visit, and, provided he kept moving, it should be possible to avoid detection.

He turned and started back along the road to the hotel. He would pack up his things and check out. There was a daily bus from New Delhi to Srinagar, and Milton thought he would be able to catch it if he hurried.

ABOUT MARK DAWSON

Mark Dawson is the author of the John Milton, Beatrix and Isabella Rose and Atticus Priest series.

For more information:
www.markjdawson.com
mark@markjdawson.com

AN UNPUTDOWNABLE ebook.
First published in Great Britain in 2022 by UNPUTDOWNABLE
LIMITED
Copyright © UNPUTDOWNABLE LIMITED 2022

The moral right of Mark Dawson to be identified as the author of this
work has been asserted by him in accordance with the Copyright, Designs
and Patents Act 1988.

All the characters in this book are fictitious, and any resemblance to actual
persons living or dead is purely coincidental.

All rights reserved. No part of this publication may be reproduced, stored
in a retrieval system or transmitted in any form or by any means, without
the prior permission in writing of the publisher, nor to be otherwise
circulated in any form of binding or cover other than that in which it is
published without a similar condition, including this condition, being
imposed on the subsequent purchaser.

Printed in Great Britain
by Amazon

30815664R00255